THEY WERE MORTAL ENEMIES
UNTIL PASSION CLAIMED THEM

With one stroke he knocked the warrior woman senseless.

The braves stood around the one who had fought so long and hard, disbelief on their faces as they watched her small form stagger to its feet. Her long midnight hair hung down her back.

"Put her on my horse," Two Shadows ordered. He looked at the woman he had defeated, his hatred for the Crow still filling his heart and soul. "She is my enemy," he said. "She shall be my slave."

Two Shadows tried to still his ragged breathing. Kalina, too, seemed not to dare breathe. For a moment, their glances met. His silver eyes probed deeply into her as though seeking out a part of her very soul. Her dark, warm eyes looked up into his face, and written in their depths was a desire to face the unknown in his arms.

He wanted this woman with every fiber of his being, and not only as a master wants his slave. He desired her warm and pliant under his hand, the feel of her silken arms twined about his neck.

Never had Kalina come so close to falling under another's spell. And then, quickly, the moment was broken, and again the Blackfoot warrior who stood before her was dark, vengeful. Perhaps this Two Shadows was more devil than man.

An owl hooted atop a mighty pine, and a lone dog barked softly in the distance. A small tear slipped from Kalina's eye. However evil he was, she felt desolate without the warrior's touch, and desired only that he reach out to her again.

P9-DTP-577

VELVET SAVAGE

KATHLEEN DRYMON

ZEBRA BOOKS
KENSINGTON PUBLISHING CORP.

ZEBRA BOOKS

are published by

Kensington Publishing Corp.
475 Park Avenue South
New York, NY 10016

First printing: September 1989

Printed in the United States of America

To my oldest sister, Mary-Jean
I am so glad that I have you.
Thanks for always being there.
Love, Kathleen

Prologue

The hidden glen was full of the wonders of Mother Earth as the fresh, piny forest smells swirled about the summer morning. All of nature seemed in perfect order.

A gentle, loving smile spread across the handsome features of the tall, broad-framed Indian warrior as his wife came to his side. His hand reached out and gently caressed her soft, golden cheek, and when her tender smile returned his affection, he sat down before the entrance of his lodge.

His silver eyes watched his wife as she started down the path along the river's edge, her midnight tresses hanging down to her waist, which was large with his child. A soft sigh of peaceful contentment escaped his lips as he relaxed, his hands on the bow he had been fashioning over the past few days. He thought of the joy that filled his life.

Two Shadows and his wife, Summer Dawn, had remained in this secluded glen at the river's edge while the rest of his tribe, which had been camped in the valley nearby, had packed their belongings and moved high up into the mountains for the warm summer days ahead. Two Shadows and his young bride had desired no company since the eve of their joining, and had gladly stayed behind for a time to themselves.

Two Shadows knew that their time alone was quickly coming to a close and that they would soon be joining the rest of the tribe, but he pushed these thoughts from his mind. Summer Dawn's time of childbirth was swiftly coming upon them. The thought of the child soon to come made his chest swell with pride. Shortly after their joining, Summer Dawn had been taken with his seed of life and though it now seemed that he had always loved the shy, innocent Summer Dawn, he marveled once again at his good fortune. The Great Spirit surely showered him with blessings. He smiled as he stroked the wood in his hands; in his mind he could already see the bow. One day, he thought with pride and anticipation, he would teach his own son this craft of making weapons.

Two Shadows glanced toward the path Summer Dawn had taken. She had gone to pick the sweet berries that grew plentifully along the river bank. For a moment the still quiet of the forest seemed to speak out to the young warrior, and his fingers automatically clutched the bow. A hawk high overhead let out a piercing scream, and a cold chill traveled the length of his backbone. He set the bow aside, leaped up, and stood at his full six-foot height, his eyes seeking out the hidden moods of the forest around him.

It was the ancient practice of his people to respect their inner feelings. As Two Shadows's moccasined feet started slowly down the path his wife had taken, some inner disquiet spurred him to a sprint, his heart racing with fear for Summer Dawn's safety.

Before he reached the river bank, a piercing terrified shriek rent the morning air and seared Two Shadows's heart. His long legs pumping hard, he ran toward the sound of his wife's torment. His pace lengthened, and his blood throbbed harshly in his veins, his heart pounding at a tremendous rate. Again and again he heard the horror-filled screams of Summer Dawn.

The scene that met his eyes as he neared the river chilled his blood. Three Crow warriors, the hated enemy of his Blackfoot people, were circling Summer Dawn, their horses crowding around her as she fought off the hands that were reaching for her. The taunting shouts of her tormentors filled the air around the panicked young woman.

Two Shadows's war cry rent the still morning air as he drew his large hunting knife from the sheath at his side and charged across the clearing. His silver eyes were filled with hatred for his enemy, but paramount in his mind was the thought that he must reach Summer Dawn's side.

When the Crow braves saw the Blackfoot warrior running toward them, his war cry filling their ears, the one that was their leader reached out a long arm and pulled up Summer Dawn across his horse in front of him. Sheer horror filled her soul as the arm circled her full waist and she was lifted from the ground. She fought with all her strength, hitting at her attacker and kicking her legs in the hope of somehow gaining her freedom.

Cries of victory filled the clearing as the Crow

9

Indians spurred on their mounts to carry them away. Two Shadows pushed his body harder, his war cry still bursting from him as he raced toward his wife.

Again and again Summer Dawn lashed out, her fists hitting the warrior in the face, the chest, any place she could strike him as she twisted her body this way and that. Her captor tried to still her, and as he reached forward to hold her down, she bit his hand, causing him to curse, gutturally. As he jerked back, Summer Dawn pushed herself from his grasp.

Two Shadows looked on, horrified, as Summer Dawn sailed through the air and fell hard upon the ground, but his steps never faltered as he raced to her side. The three on horseback gave thought for a second to attacking the lone warrior, but they knew that they were only a few, and were too close to their enemies' home territory. At a shout from their leader they spurred their mounts onward, leaving only the quiet of the morning behind them.

Two Shadows stood gasping over Summer Dawn's still body, lying so quiet now on the soft earth. Slowly he bent, and with a trembling hand he turned her over. When he saw the line of blood coming from a wound at the side of her head, the warrior clutched the still, warm body of his young wife to his chest with a ragged cry, tears coursing down his cheeks as he gave vent to his agony. He had been raised not to show emotion, but he could not suppress the searing pain that shattered his very soul.

He screamed her name aloud with numbing pain. His cries were lifted on the gentle summer breeze and dissipated throughout the lush, green valley around him.

Chapter One

Two long winters had passed while the Blackfoot tribe camped in the peaceful shelter of the valley. There had been small skirmishes with the white man during this time, but it was mainly the Crow who had been the adversaries of chief Star Hawk's tribe. The Blackfoot protected and guarded their lands fiercely, and any intruder was quickly punished. Most of the white men respected their strength, but the Crow, Indians known more for their bravery in battle than for their good sense, often invaded the Blackfoot lands, and found there either glory or death.

During this time the fiercest foe of the Crow Indians was Two Shadows, the feared son of the mighty Star Hawk. He seemed to strike terror in the bravest opponent as he swept down on his enemy with a lethal hatred. His war cry was feared throughout the land, and the stories of his bravery were told with much awe around the campfires.

Now, as the season of the falling leaves settled on Mother Earth, chief Star Hawk approached Two Shadows. Star Hawk's heart went out to his only son as his ebony eyes studied the handsome features across from him. They were so much like his own—the same breadth of shoulder and large frame, the gold of his skin shimmering in the firelight. His long ebony hair hung straight down over his shoulders in the front and was braided in one long length down his back, a leather headband tied around his forehead. His features were almost exactly those of Star Hawk, as if he looked into the white man's mirror, except for the silver eyes, which were a gift from his mother. But as Star Hawk looked into those silver eyes he saw none of the warmth and love of the giver. The eyes before him seemed old and tired, almost chilling, but with an inner fire. It had been two years since the death of Summer Dawn, since the death of the joy in his own son. "The time has now come, my son, for you to set aside your grief and face life once more." Star Hawk's voice was gentle and full of the love a parent feels for a child who is deeply hurt.

There was no answer as Two Shadows looked up from the gold and blue flames of the fire that was kept continually alight in Star Hawk's large tepee. He had no answer to give his sire. His life was centered on one thought: revenge against his enemy. He sought a means of escape, to somehow find peacefulness in death itself, to still his miseries of a love now long shattered.

"Your mother and I have waited with patience for you to come to terms with your life, my son."

12

Star Hawk paused for a moment, thinking of the pain that tormented his son. He had witnessed the agony on Two Shadows's face the day he had come to their village, high in the mountains, with the dead body of his wife. He had been at his side throughout the ordeal of preparing Summer Dawn for the burial grounds of their ancestors. He had shared his son's pain as his own, knowing that he would have been in the same state if his own wife, Silver Star, had been killed in a like manner. So he had given his son these two years in which to cleanse his soul of the hatred and hurt that seemed to live in him day and night. Now it was time for Two Shadows to face the paths of his life. "You have been trained from birth to lead your people. You have learned all I could teach you, and have also learned much from the white man. Now you must give this knowledge to your tribe. Do not let the years when you were away from your family count for nothing."

"You would have me forget my wife and child?"

"There are things in this life, my son, that we can never forget. But we must accept and go on. A life lost, a love known fully and then taken suddenly — are these not better than the silent murmurings of nothingness? Allow your wife to travel down the ghost path without your thirst for revenge hindering her footsteps. She would not wish your life to be wasted. She knew of the great need of your people, and that one day they would depend on you." Star Hawk had spoken like this to his son shortly after Summer Dawn's death, but Two Shadows had heard little of his father's wise counsel.

The silver eyes, so much like his mother's, looked up once again from the embers of the glowing fire. Two Shadows slowly nodded his dark head. "I will heed your wise words, Father, for our people mean much to my heart. But it will be hard to forget, for our enemies the Crow are still trespassing on our lands and pillaging our villages." As he spoke of his hated foe a look of dark vengeance crossed his handsome features.

With a sigh, Star Hawk slowly nodded his head. "Your words are true, my son; our enemies are more daring with each moon that passes. But they have felt the mighty hand of the Blackfoot, and those that trod on our lands have felt our strength. You, my son, have been a fearless and wise war chief in this past year. There is not a brave in our village who would not willingly follow wherever you lead. But this day there is concern in my mind for more than the Crow. Word has come to my ears that the white man is building a fort for their bluecoats only a few days' ride away."

"How did you hear of this, my father?" Two Shadows asked.

"A band of our young braves was hunting and watched from the cover of the forest. Many men were seen building a group of small wooden buildings with a high wall around the outside. I have spoken of this with your mother and she agrees that it must be a fort for the bluecoats. Our braves saw many bluecoats around the area, working on the buildings."

"You would have me go to this fort and find out

14

what they are doing so close to our lands?"

Star Hawk smiled at his son. "You have traveled as a white man in the past, going to your mother's plantation, Sweet Oaks. I have thought this over carefully. You should again dress as Heath Coltin. If you go to this fort of the white man's, perhaps you can learn what is in their minds."

"When would you have me leave?" Two Shadows asked, no thought in his mind of disobeying his father's wishes. All his life he had been trained to lead and help his people and now, if there was such a close threat as his father was saying, he would leave his village as soon as possible.

"With the sun of the new day you will leave. Several of our braves will ride with you and await you in the forest near the fort. Learn all that you can, my son, for the lives of our people may rest on what you learn. To have the white man so close to our village bodes ill for us."

Two Shadows nodded his head thoughtfully in agreement. But before he could speak further on the subject, a young Indian maiden of very rare beauty entered the lodge, and both men's eyes were drawn to her.

She was tall and willowy for an Indian maid. Her straight black hair was left unbraided and lay in shimmering strands down her back. Her gentle features were set in a heart-shaped face with creamy skin, high cheekbones, and a berry-red mouth. She smiled at the men, her silver eyes filled with love.

"It is good to see that my brother is home once again." Her soft, lilting words filled the large tepee. "It is too often now that you are gone from your village, Two Shadows."

Two Shadows rose to his full height, and with a grin went to the maiden's side. "Each time I see you, Sky Eyes, you seem to grow more lovely." He kissed her soft cheek and lightly ran a finger over her jawline.

The girl's eyes sparkled with adoration. "You compliment yourself, brother. All say that we look much alike." A small giggle escaped her soft lips.

"Perhaps," Two Shadows responded. "Or it could be that I flatter you because I am hungry for some of these wild strawberries in your basket." He reached out and took a handful of the luscious, sweet berries and popped them into his mouth.

Chief Star Hawk looked at his children with delight. They had been born within minutes of each other, and had always loved one another. Even as children they had watched out for each other, always protecting and shielding one another from harm. Indeed they did look much alike. His own Indian features, combined with his lovely Silver Star's beauty, had created two very handsome people, Star Hawk thought.

"Walk with me, little sister." Knowing that his talk with his father was over, Two Shadows took Sky Eyes's basket of fruit, set it down, and started from the lodge. Sky Eyes was only steps behind him, as she desired nothing more than to be in his company.

They walked through the village, enjoying the sights and scents of their everyday life. Neither spoke until they neared the river and then, softly,

16

Sky Eyes asked, "You will leave again shortly?"

Two Shadows looked keenly at his sister. "Have you seen this in a vision, or are you only asking me, little one?"

"I have not seen this in a vision, but already I feel the loneliness of your leaving. Do you go again into the enemy's land?" She remembered all the times she had forced her fear from her when her brother had ridden out of the village with a group of braves to strike out at their enemy.

"Father sends me once again into the white man's land. He wishes me to find out some information as Heath Coltin." For a moment Two Shadows thought of the three years during which he had been gone from his village, across the great sea, in the far-off place called London. He had stayed in the large city with his father's friend, Ollie Benjamin, and had gone to school and learned as much of the white man's ways as he could. He also remembered the heartache he had felt each day—the desire to be home, to feel the earth beneath his feet, and to be able to breathe deeply of the pine-scented forest.

For a moment Sky Eyes did not speak. She sat down on a large, smooth, flat rock, her thoughts swirling with his words. It had been her own hope to one day live among the white people. Her mother had told her so many stories of her own life that Sky Eyes could almost see the plantation, Sweet Oaks. She could imagine the splendor of this unknown world. It was as though the white world beckoned to her with an outstretched arm. "Do you go once again to our mother's plantation? Do

17

you think that I could go with you this time?" Her excitement was evident in her voice and in the sparkling lights deep in her silver eyes as she looked up at Two Shadows.

"Little sister, why do you seek the ways of the white man? Is it our mother's past that pulls at your thoughts? It is not as you would like in the white man's land. There is not the peace and beauty that you now find around yourself." For a moment he looked at his twin and wondered if there was more to her desire to travel among the white man. "Have you had more dreams of the white man?" He remembered all she had told him of her visions before he left for London. All that she had spoken to him, he had seen with his own eyes, for Sky Eyes had a rare gift among their people. Her dreams or visions about the future always came to pass. She had told him of the great water that he would cross, and of the large ship that he would sail on. She had told him of the many people in the white man's land, and even how some of them dressed. All she had dreamed and told him had come true. And now he wondered if there was more than she had seen of late.

His eyes sought out hers as though he could read her thoughts. "It is not my visions that pull me, Two Shadows. There is more. A part of me knows that I will never be satisfied until I visit this place of the white man. I must see for myself what I know awaits me."

She did not tell him of the dream that had come to her often over the past year. At first she had pondered the dream and its meaning. She had seen a golden-haired man with eyes the color of the greenest grass. In her deepest thoughts his smile had seemed to quicken her heart, and her inner being had become tranquil with his presence. But she still did not know why this dream had come to her while she slept. Was this man to come to her and change her life, or was she to go to the white man's land and seek him out? All she knew was that he had some strange hand in her destiny.

"I am afraid your wish will have to wait for a time. I go not to Sweet Oaks, but a few days' ride to a place where our father sends me to seek out information." Seeing her downcast look, he lifted her chin up with a finger. "But perhaps on my return I can talk our father and mother into letting you go for a few days to the plantation." But although he spoke the words, deep inside he doubted that they would come to pass. If, in fact, the braves' report to his father was correct, and there was an army fort so close to their village, he knew that he would not be able to leave his people even for the time it would take to escort Sky Eyes to his mother's plantation and allow her to see for herself that the white man's life was not what she truly desired. Two Shadows could not fathom why anyone would wish to trade the life they now lived for that of the white man.

Excitement raced through Sky Eyes's veins as easily as disappointment had a moment past. "You will ask them? As soon as you return from your trip, you will take me to Sweet Oaks?" She jumped to her feet and kissed her brother on the cheek. "I love you dearly, Two Shadows."

A dark shadow came over his silver eyes with her words. His sister and Summer Dawn had been close friends, and now he remembered the times when his wife had been filled with this same excitement, and had kissed him and spoken of her love for him.

Sky Eyes, always sensitive to another's mood, saw the pain that crossed her brother's face. "Come, let us hurry back. Mother will be wondering where I have gone, for she will need me to help her with dinner and she will wish to see you also, Two Shadows."

Two Shadows nodded his dark head and allowed himself to be pulled along behind his sister. "Have you not found a warrior among our tribe who has stirred your heart, little sister?" he asked as they neared their father's tepee.

Sky Eyes shook her long, glossy mane of dark hair in the negative. "No, my brother. There is none I would care to be joined with."

"But surely you could care for Night Rider or Yellow Hawk?" He named two of his own closest friends, knowing them to be strong and handsome warriors. He would be proud for his sister to choose either one of them.

"They have courted me as well as others, but I have not found the love in my heart that should exist between me and the brave I would choose." Once again, unbidden, the image of the golden-haired white man of her dreams came to her thoughts.

Two Shadows could well imagine the many young warriors who had come to his father's lodge in the

20

past years to court their chief's daughter. Not only for his sister's family rank and wealth would they have come seeking out Sky Eyes as a bride, but also for the young woman herself. She was beautiful, her heart generous and kind. She was always willing to work or to help others. "Perhaps Father should seek among the other tribes and see if he can find one worthy of you." He spoke in jest, but she took his words seriously.

Sky Eyes stopped in her tracks and looked at her twin. "Our father would not choose a mate for me. He wishes my happiness, and I will only find that with the man whom I will one day love. He would not seek out such a man for his only daughter."

Seeing the serious look on her face, Two Shadows reached out and lightly caressed her jawline. "I jest with you, little sister. I know well that our father would only wish your happiness."

A smile of relief came over her face as her brother grinned down at her. "Perhaps" he teased, "*I* should be the one to find the man who can fill your heart with this love that you desire."

Stamping her dainty foot in irritation, Sky Eyes glared at him. "I will find the one of my heart myself, without your help or any other's."

Two Shadows chuckled deeply and wrapped his arms around her. "The man that captures your heart, little sister, will be a lucky man indeed."

Knowing that he was only having fun with her, Sky Eyes nodded her head in agreement and followed him into the cool shelter of the lodge.

Dinner in the chief's lodge was a happy affair, with the family gathered around the large center fire. Star Hawk leaned against his backrest and let his dark eyes rest on each member of his family. It warmed his heart that they were all once again around him. Too often, of late, his son was missing from their family group. His wife smiled at him as she filled his bowl again with stew. "Do you wish your husband to grow fat, woman?" He grinned at her as he lifted the bowl up and spooned out a piece of the delicious meat.

"You will never grow fat, my husband." Her smile set his heart alight. "You look as you did the first time I laid eyes on you."

"You are a good wife, Silver Star. A man needs a woman who says the things he wishes to hear."

Two Shadows and Sky Eyes both grinned at their parents, happy to be near them and to share in the love that radiated from them.

"Your father tells me that you will leave again in the morning, Two Shadows. I had hoped you would stay in the village for a time. I have missed you around your father's lodge."

Two Shadows looked at his mother. She was still so very beautiful, he thought, as her silver eyes and golden hair glimmered in the firelight. Her creamy, smooth skin was such a contrast against the bronzed-skinned warrior sitting next to her.

"Yes, I leave with the sunrise, but we should be gone only a few days. When I return I promise that I shall not leave as often as in the past. I thought that with my return Sky Eyes and I might be able to go to Sweet Oaks for a few days."

With his words all eyes turned toward Star Hawk. The chief felt those around him awaiting an answer, and his eyes turned to his daughter. "We shall talk about such a trip when you return, Two Shadows."

Sky Eyes smiled at his reply, but as her eyes turned to her mother she glimpsed the concern in her face. She knew that there would be much discussion on this subject between her parents.

When the meal was finished, a call came for Sky Eyes from outside the lodge. The young girl recognized the masculine voice as that of Thunder Spirit, and she grimaced.

Star Hawk and Silver Star both smiled as they also recognized the voice. A nod in their daughter's direction excused her to go to speak to the young warrior waiting outside.

Slowly Sky Eyes made her way out of the lodge. Two Shadows also excused himself, for he knew he must find his friend, Night Rider, and make sure all the warriors would be ready to leave with the first light of morning.

Silver Star settled her small body next to that of her husband. "I hope Sky Eyes will find some favor with Thunder Spirit or one of the other braves of the tribe," she said lightly as she moved her husband's bowl away from him and her hand lightly rubbed his muscular arm.

"I have seen the way her eyes seek an escape when he comes around her," Star Hawk replied. "I think he shall not be the one to claim our daughter, my love."

"Perhaps you are right. I only wish she would

decide soon on the one she would join with. Her desire to go to the white man's world sits ill in my mind. Though they are my own people, I fear for my daughter in the midst of those who would not love her as we do."

Star Hawk bent and brushed a kiss on the soft lips before him. "I do not wish her to leave either, but we must allow her to seek out her own path. For myself, I found the greatest treasure in the white man's world." His large hand caressed the soft flesh of her cheek.

"We were meant to be together from the beginning of time, my husband." She cuddled against him, feeling alive under his masterful touch. "But our daughter is so young and innocent, and she does not know the ways of the white man, the evil that can lurk in his heart."

Star Hawk well remembered when he had first met this woman of his heart, Jessica Coltin, his Silver Star. It was true that there had been many evil men they had had to face and withstand. There had also been those who had become trustworthy friends. "Our daughter is wise, my love. She has learned much and has always seen easily into the hearts of those around her. I have much faith in our children."

"I do also, Star Hawk. It is only that I fear for them. There is so much that can hurt them." She thought of her son's great loss and the pain that was still reflected in his handsome features.

"We can but seek the Great Spirit and ask that he guide their steps, my sweet. It was he who brought you to me, and he has guided our paths from the first day we met. He will do no less for our children."

Silver Star sighed at his great understanding, feeling contentment and love in the shelter of his arms. All talk of children and problems halted as Star Hawk softly touched his lips to his wife's. The pair slowly lost all sense of worldly reality as they slipped into the world that was set aside only for them, their passions fired as in their youth, their hearts blending as Star Hawk gently lifted his wife into his arms and carried her to their soft sleeping couch.

Outside the lodge, Sky Eyes faced Thunder Spirit. "I have told you already, Thunder Spirit, that I do not wish to accept your gift." She handed back the finely worked headband that he had placed in her hands.

"I had thought that with the time I have stayed away from your father's lodge, you would have realized that you should become my woman." The large, broad-chested Indian brave spoke boldly, ignoring the hand that reached out to give the headband back to him. He had spent much time making the beaded leather piece, for he had wished to please this woman with his workmanship.

"I do not need time, Thunder Spirit. I have always known that I cannot join with you."

"Your words are foolish, Sky Eyes. You speak of a deep love in the heart. Do you not know that in time you will learn to feel that love? When you watch our children laughing and playing in my lodge, when you cook my food and lie on my sleeping couch, you will feel all that you seek." His dark eyes flashed with unclaimed passion as he watched her.

"I do not wish to *learn* feelings of love. I want to know them now, and I shall never know them with you, Thunder Spirit." She spoke strongly, hoping to deter him from his pursuit of her.

"You will know them from no other, Sky Eyes." The words were a soft caress on the night breeze, but sent a shudder down the Indian maiden's spine.

Slowly shaking her head, Sky Eyes backed away from him a step, feeling a menacing presence in his stance. Gaining courage from the fact that she stood before her father's lodge, she said firmly, "No." She started to turn around.

A strong hand took hold of her upper arm. "I go with your brother in the morning. Take this time to think of my offer. I will bring your father the horses I have captured and the furs I have been gathering. I have even gained one of the white man's rifles, which I will offer to your father for your bride price." As she shook her head to deny what he was saying, he added, "You will know no other as your mate. I have waited long enough, and when I return I will have your answer." With this he released her arm and strode away into the dark night.

Sky Eyes was left standing before the lodge, still holding the headband, her limbs shaking from the fear that always came up on her when she was in the presence of Thunder Spirit. She had put him off often in the past, but now she sensed a harsher side to the Indian brave, a side that would not take no for an answer. She reminded herself that her father was the only one who could force her to wed, and she tried to still her trembling.

She would give Thunder Spirit the same answer on his return. He would have to accept it, and then perhaps he would turn to another.

Chapter Two

The sparkling morning dew was still lingering on the tall grass when Two Shadows donned his white man's clothes. His midnight hair was pulled back tightly with a strip of leather and tucked beneath his shirt, his jacket collar pulled up so that none would notice the length. He set out slowly from the thick woods, leaving the group of warriors that had ridden with him for the past few days within the shelter of the tall pines to watch and await his return from the army fort.

They could easily see the fort that now stood sentinel over the tall prairie grass surrounding it. When the braves of the village had reported to their chief about this army fort, they had seen the blue-uniformed men building it. Now it stood completed, the thick, high walls surrounding the inner buildings as though to ward off any who would dare to intrude.

Two Shadows sighed aloud with mistrust and

worry over what these white men were about. There had only been few incidents in the past years between his village and the white men, but with the building of an army fort so close, he knew that the danger could be tremendous to his tribe's very existence.

Two Shadows's buckskin pony slowly made its way toward the fort. As they approached the gates, a shout rang out across the lookout, and a large man dressed in blue waved him forward.

There was much activity about the fort. Soldiers tended to their duty or stood about, and trappers roamed the area, a group of them gossiping in front of the mercantile and drinking the whiskey they had traded for their furs.

Before this group of men Two Shadows halted his horse, and with a glance they accepted him as one of their own.

Two Shadows dismounted and spoke to the group. "I've been trapping in these parts some years now, and this is the first time I have run into an army fort," he said.

"We're as surprised as any that we got these buildings and walls up as fast as we did." A soldier leaning against the mercantile responded first and several of the other men nodded in agreement.

"Yeah, with Major Thatcher standing over your backside, you don't get much chance to do anything else but work," another tall, slender man added.

"The man in charge of this fort is Major Thatcher?" asked Two Shadows. "Why would the army build a fort out here in this wilderness? There hasn't been any trouble with the Indians, has there? Has there been an uprising I haven't heard about? I have been so long up in the mountains, I don't know what year it is sometimes." Two Shadows grinned good-naturedly, winning the group's confidence.

"Naw, there ain't been no trouble yet." The tall, slender man spoke out again, and pushing a bony elbow into the ribs of the man closest to him, he added, "But that be only so far, hey, Johnny? I heard tell that our major enjoys nothing more than a morning's sport of hunting down some red savages before breakfast. I reckon that's the truth of the reason we're out here in this godforsaken wilderness. I hear there's supposed to be more reinforcements coming any day now."

Two Shadows listened intently to the talk around him, his silver eyes turning to flint at talk of the callousness of the man in charge of this fort. "I haven't heard any talk from the other trappers up in the mountains. I haven't heard of any Indians kicking up their heels lately. What tribe do you think he is after?"

The slender man was again the one to respond. Slowly shaking his head, he said, "I heard from old Bizzy the cook that he heard the corporal saying that some of them young bucks from the Blackfoot tribe of chief Star Hawk had been raising up some dust."

"Star Hawk?" Two Shadows repeated the name to see if anything else would be said about his people.

"Yeah, they say he's the most feared in this area."

One of the trappers, who was sipping from a bottle, spoke up. "I heard a tale some years back about two trappers." His light blue eyes focused on Two Shadows as though he were giving a warning to the younger man. "I was told that this chief Star

30

Hawk was a fierce one when he was a young buck, and some say he's even worse now that he's older. The story goes that he came upon these two trappers, alone in the woods, stripped them naked, staked them out, and cut them up real good. Then he left them there on the ground, staked and still screaming, for wolf bait. They say one of the trappers lived for a few minutes after some white men come upon them, and he told the story of bloodthirsty Star Hawk. Then he died." The trapper spat a stream of tobacco juice in the dust at his feet, his contempt for Indians obvious in his manner and speech.

Two Shadows did not respond. He had heard the full story of the two trappers, and how they had kidnapped his mother from his father's tribe and sold her to her ruthless cousin. Two Shadows felt that the trappers had deserved everything his father had given them.

"Yeah." The one called Johnny spoke up, "He's a bad one, this Star Hawk. And the way he holes himself up in them mountains and that valley of his, they claim he won't let anyone intrude on his lands. He thinks he's a king of some kind."

"I was told that his valley holds more gold than all of California," the old trapper grunted. "But as it is, I sure wouldn't be the one going in there and looking for it. No gold's worth getting your throat cut for."

Two Shadows had heard enough to satisfy himself of the intent of these men. What he needed now was to get a close look at this Major Thatcher, and then report back to his father. "Where is your major's office?" he asked a uniformed man who was sitting on a barrel.

"Near the end of them buildings over there." He nodded toward a group of wooden buildings that looked like officers' housing. "I 'spect he probably would be there at this time of the morning. His nephew came a-traipsing in here yesterday afternoon. They say he come all the way from London and I 'spect they be right, with his fancy duds and all."

Two Shadows nodded to the group before him, mounting his horse and kicking its sides. He did not linger in front of the mercantile. The trappers had told him all they knew; now he had to face the one in charge and see if he could find out anything else. It was only a short ride across the dirt yard. Tying his pony outside the first wooden building in the row of small houses, he knocked at the door.

"Come in!" came the loud shout from within.

Entering, Two Shadows looked around. The front room was set up as an office, with comfortable-looking chairs and a large oak desk. Another door led to another portion of the building that was probably used as living quarters.

The gray-haired older man behind the desk looked at the tall, dark stranger with keen eyes, taking in his fur jacket and traveling garb with a single glance. "What can I do for you?" he asked.

"My name is Heath Coltin," Two Shadows replied. "I trap out there in the mountains." He jerked his head in the direction of the tall, snow-capped mountains that reigned over the area.

"What is it you want?" the major asked, relaxing in his chair now that he knew the young man's name and was assured that he was really a trapper.

"I have been trapping in this area for some years

now, and this is the first fort in the area. Is there some trouble I should know about?"

"We are here to protect anyone who needs protection," the major replied. "You can stay here at the fort if you like. We can always use a good man. If you know that forest and the mountains well, perhaps you would like to scout for us. There would be a salary at the end of each month, and three meals a day."

The older man's eyes glinted with this thought. The fort would need good scouts when they went out on patrol. Thus far, all they had been able to hire were a few Crow Indians, and Benjamin Thatcher trusted no red man, be he Crow or Blackfoot.

"And what would I be scouting for? I haven't heard of any trouble lately with the Indians, and I can't see what else an army fort would be here for."

"You're right, Mr. Coltin. We would only be here to put down an Indian uprising."

Two Shadows felt his chest tighten. He listened as the major went on.

"There have been several incidents with a tribe of Blackfoot Indians. Their chief is called Star Hawk. If you've been in this area for a long time, you must have heard of his tribe." When Two Shadows nodded his head, the major added, "He's a savage and a bloody killer, and he's been threatening this area long enough. Washington wants peace at any cost, and that is why we are here."

"I can't say I have heard of Star Hawk's people causing any kind of problem lately." Two Shadows felt the full enormity of the situation now.

"Washington wants these lands opened up. Travel

33

time could be cut in half if settlers could pass through the valley that savage claims as his own. He's got his winter camp there now. And I am the one to see that he settles elsewhere."

"But their tribe has always settled in that valley during the winter. He will fight to the death to protect what he feels is his own." Two Shadows's anger was mounting by the second, and now he was giving fair warning to this gray-haired man who was going to try and force his people from their lands.

"And another thing," the major continued. "A rumor has reached my ears that this Star Hawk is keeping a white woman in his tribe. This is an outrage! The filthy savage holding one of our women!"

Two Shadows's anger became full blown as Benjamin Thatcher spoke of his mother and implied that she was being held against her will. He could have reached out and choked the life out of this self-righteous, inhuman army major, but as this thought went through his mind, the door to the next room was thrown open and a young man with wide shoulders and of towering height stepped into the front office.

The second the large, golden-haired man entered the room, Two Shadows was immobile, not believing his eyes.

As the young man looked at his uncle's guest, he also stood still for a moment. Then, when he regained his senses, a grin covered his handsome face. "Heath? Is it truly you?" As he started across the space between them he said, "I couldn't believe my eyes when I saw you standing there. What are you doing here at Fort Edwards? I remember you told me about your mother's plantation, and I thought I would soon try to find you. But I would never have expected to find you here in my uncle's office!"

Two Shadows clasped the young man's hand tightly in his own, remembering well how this man had been his friend when he had needed one so badly at school in London. But now he was feeling a need for caution. Nicholas Prescott was one of the few white people who knew of Two Shadows's true identity. "It is good to see you, Nick. I have been out trapping and stumbled upon the fort." He tried to discern, in a single glance, if this man before him was still his friend. It had been some years since they had roamed the streets of London together.

"Well, I'll be double damned!" Nicholas threw a large arm around Two Shadows's shoulders. "One of the main reasons for my coming to America, besides visiting my uncle Benjamin here, was the hope that I would run into you, old friend. I have missed those good times we shared."

"You know this man?" The major's voice broke into the happy reunion.

"Aye, uncle. Heath and I went to school together. Those were some great times." He turned toward Two Shadows once again. "Remember when we went to Madam Charlotte's house? I swear I thought that old man you lived with was going to skin us alive when he caught us coming down the back stairs the next morning."

Two Shadows chuckled at the remembrance of that morning, and the preceding evening spent in the arms of a lusty-red-haired vixen. "I thought Ollie would send me home for sure over that one." He grinned.

35

The major sat back down behind his desk. Waving his hand, he dismissed the pair. "I have plenty to do today. Tomorrow afternoon more men should be arriving, and I must see that all is made ready. It looks as if the two of you have much to catch up on."

"Thank you, Uncle. Heath and I will go out into the compound and stay out of the way." Nicholas started toward the door with Two Shadows on his heels.

As they stepped away from the major's office and out into the dirt yard of the fort, Nicholas was quick to come to the point. "Do you remember, old friend, the times when you talked of your people, and how you asked me to visit you when I could?"

"We were younger then, Nick." Two Shadows spoke truthfully. Now that they were alone, he had to find out if his friend was going to give him away. "I was in a country that was strange to me and you were the only one I could trust, besides Ollie."

"So are you saying that things are different now? I thought we were friends and would remain so forever." The green eyes looked deeply into Two Shadows's silver ones.

"What is it that you wish, friend?" Two Shadows slowly nodded his head, admitting that the time that had passed had not altered the friendship he felt for this man.

"I will speak truthfully to you, Heath." Nicholas swallowed hard, as though bracing himself, before he went on. "There are people who are concerned over what is going on here. They wish to know the mood of your people, and they wish to make sure that something unnecessary does not happen at this fort."

Two Shadows was taken aback for a moment as he looked intently at this young man. "Who are these people you speak of?" he softly inquired. "Why would what happens here in this wilderness concern you or these people you speak of?"

"There are men in Washington, regardless of what everyone else thinks, who are truly concerned about the plight of the Indian, and wish for things to remain on a peaceful basis. Senator Willis is one of those I speak of. He and a group of his friends have been working hard to protect the rights of the Indians. There has been too much bloodshed already between the white man and other Indian tribes. So far, your people have remained quietly out of the way, but with this fort so close to your hills, Senator Willis suspects foul play. There are white men in power who have the wealth to manipulate things to their own liking and their own gain. And if they wish to open the Blackfoot lands they will stop at nothing."

"All my people want is to be left in peace."

"I know this, and that is why I have come here. Senator Willis has asked me to watch and to report back to him. He hopes he will be able to stop anything bad from happening with the information I can bring to him. I have already found out all I can here at Fort Edwards. My uncle does not suspect me. He thinks I am just a bored, rich relative, looking for adventure. And I have allowed him to think along these lines. He has spoken openly to me about you Indians, and I am afraid that with his hate and distrust for your people, the situation could easily become serious here."

"I, myself, have come to find out why the army would build this fort here. I also believe that your uncle is the wrong man to be in charge here, if it is peace that the white man desires. What is it that you wish of me?" Two Shadows was still wary. Things seemed to be happening much too quickly, but if there was a chance that this friend could help his people, he could not walk away from it.

"I want to go to your village with you." As Nicholas saw the frown settle on Two Shadows's features, he added, "I will keep to myself; none need know why I am there. I just want to get information for the senator as soon as I can. Perhaps with some luck he will be able to stop anything from happening."

"I will have to tell my father," Two Shadows said. He would not hide from his father what he had heard, for upon it could depend the survival of his people.

"That is fine, for I wish also to talk to Star Hawk. He will understand that Senator Willis and I want peace, and that there are those who wish no more blood to be spilled between the Indian and the white man. You can tell him all and let him decide if I can stay for a time among your people. There is a rumor that several of the Cheyenne tribes are banding together, and Senator Willis needs to know the feelings of the Blackfoot nation. A lot of foolish men in Washington would do anything for their own gain and not reflect on all the lives they could affect."

Two Shadows slowly nodded his dark head. "I will leave shortly. A small group of warriors waits for me in the forest on the edge of the prairie."

Nicholas grinned widely, and slapped Two

38

Shadows on the back. "This will be just as I imagined when we were younger and you told me all the stories of your people. I won't be long. I'll tell my uncle that I am going trapping with you, and gather my things. He will probably be relieved at my going. It will mean less worry about me and more time to worry about this fort."

Two Shadows waited by his pony for his old friend and wondered if he was making the right decision. There had been few white men in his village, and those who had been allowed to spend time in their tribe had remained only a short time and then hurriedly gone on their way. How would his father and his people treat Nicholas Prescott? Would his father believe his words, or would he read evil into their meaning? Perhaps evil that Two Shadows was unable to discern? What if Nick was in truth an enemy, as was his uncle, and only wished to get into the Blackfoot village to learn of its strategic points? Though they had been good friends, that had been five years ago. A lot could have happened in that time to change a man. Two Shadows promised himself that he would watch his old friend very carefully. If Prescott's heart carried evil within it, he would sooner or later show his intent.

Less than an hour later, the two rode slowly out of the fort's front gates. Two Shadows quietly studied his friend and listened to all he told him of London, and how he had met Senator Willis and had quickly formed a strong friendship.

"I remember you always speaking of your family home with such fondness. I would have thought you would have stayed there and lived a peaceful life,"

Two Shadows said as they neared the forest where his warriors were awaiting him.

Nicholas grinned widely. "I admit that I thought the same thing. If it were not for Senator Willis, I would still be at Rosebriar. But there comes a time in a man's life when he must fight for something. All the images you evoked in my mind, of your life here in the forest, never truly left me. When Senator Willis told me of the fight that faced those of your kind, I could not sit before my great hearth with my feet propped up on a satin stool and act as though all was well."

"If you speak the truth, you are a true friend."

"There have been plenty of times, I must admit, when I have longed for Rosebriar," Nicholas said. "I am afraid that I am at heart a gentleman, used to the comforts of my home and family."

"I am glad I came to the fort when I did and found you again. I also think often of those days in London and the closeness we shared."

It was some surprise to Nicholas that as they entered the forest they were swiftly surrounded by a group of fierce-looking Indian braves. Their faces were painted with war paint, and their bodies glistened, naked and bronzed. They brandished their weapons threateningly as though at a given signal they would set upon the white stranger riding with their chief's son.

With a call, Two Shadows halted the warriors' intent. "This is an old friend from the days when I lived with the white man across the mighty waters. He is called Nick Prescott. He is coming with us to our village to speak with my father."

Several scowled darkly at the white man, but none would dare to question Two Shadows's authority. He had proven himself strong and wise. It was Night Rider, though, who sidled up to Two Shadows and softly said, "Do you think this wise, with the white man's fort so close by? Would it not be better to keep the white man far away from our village?"

Two Shadows smiled at his friend. "I had these same thoughts, for the years have been long since I last saw this friend. But I am sure that his heart is true, and he wishes to help our people." Though Two Shadows stated this for all to hear, he still warned himself to use caution where Nicholas was concerned.

Night Rider did not argue. Whatever Two Shadows decided, he would back him all the way. He and Two Shadows had been as brothers as they grew up, and since the death of his wife, Summer Dawn, Two Shadows had drawn closer to him. They were blood brothers, and Night Rider trusted his feelings as he would his own.

Dismounting from his horse, Two Shadows quickly pulled off the white man's garb and once again donned the breechcloth and leather leggings of his people. His long hair hung down and swiftly he braided two long strands at each side of his face with white eagle feathers hanging from the leather band about his forehead on either side.

Nicholas looked at his friend with incredulity, not believing the transformation that had taken place. Now Heath Coltin indeed looked like the Indian called Two Shadows, only his light silver gaze showing his white blood. With a loud laugh Nick pulled off his jacket and tied it to his mount's rump. "I feel somewhat overdressed compared to the rest of you."

Two Shadows grinned. "Do not worry. If you decide that you wish to become one with us, I have similar clothes that you can wear." He was joking, but something in the green eyes looking at him held him at his word.

The first two days were uneventful, as the small band moved quickly through the forest; but late the second evening, one of the scouts reported to Two Shadows that a band of Crow warriors was camped ahead of them, a few miles down the river.

The dark glaze of hatred that filled Two Shadows's eyes was not lost on Nick as they sat around the small campfire, where they had been talking of old times. His friend suddenly turned into a hate-filled savage before Nicholas's very eyes, and began to give out orders and to throw dirt on the fire. Nicholas rose. "What can I do? Tell me, Two Shadows."

"We will do nothing until the first break of sunlight. You can stay here at this camp, and I shall send one of the scouts back to you when we have finished."

Nicholas quickly understood what was going to take place: the Crow were the enemy and they intended to attack them. "No. I came along and wish to be one with you as you were with me in London. Who knows, there could be a good story in this to tell my grandchildren one day."

Two Shadows's heated gaze rested on his friend, and then slowly a small smile broke his hate-filled features. "It has been a long time, Nick. If you desire to ride with me and my braves, see that you keep to the back. I would not wish to have to tell your uncle that you were killed at the hands of an Indian."

A burst of laughter filled the small clearing. "I can see my uncle's face now with such news. He would have the very excuse he is looking for. Do not worry, friend. I will be careful."

Before daylight the group of warriors readied themselves and quietly slipped through the forest. Their mounts were trained to step quietly and not make a noise that could give them away.

The band of Crow had only just awakened, and were starting to stir about when the first war cry of the Blackfoot filled the area.

It all seemed to happen so quickly that Nicholas was caught up in the heat of the moment. His arm struck out at a large Indian who threw himself at him and tumbled him from his horse. Automatically Nicholas drove the knife Two Shadows had given him into the Indian's chest, for the fierce-looking features above him held only hate and death.

There were more than a dozen of the Crow and only six Blackfoot—seven, including Nick—but with the art of surprise and strength against them it was soon evident that the Crow were outmanned and overcome. Two of the enemy, seeing the defeat of the others, ran into the forest as they saw everyone around them fall in death.

With some surprise, Nicholas watched as a small-framed warrior with long hair hanging down his back and over his face fought on against the odds. First one of Two Shadows's braves, and then another, attacked him from each side, and still the smaller warrior fought on, teeth bared and knife held high and threateningly. As Nick stood to the side and watched, something in the warrior's manner struck him. My God, he thought, it is a woman! As quickly as his feet could get him across the clearing, he ran toward the group of Blackfoot warriors as they circled their enemy. He shouted out for them to stop, and his hand reached out to stay one from plunging his knife into the lone opponent's heart. He pulled his arm back and found it cut down its length. With stunned amazement he watched the woman turn and jump on one of Two Shadows's braves, her teeth biting deeply and spitting out blood, her arm raised, with the steel of her knife glistening brightly as she would have brought it down into the warrior's heart.

It was Two Shadows who finally turned and realized that the one his braves were attacking was a woman. With quick strides he was at the side of the warrior she was pummeling, and with a stroke he knocked the woman senseless with a hard blow to the side of her head.

All stood around the one that had fought so long and so hard, disbelief on their faces as they looked at the small form dressed in a breechcloth, leather leggings, and a leather, fur-lined vest, tied together with thin strips of rawhide. Her long midnight hair hung down her body.

"Put her on my horse," Two Shadows ordered quickly, as he looked at the bodies of those he had defeated, his hate for the Crow still filling his heart.

As Nicholas looked around at the destruction of the camp, he started toward his own horse, wrapping his handkerchief around his bleeding arm. A tall, formidable-looking brave approached him. "Never come between my blade and my enemy again, white man. The next time, my knife shall find your heart."

It was Thunder Spirit who spat out the words, and as he walked away, Nicholas again warned himself to beware of the young brave. He had already learned in the past two days that some of Two Shadows's group were not pleased with his being among them. The looks of hate that had pierced him often came from Thunder Spirit, and had shown that he would be the first, if given the signal, to jump on the white man.

Two Shadows's band of warriors left the area quickly and started again on the trek toward their village. Their captive was still unconscious on the rump of their leader's buckskin pony.

Scowling darkly, Two Shadows wondered what he was going to do with this enemy woman. It was not unusual for members of his tribe to take the enemy as their slaves, but as he remembered how the small, fierce-looking warrior woman had brandished her knife, he wondered at the folly of his actions.

Perhaps he would free her into the forest when she came to her senses, he thought. It was plain that she would never be one to be trusted, and he would feel responsible if she were to harm any member of his tribe.

It was not until late in the day, when Two Shadows had halted his band near the river's edge to rest and water their horses, that the woman on the back of his horse roused herself, slowly coming to her senses and

45

taking in her situation.

As Two Shadows lowered his large frame from the back of his mount, he pulled his captive to the ground. Standing over her, he watched her shake her head to clear her thoughts. With this movement she winced from the pain of the bluish bruise along the side of her cheek, where Two Shadows had struck her to overpower her.

Her dark, piercing eyes slowly rose to meet those of cool silver. In their depths was a hatred and cunning equal to that of Two Shadows.

When she did not move, Two Shadows bent toward her and spoke in the Blackfoot tongue. "What is your name?"

When she did not respond, he reasoned that she did not understand the Blackfoot language, so he proceeded to use sign language. Pointing to himself he slowly pronounced his name, and pointing to her, he raised his eyebrows questioningly.

This did not work, though. For all his patience in trying to speak with her, she only glared at him with dark, hate-filled vengeance.

The rest of the group of warriors tended their mounts and quietly watched their leader with the beautiful young captive.

Feeling his patience beginning to diminish, Two Shadows reached out to grasp the woman's forearms and pull her to her feet. But as he touched her, he was pulled up short as she jerked from his grasp and jumped to her feet, ready to defend herself, her breasts heaving with her fear of the moment, her hands curled into fists, and her small, white, perfect teeth clenched together.

For a moment Two Shadows looked at his beautiful prisoner. For the first time he noticed her rare beauty, her womanliness now plainly apparent even though she stood ready to defend herself. For an instant, something deep in his chest quickened, a spark that had been lying dormant these past two years. But as quickly he saw her as the enemy, one of the same blood that had taken his wife and child from his arms. As a deep rage beset him, Two Shadows boldly stepped toward the woman and, with a low growl, he pulled her up tightly against his chest, wanting to prove his mastery over her.

With a small squeal of fear, the warrior woman began to strike out against her attacker, her fists pummeling his jaw. With his grunt of pain, her attack increased, her small hands hitting against his chest and upper body, her legs kicking out, and more often than not, striking their object.

Holding onto his quarry as he would hold a fighting wildcat, Two Shadows felt her fist on his jaw and then her moccasined foot hitting his shin time and again, her slim body pulling and wriggling in his grasp and all but winning her release. And as Two Shadows heard the soft laughter of those in his band, he felt his anger mount again. With a strong hand holding one of her arms, he reached with the other and grabbed a handful of her lustrous black hair. Pulling her head up closely to his own, he gave a small jerk that stilled her movements. "That is enough!" he hissed between clenched teeth. But in return the woman's dark eyes glared out her own hate, and on impulse she spat into his face.

Picking her up with ease, Two Shadows turned and

47

let her fall into the river. She splashed and sputtered, out of breath from her exertions, now drenched and gasping. Two Shadows stood over her, his face an angry mask as he spoke in a hard, unyielding voice. "*Never* again dare to spit on me or strike me! For the next time you shall not get off so lightly!"

His meaning was clear to all. Even the woman knew that to dare such a thing again would mean a beating. With the loud, harsh laughter in her ears of the group now standing on the river's edge looking at her wet beauty, the warrior woman felt her face begin to flame. Slowly, she lowered her head.

Sensing her shame, Two Shadows stepped out of the cool water. Without a backward glance at the woman he began to tend his horse. Taking up handfuls of grass he began to rub him down.

"What do you intend to do with her?" Nicholas stepped to Two Shadows's side. Glancing from the woman still sitting in the water to his friend, he wondered why Two Shadows would bother with the girl.

At first Two Shadows did not reply as he tried to regain control over the emotions that had assaulted him. Working with horses had always eased his raging spirits, but now even this job did not seem to calm him. Something about this small spitfire of a woman overrode all his reasonable emotions.

"Why do you not just let her go, Heath? I am sure she will be able to find some of her tribe." Nicholas could easily see how this woman was affecting his friend, and he wished to offer some help.

This was exactly what Two Shadows had intended to do with the woman earlier; but now, hearing the words, he could not set the act into motion. As his hands stilled and he turned to face his friend, Thunder Spirit approached the two.

"I would take this woman that so insults you, Two Shadows. She is worthless and will be hard to manage, but I would have her for my lodge. I will soon take a wife." He left out the fact that the one he desired as his mate was this tall warrior's sister. "I would have this woman as my slave to tend my lodge and to make things easier on my wife."

Two Shadows did not answer right away. He looked carefully at Thunder Spirit. He had ridden with Two Shadows on many raids and hunts, but his hard ruthlessness had prevented a close friendship between the two. Two Shadows had seen a cruelty in Thunder Spirit as he had dealt with his enemies and had heard rumors throughout the village of his heavy hand with women. Slowly he shook his head, and his silver eyes looked back to the river. He watched as the woman began to pull herself from the water, her hands reaching up and wringing the water from her long hair. That Thunder Spirit would soon quench this woman's bold spirit, there was no doubt in his mind. But this thought gave Two Shadows no pleasure as he allowed his gaze to roam over her perfect form, which now was plainly revealed through her dampened vest and breechcloth. "The woman is mine," he answered finally.

Thunder Spirit also looked at the woman, and his heated look saw all that Two Shadows saw. With a lustful heat growing in his loins, he ventured, "I would offer you two of my prized horses for the woman. She is not worth even this much." His mind filled with visions of this woman on his pallet at night. He would use her until he could claim Sky Eyes, and then he would give her to his wife as her slave. Perhaps he would even still bed her after his joining with his chief's daughter. There were many in his village who did the same.

"I will not trade her. She is mine!" Two Shadows directed his gaze full on the other warrior. "Do not question me further." He turned back to his horse and finished rubbing him down.

For a moment Thunder Spirit thought of offering more, but Two Shadows's back was now given to him, and as he looked at the white man at his side, he scowled darkly and strode back to the group of braves where they sat eating dried venison.

"I am glad you refused him, Two Shadows. There is something about that one that does ill with me. But are you sure you wish to keep the girl?" To Nicholas, it appeared that the easiest way out of the situation would be to free this woman and finish with her.

"She is my enemy. She will be my slave." Two Shadows turned toward his friend, having heard enough on the subject of the girl. He threw down the grass in his hands. "You had best get yourself something to eat, for we soon ride again. There are still a few hours before dark."

Knowing when he was dismissed, Nicholas left Two Shadows to his brooding thoughts and sought out his meal.

A short time later the group mounted their horses and started through the forest once again. Two Shadows was in the lead, with the warrior woman behind him on his buckskin pony. With her warm body pressed tightly to his back, her full breasts pushing against him and her slim legs bent and molded to his own, Two Shadows moaned inwardly. Was it foolishness to keep her for himself? Perhaps he should have freed her or traded her to Thunder Spirit; but with such thoughts his heart seemed to skip a beat. Something about this willful woman pulled at his soul. Her beauty was obvious to all, but her inner strength and her fearless stance in the face of her enemy touched off some pleasure deep within him. She was like no other he had ever seen. Other women in his past had been soft and giving, like his Summer Dawn. This woman was as fierce as any warrior he had stood before, backing down to none. Perhaps this alone was the attraction, for since Summer Dawn no woman had come near to piercing the hard covering around his heart. No other's sweet words and swaying hips had penetrated his mind. But this woman, with her warrior's dress and fighting ways, had sparked something deep within him. But with tight control, he forced these thoughts from his mind. She was the enemy and he was her master. He would make her pay, and pay dearly, for her very presence near him. She would receive little more from him than was her due.

Chapter Three

The Blackfoot village was teeming with activity when Two Shadows and his band of warriors rode into the midst of the shouting children. Men and women stepped out of their tepees when they heard the shouts that the band was approaching.

The villagers noticed the large, golden-haired white man who rode at Two Shadows's side, then the Crow Indian woman, wearing a warrior's clothing and clutching the waist of their chief's son as she sat on the back of his horse. The shouts and murmurings increased.

Nicholas watched all this with mounting excitement. He had tried to envision all Two Shadows had told him about his people and his way of life, but nothing had prepared him for what was before him. Tepees of various sizes, colorfully decorated, were set out in a large circle on the bank of the river that ran through the valley, and all faced each other. The men, women, and children had features much like those of Two Shadows—bronze skin and long, shiny black hair. Their clothing, of bleached deer hides and moccasins, was also a variety of colors, depicting the status of the wearer in the village. Dogs were barking and the smaller children chased after the heels of the warriors' horses as they rode through camp.

The woman on the back of Two Shadows's buck-skin pony did not share Nicholas's wonderment. She saw around her only her enemies, the fearless Black-foot. There was no joy or excitement in her heart. She had been taught the ways of the Crow warriors: how to fight and shoot a bow with pride and accuracy in order to protect her village from attack and invasion. Now all she had to look forward to was the shame of being a prisoner. And her deepest shame lay in her feelings about this man before her.

The night before she had been forced to lie upon his sleeping pallet with him, the heat of his large body, the very beating of his heart filling her senses and leaving her trembling with fear. It was a fear that she had never known before, but thus far she had to admit that it had been unfounded. Besides throwing her in the river after she had spat on him, Two Shadows's punishment had been small compared to what many others would mete out to an enemy. He had not touched her, but had only forced her to share his sleeping mat and to ride behind him. But she was not foolish enough to believe that this would last for long. She had pretended not to understand the tongue of her abductor, but in truth his words had come into her mind as if through a fog. Somehow she knew his tongue, remembered it from another time, long ago in her past. She had heard the others talking among themselves about how one of the braves in Two Shadows's band had offered to buy her from her captor, and she had heard how he had refused, claiming that she was his and would be his slave. She, Kalina of the Crow tribe, would become the lowest woman, having no rights and used by this man as he desired. A single tear escaped her eye and, taking her hand from around Two Shadows's waist, she dashed it away with a swift movement, forcing herself to conceal her fear and shame. When Two Shadows glanced back at her, she glared. She would never let her inner emotions be seen by this cold, heartless man who now laid claim to her.

Two Shadows halted his horse before the largest of the tepees. A large man with features similar to his own stepped out, and Two Shadows greeted him with warmth. "It is good to see you, Father. I have returned with a friend and a captive." As he said this he looked first at Nicholas and then at the woman behind him.

Star Hawk did not speak, but nodded his head, his dark piercing eyes looking upon the golden-haired, formidable man with the eyes of the clearest green, and then on the woman sitting astride his son's horse. His eyes rested a moment as he studied her beauty and her strange clothing. There would be a very interesting story here, he thought, noticing at once that her headband was of Crow design.

"I will take my friend and this woman to my lodge and then I will return to you. There is much I have learned, and Nick also wishes to speak with you."

Again, only the nodding of the regal head indicated that the chief had heard his son. Without another word, Two Shadows kicked his pony and started toward the outer circle of the village.

Two Shadows's lodge was near the river, and had once been the lodge of the old healing woman, Cloud Dreamer, who had taken his mother in as her own daughter when Star Hawk had first brought Jessica Coltin to his village. Before the old healing woman died, she had told the shaman of their tribe that she did not wish her lodge to be destroyed, as was the tribal custom; but instead she wanted it to be left, as she had kept it, for the son of Silver Star. This wish had been observed, for the healing woman had been revered in their village. Though Two Shadows had shared another lodge with his wife, Summer Dawn, and after her death had spent most of his nights in his father's lodge, many times he had stayed here in Cloud Dreamer's tepee. He seemed to draw strength from her possessions, as though they held a mystical power to lend him inner wisdom. And it was to this lodge that he took his friend and the woman who had affected him so strongly from the moment he had first set eyes upon her.

"The lodge fire has not been lit in some time," he said as he dismounted. He reached up to help the woman from the back of his pony, but as his hands went to circle her small waist to help her to the ground, Kalina jumped from the pony and away from his hands.

Two Shadows sighed aloud, turned his back as though ignoring the woman, and waited for Nicholas by the entrance flap of the tepee.

Nicholas observed what went on with this strange Indian woman and his friend. The warrior woman

55

was strong willed and fiercely independent. He had no doubt that she would flee the first moment that Two Shadows was not about, and, thought Nicholas, this would be for the best. Over the past day he had observed the woman closely, and to him she was as wild as the forest about them, as untamable as any animal of the woods. Who could capture and hold such a spirit, without breaking it forever? And there was something else he had noticed—a look deep in her dark eyes that he had glimpsed at unguarded moments. That look told of past sadness, and a desire to love and be loved. Would it be fair for any man, even this friend of his youth, to take and break such a one as this? Her spirit reminded him of a story his mother had told him when he was a lad, about a gentle wood nymph who had been captured and locked away in the body of a ravaging beast. As he entered the lodge and looked at the girl standing across from him, he could only hope that the outcome of her life would be as happy as that of the heroine of his story; for she had been loved by one who could see through the beast, and had freed her spirit. Would that be the outcome for this warrior woman? he wondered.

The lodge was dark and cool inside, and quickly Two Shadows set about starting a fire with the small supply of wood that was stacked in a corner. "There is a pouch for water over there." He nodded his head toward several clay pots and a hide pouch on the opposite side of the lodge.

Kalina paid no attention to what Two Shadows said, and stood as though uninterested in what was taking place around her. Suddenly Two Shadows was standing before her and placing a light hold upon her arm. Her dark eyes now were forced to pay attention to this tall, bronzed man towering over her.

Two Shadows pulled her along with him to the water pouch. Picking it up, he handed it to her, and using sign language he instructed her to go to the river and get water. "I will have my mother and sister bring some food for this evening's meal. After that, you will see to the meals in this lodge." He said the words sharply, showing his irritation at not getting through to her.

Pulling her arm away from Two Shadows's grip, Kalina started sullenly toward the entrance flap. She had, of course, seen the river when they had ridden to the lodge, and she thought now that going to the river would give her a chance to escape.

When she had gone Nicholas looked at his friend, noticing Two Shadows's anger. "You still think it wise not to let her go back to her own people?"

Two Shadows sighed wearily. "Perhaps you were right, my friend; but what is done is done. She will serve me as my slave. I admit that she already tries my patience, but with time she will learn."

"Do not fool yourself, Two Shadows. She is not the kind to bend easily. I guarantee that right this moment your little girl is out there scouting about for a way to flee from you."

"I would expect little more. I would do the same in her place. But she will do nothing this day. She knows that the whole village is watching with curiosity, and that if she were to make a move away from the village, I would be called and I would have her back within moments." However, although Two

57

Shadows spoke with much confidence, he finished with the fire hurriedly. Then, going to the entrance flap, he told Nicholas to make himself comfortable, for he had to go and speak with his father. But first he went to the river and sought after his captive.

He spied her bending down at the bank of the river, filling the water pouch, her eyes not watching what she was doing but looking up and down the embankment of the river. Two Shadows knew what was in her mind. Nicholas had been right; she would try to make an escape and return to her people at the first chance she gained. And with this thought, Two Shadows felt a swift pang of posessiveness. This woman belonged to him now. She was his slave, and he would make sure that she stayed under his care. Going to her side, Two Shadows stood behind her quietly and, as she rose, took the pouch of water from her hands. "You will never escape from me, for I will track you down and always bring you back." His words were spoken more to himself than to the girl, but his meaning was not lost on Kalina.

She had, indeed, thought of nothing else but escaping. She had thought that perhaps with the darkness of night she would be able to slip out and make her way through the forest to some of her own tribe. But when she heard his heated tone of voice, she had second thoughts. She would have to plan carefully for her escape, for there was no doubt this man would not allow one of his possessions to slip away from him without a fight.

For a few moments the pair stared into each other's eyes, each taking full measure of the other. Then, as Kalina could stand no more, she lowered her head from those piercing shards of glimmering silver.

Two Shadows pointed back toward his lodge and spoke softly. "Go back to the lodge and stay there until I return. I go to my father, and will have my sister bring you clothing to cover yourself." Again he felt the strange heat coursing through his body as he let his eyes roam over her barely covered breasts and across the breechcloth that covered only a small area of her lower body.

As his eyes rose back to her face, Two Shadows saw the dark eyes clouded with anger, as Kalina responded with her own burning fury. He would have his sister bring her clothing indeed! And what was wrong with what she wore now? She dressed like this in her own village and when she went on a raid with the warriors of her tribe. Her clothing was like a man's, unrestricted, so that she could hunt and protect herself without constraint. Pointed Arrow had raised her along with his own two sons, and he had made little mention of her sex. He had taught her the arts of defense and hunting, and he always allowed her to dress as she pleased. Everyone in her village had respected her strength and valor, and none had dared to insult her as this man did now.

As Two Shadows handed her back the water pouch, she let it slip from her hand to her feet, where the contents spilled upon the earth. Her glare was still directed at him, a fire of black ice.

Again Two Shadows felt his rage come boiling to the surface. Was her only intent to make him furious? Pointing down to the water pouch, he harshly spoke. "Pick it up and refill it!" He kept his finger pointed to the pouch so that she could not misunderstand his meaning.

With a quick negative shake of her head, Kalina stood her ground, her teeth clenched, though her body was trembling with rage and fear.

Grabbing hold of the pouch and taking her by the wrist, Two Shadows dragged her back to the water. Pulling her down, he bent over her, trying to force her to refill the pouch. His insistence on punishing her was of no avail, however, for he was boldly pressed against her backside and could smell the sweet, musky-flower scent of her long hair. With a curse at his body's inability to keep his response to this woman under control, and at his anger with her for forcing him to berate her in this manner, Two Shadows released her and rose to his feet. "Get back to my lodge!" he shouted, before turning his back upon her and starting through the village to his father's tepee.

Kalina, too, rose, and watched his straight back as he walked away from her, her thoughts confused as she wondered at his manner. She had refused him, and he had simply forced her to do as he wished. She had spat upon him, and he had merely dumped her into the river. Her own father would have beat her for her disobedience and disrespect, but this man, her abductor and captor, had not laid a hand upon her in anger. Slowly she bent back down and refilled the pouch, shaking her head as she started back to the lodge. There was much for her to think upon. She felt several pairs of enemy eyes upon her, and she straightened her backbone. She would soon flee this place and be away from the madness this tall silver-eyed warrior wished to inflict upon her. Kalina was not one to take orders or endure the cruelties of another for long.

Two Shadows walked through the entrance flap of his father's lodge and was greeted with a warm smile from his mother. He kissed her lovingly on the cheek, his large hand lightly caressing her copper curls.

"It is good that you are home again, my son." Silver Star smiled and thought to herself how much this young man was like his father—so loving and warm to those who were close to his heart. "I have prepared the evening meal and have plenty to send to your lodge." Star Hawk had already told her that Two Shadows had brought a white man back to the village, and a woman from a Crow tribe. Neither she nor her husband questioned her son, knowing that in his own time he would tell them all.

"Thank you, Mother." Looking about, he asked, "Where is Sky Eyes? I would have her bring the meal, and one of her dresses for my slave." He also had hopes that perhaps she, with her kindness, would be able to form some kind of friendship with his captive, for it was wearing on his nerves that the girl fought him at every hand. Perhaps if nothing else Sky Eyes would be able to teach her their language.

Both Silver Star and Star Hawk looked at their son with wonder. Never before had he brought a woman to their village. Neither Star Hawk nor his son had ever forced another into servitude.

"Your sister sits with the daughter of Falling Leaves. I have been there the day through, for the child has a high fever. I have only come to your father's lodge to prepare the meal, and then I shall return to tend the child. I shall have Sky Eyes come

61

to you as soon as I relieve her."

Two Shadows thanked his mother, and was soon sitting at the pit fire next to his father, telling him all he had learned at the white man's fort. "We must prepare for an attack, for the white major hates Indians, and he also spoke angrily of a white woman being in our village." Two Shadows said this aloud only after his mother had left the lodge.

As Star Hawk leaned against his backrest and listened quietly to his son, he let out a large sigh. "The time has come that my father spoke of often in the past. He warned of the white man coming upon our lands and trying to force us from what we now claim. The Great Spirit gave visions of the day when the white man would cover our lands like the number of a mighty buffalo herd. I will think on your words and prepare for what shall come. The full moon approaches and the young braves talk of preparing for the sacred sun-dance ceremony. This will strengthen our village and give us victory."

"I wish to participate in the ceremony," Two Shadows said. "It seems as though a lifetime has passed since I hung upon the sun-dance pole. I also seek the wisdom of the Great Spirit and I have thought upon this and wish to join the others."

"You must seek out the shaman, then, and let him guide you with this undertaking. When you were younger you sought out the Great Spirit for strength and endurance to face the enemy. You have been a brave and mighty warrior for our village. Now you are older and you must call out to the Great Spirit and the fathers of days long past to lead you, to guide you in the right steps, for you will one day lead the people as I do now." As Star Hawk thought about this, he realized that it would be good for Two Shadows to participate in the ceremony. He agreed with his son that much time had passed since he had borne the wounds upon his chest in the sun-dance ceremony. He had already gone through much in his young years, suffering a great loss and having his life filled with so much hate and vengeance. Perhaps the Great Spirit would help him cleanse his soul of anger and need for revenge upon those who had brought about such destruction in his life.

Next Two Shadows broached the subject of Nicholas Prescott. He had told his family of the young man who had befriended him while he was away at school, and now he told his father the true reason for Nicholas being here amongst them.

Star Hawk listened patiently to what his son had to say, asking questions often and also seeking Two Shadows's own thoughts upon the trustworthiness of his friend.

Two Shadows answered truthfully, not leaving out his doubts about Nicholas being here in their village. But he also spoke of what he knew of the white man's heart.

"I will talk with this white man soon," Star Hawk pronounced, "but with the morning light I will take several braves and go to the other tribes and speak to them of what you have learned. We will need the united strength of our nation to defeat this enemy, and I would have those that are our friends join with us."

Seeing the wisdom in this, Two Shadows nodded his head in full agreement. "I will not go with you on this mission. I will stay in the village and see that my friend is what he claims."

"Is it the white man or your new slave that keeps you here, my son?" Star Hawk asked, at last bringing the woman into their conversation.

"The braves I rode with call the woman 'warrior woman.' " At Star Hawk's raised brow, he continued. "We came upon a band of Crow warriors and attacked them. She was the only one left standing when the battle was over. She fought as any brave, she wore the clothing of a warrior, and her strength is equal to that of any brave that I have known."

"And you would keep such a one as your *slave*?" Star Hawk saw little wisdom in such a decision.

"At first I thought to set her free and allow her to return to her own tribe. But I cannot. Each time I am near her she sets my anger on fire. I cannot free her."

Two Shadows had spoken softly, his silver eyes gazing into the lodge fire as though the answers he sought lay in the blue and amber flames.

For a time Star Hawk did not speak, allowing his son a few moments to search out his own answers. "Keep her, then, to tend your lodge. If she does not please you, you can always trade her or let her go back to her own people."

The eyes that looked back at Star Hawk showed a touch of anger in their depths at the words that his father had spoken. "I will *not* let her go!"

Was his son keeping this woman to avenge himself once again upon his enemy, Star Hawk wondered, or was there something about this warrior woman that had touched his spirit where no other had been able to in the past two years? Could she bring about peace in his son's soul, or would she be the one to suffer and thus remain unable to help his son?

At the end of their talk Star Hawk spoke again, as Two Shadows stood to his full height. "Your mother has already gone back to Falling Leaves's lodge. Your sister will bring you food and the clothing you desire for the warrior woman. Tell your white friend that I will speak with him soon. If what he claims is true, perhaps many will be spared."

It was a star-bright, cool evening as Two Shadows slowly made his way back to his lodge. He wondered about his own actions. There was much that he needed to do to prepare for the threat of the white man's army, but all he could think about was the beautiful captive in his lodge. He could remember the feel of her soft limbs next to his own upon his sleeping mat the night before, and vividly recalled the feel of her trim backside pressed so tightly against him when he had forced her to get water at the river. It felt as if each time he tried to punish her for her outbursts or refusal to obey him, it was he who was being punished. Once again he acknowledged that it would have been best for all concerned if he had set her free, or even traded her to Thunder Spirit. But these thoughts did not ease his mind. There was something about this woman that confused him. She was so different from his Summer Dawn and all the other women he had known. For a moment, as a soft breeze caressed him, he longed for the soft, warm body of the woman he had loved so well. But all his longing over the past two years had been to no avail—she and his child could not be called back from the Great Spirit's keeping. They had traveled down the star path without him, and only with his own death would he once again be with them.

It was only a short time later that Sky Eyes, her arms full of food and clothing, called from outside Two Shadows's lodge. Entering, she first sighted Two Shadows sitting next to the small pit fire in the center of the lodge, seemingly in a brooding mood. "I have brought you some stew, and the clothing you told our mother you needed." She went to him and bent down to place the pot of stew next to the fire. As she straightened she saw the woman sitting next to a sleeping pallet.

Sky Eyes had heard the rumors circling throughout the village about her brother bringing back a white man and a strange woman, and now with a soft smile she approached the woman. "I have brought you a dress. I hope it will fit." She stretched out her hand to give the girl the deer-hide clothing, but the look of hostility on the beautiful face froze her hand in midair. Turning around, she started to question her brother, but her eyes caught a movement in the dimly lit lodge and she glimpsed a large man with the glistening of gold upon his head.

Her heart seemed to have stopped in that small space of a moment as she stood and gazed across the lodge into the face of the man her brother had brought to their village. Without having to see him closely, she knew he would have a handsome face and the greenest of eyes. This was the man in her vision. This was the one who would change her world.

Two Shadows slowly came to his feet, misunderstanding the strange look upon Sky Eyes's face. Usually his sister was able to handle any situation, but with his mind so distracted he unreasonably thought that she had been offended by the warrior woman's refusal to take the clothes Sky Eyes had tried to give her. Quickly he went to her side. "She does not understand our words, Sky Eyes. Do not feel hurt by her manner. I will make her understand about the gift that you have brought to her." He took the dress from her hands and turned toward Kalina.

Sky Eyes did not even hear her brother; the beating of her heart filled her ears with a mighty throbbing. Her eyes remained focused upon the one across the lodge. As she stood, he came closer toward the small fire, his lips parted in a smile that went straight to Sky Eyes's heart.

"You must be Sky Eyes," he said softly. He, too, had the feeling that no one else existed but himself and this woman who was staring at him. "Heath has spoken to me often about his sister. He told me many times in London about your beauty and gentle ways. And now I see for myself that all he said is true."

Sky Eyes felt as though she had known from the beginning of time that his voice would hold this gentle, masculine tremor and would fill her mind with joy. Not realizing it, she was moving toward him. "My name is Mary Jean. My mother named me this at birth, as my father named me Sky Eyes."

"Mary Jean." The name came from Nicholas's lips as a feather soft caress. Sky Eyes smiled fully, knowing that she had never heard her name sound so wonderful.

Two Shadows, after giving Kalina the dress and not

67

allowing her to refuse the gift, turned back toward his sister. "This is my friend, Nick Prescott. I told you of him when I returned from the white man's school, Sky Eyes." He approached the pair, leaving Kalina for the moment as she sat with her dark eyes focused upon the dress in her lap.

Her brother's words seemed to pull Sky Eyes back somewhat to her senses, and turning to him she smiled. "I am glad that you brought your friend to our village."

His sister always seemed to hold an unusual sweetness, Two Shadows thought, but at this moment she seemed more womanly and beautiful than ever. Remembering the promise he had made to her before he left the village, he started to explain. "I know that we spoke of going to Sweet Oaks upon my return, Sky Eyes, but I am afraid that this trip will have to wait. I will have to stay near the village until the threat of the white man is past."

Still gazing at the golden haired man, Sky Eyes smiled. "It no longer matters, I am content here."

Surprised at her words, Two Shadows looked more closely at his sister. It was odd that she would change her mind, for lately she had spoken of little else to him but the desire to go to the white man's land. What could have changed her mind so quickly? he wondered.

Feeling herself beginning to flush from the two pairs of eyes upon her, Sky Eyes lowered her head and softly spoke. "I must return to our father's lodge. Our mother will worry if I linger much longer." She started toward the entrance flap. "I will return in the morning and perhaps"—she turned now toward the girl across the lodge, not knowing what she should call her, for she had not heard the strange woman's name—"perhaps I will come and help your slave learn her duties." As she said this her eyes drew away from the other woman and went to her brother. She felt very uncomfortable calling another person a slave, and she could not bear to feel her brother's ebony eyes upon her while she spoke.

Without thinking, Nicholas volunteered, "If you don't mind I will walk you back to your father's lodge."

Both Two Shadows and Sky Eyes were surprised at his offer, but as he started to follow her out of the tepee neither objected. Two Shadows had his own problems, and Sky Eyes was too thrilled by his offer to deny him.

As they walked through the village, Sky Eyes told Nicholas about their life and he told her a little about his home in England. What the pair left unsaid it seemed impossible to speak aloud. They both felt a pull upon their senses, each drawn closer to the other.

"Will I see you again tomorrow?" Nicholas ventured as he stood outside Star Hawk's lodge, hating the thought of leaving her when they had only just met. Her graceful beauty held him enraptured, and he loathed to walk away from her presence.

"I will come to my brother's lodge in the morning." Sky Eyes spoke softly as she felt the pounding of her blood rushing swiftly through her veins.

"I will see you then." Nicholas hated to let her go into her father's lodge and leave him, but he could think of nothing to say to detain her. From the moment he had set eyes upon her when she had entered Two Shadows's lodge, he had been drawn to her. He had watched her trim, softly shaped form walk over to the warrior woman, and her sweet, lilting voice had filled him with a searing thrill. She was so beautiful, with her silver eyes and long, flowing midnight hair. Two Shadows had often told him of his sister, but Nicholas would never have imagined that any woman could possess such beauty.

With a sweet smile, Sky Eyes bent and entered the lodge, leaving Nicholas to the cool night air and his own tumbling thoughts.

With the leavetaking of the two from his lodge, Two Shadows had returned to his brooding near the fire. There was much that plagued his mind. He would go to the shaman tomorrow and seek his wisdom and direction for the sacred sun-dance ceremony, for he would need much strength and wisdom in the days ahead, both for himself and his people. As he thought about all he would need to do to prepare for the sacred ceremony, a small noise behind him drew his attention away from the fire and toward the woman who was sitting near his sleeping pallet.

Kalina was so tired from the day's ordeal, and from the emotional strain of all she had endured, that when Nicholas and Sky Eyes left the lodge, and quietness encased her and Two Shadows, her eyes grew so heavy that she could not hold them open. She had not wanted to let sleep overtake her, for she feared what this night would surely hold. She was sure that this large, brutal man would show her no mercy now that they were in his village and alone in his lodge, and she dreaded what was certain to come. She would fight him with all the strength she possessed, but she had seen already that her powers were little compared to her large, strong captor's. But even with these horrible thoughts filling her mind she felt herself losing hold. Sleep cannot always be eluded, and as slumber overtook her, Kalina slipped to the floor.

Two Shadows heard her fall from her sitting position and, rising to his feet, he stood over her supine figure, gazing down at her radiant beauty. She lay with her long, black tresses wrapped about her and fanning out upon the floor of the lodge, the soft deer-hide dress still clutched in her hands, and her cheek pressed against the material. In her sleep she seemed vulnerable and innocent. The proud black eyes were now shut, and the stubborn tilt of her jaw had eased with her slumber. Without a thought Two Shadows bent and picked her up in his arms, laying her upon the soft furs of his sleeping couch, and then gently pulled the furs about her.

Kalina was so exhausted she did not awake with this movement. In the deepest recesses of her mind she felt safe and sheltered in strong arms, and was being protected from the outside world. She had always presented a strong front. She had to appear as brave and hard as Pointed Arrow had instructed her from her earliest childhood; but now in sleep she could let all those demands slip away. She felt a light caress upon her cheek, and a small smile flitted across her lips. She did not have to be on guard; another would watch over her.

Two Shadows touched her soft cheek, where he had struck her. A bruise stood out plainly. Two Shadows marveled at the sheer beauty of the smile his caress had caused. He knew that she was deep in sleep, for otherwise she would never have allowed such a gentle look to steal over her features. With a ragged sigh, he turned from his sleeping couch and left the lodge. He would go for a swim in the river. The cool water would help rid his mind of his plaguing thoughts and bring his senses back under control.

It was only a short time later that Two Shadows returned to the lodge to find Nicholas sleeping on a pallet on the floor. Kalina was still upon his sleeping couch. Upon silent feet he went to his pallet and eased his large frame down next to her on the soft furs. With an effort of will he held himself away from the woman at his side, but he could not hold himself away from the remembrances of her soft, beautiful body as she had lain next to him the night before and of the feel of her against him today at the riverbank.

Early the next morning Two Shadows awoke with a feeling of total contentment, his large frame molded against Kalina's and her soft, pliant form and slim limbs wrapped around his own. For a moment he forgot reality and allowed his body to indulge in the soft warmth of the woman next to him, his nostrils filling with her sweet scent, but all too quickly, and with an inner curse at himself, Two Shadows quietly disengaged himself from her. As he pulled on his breechcloth he stood to the side of his sleeping couch and looked down at the woman in his bed. In her sleep she buried herself deeper into the furs, seeking more warmth now that she had been deprived of his. Feeling his anger beginning to boil within his body, Two Shadows raged at himself for his weakness. This woman was the enemy — he should not be feeling this softness toward her. She was here in his lodge for one reason only, and that was to tend to his needs. She belonged solely to him and he could do with her as he wished. This moment, if he desired, he could take her, here upon his sleeping couch while she was lost in sleep. But with a scowl on his handsome features, he turned from this thought and instead went to Nicholas. Touching his arm, he stirred him awake.

Nicholas, always an easy sleeper, quickly arose, pulled on his breeches, and followed Two Shadows out into the cool morning air. "What is it, Heath?" he asked, wondering if something was wrong.

"I thought you would like to go hunting this morning." Two Shadows suggested, seeking a means to put the thoughts of the woman from his mind.

The first thoughts in Nicholas's mind were of Sky Eyes, or Mary Jean as he now thought of her. She had said that she would be at her brother's lodge this morning, and he had hoped to find a few moments alone with her. His dreams last night had been filled with her lovely presence, her beautiful face and soothing voice remaining with him throughout the long dark hours. Nodding his head toward his friend, he grinned widely. "Sure, Heath, hunting sounds fine." There would be plenty of time for him to get to know Mary Jean, he reasoned, happiness filling his soul.

Sky Eyes was also up early this morning, helping her mother to gather her father's things and to prepare the morning meal. She smiled fondly at her parents as she set about filling the bowls with the savory breakfast that would start their day. She felt a completeness this morning that she had never felt before. With a small sigh, she thought again of her brother's friend, Nicholas Prescott. In her sleep the night before she was again visited by a vision, but she was not disturbed over its meaning as she had been in the past. Nicholas had come to her, and with the beauty of the forest around them, he had taken her in his arms, his lips gently covering her own, his tender voice filling her ears. Her heart sighed with a gladness that carried her high upon the tops of the clouds. He was the man of her heart, the one of her destiny. And somehow she knew he felt the same. Deep in his heart, he must also know that she was the one for him.

The meal was hurriedly eaten and soon, standing outside the large lodge, Sky Eyes and her mother waited to send Star Hawk and several braves off on the journey. As Star Hawk drew Silver Star away for a private moment, Sky Eyes smiled at the love between her parents.

Without warning, Thunder Spirit approached Sky Eyes when he saw that she was standing alone. "Once again I am called away. Perhaps I shall have the chance to approach your father when we are returning from the other villages." His dark eyes seemed to devour her with heated intensity.

Sky Eyes gasped aloud at his words, having forgotten completely that Thunder Spirit had promised to seek her father's permission for their joining. "Do not ask my father anything." She spoke softly, so that the others could not hear. "I have told you already that I will not be your wife, and my mind has not changed." She thought to herself that after meeting Nicholas Prescott last night, she would deny Thunder Spirit now more than ever.

"And I have told you that you shall be mine. No other shall ever claim you." Before Thunder Spirit could say any more, Star Hawk mounted his horse and called his warriors to follow. "There is much that we shall speak of on my return. Do not forget my words, Sky Eyes. You belong only to me."

Sky Eyes turned around and went back into her father's lodge. She would never belong to Thunder Spirit, she vowed inwardly. And then the image of Nicholas filled her mind again, and with thoughts of the white man, she found herself calming down. Even if Thunder Spirit did speak with her father, Star Hawk would never agree to their union unless she approved. And she did not. She would never agree to become his wife. There was only one man she could ever belong to—her brother's friend, Nicholas Prescott. The threats that Thunder Spirit had uttered about her never belonging to another drifted from her mind. All thoughts, except those of Nicholas, vanished, unimportant.

Chapter Four

Two Shadows returned to his lodge late that afternoon. As he and Nicholas dismounted before the tepee, Sky Eyes stepped out of it, her smile radiant as she looked at the white man at her brother's side.

Two Shadows sighed, relieved. He had thought of nothing all day but the warrior woman he had brought to his lodge to be his slave. He had not been able to concentrate on his hunting, and had allowed a large buck to get away from him. His mind had not been on what he was doing, and he had stepped on a twig that had snapped loudly and sent his prey running through the brush. It had been Nicholas who had brought down the buck. He had jokingly laughed that Two Shadows would have to get up even earlier the next time they went hunting, if he thought to out-shoot him. Two Shadows had smiled at his friend, still not truly attentive to the hunting. His thoughts kept returning to the woman in his lodge. Now, seeing Sky Eyes coming from his tepee, he felt cheered. He had hoped that his sister would come, as she had promised to the night before, to teach his slave her duties. He had been afraid all day that he would return to his lodge to find that the warrior woman had fled.

"I was on my way to get fresh water for your lodge, Two Shadows." Sky Eyes smiled at her brother, her thoughts also on the woman in her brother's lodge. All day she had not been able to get through to his slave. The girl had looked at her as though she did not understand either her words or her signaling, and she had refused to do any of the work in the lodge. With a small sigh, Sky Eyes now turned from her brother, leaving the matter in his hands.

"I will walk with you," Nicholas said quickly as Sky Eyes started to leave. He, like his friend, had also carried the image of a woman in his mind throughout the day. But his thoughts had been warm and sweet as he thought of the girl he had met the night before. And now, not wishing to be away from her any longer, he started after her.

Not sparing his friend nor his sister a second thought, Two Shadows reflected on the warrior woman in his tepee. The slight frown that had creased his sister's brow had spoken much to him: all had not gone well this day between Sky Eyes and his slave. Throwing back the entrance flap, he boldly strode inside. In seconds his eyes adjusted to the dimness of the interior. Looking across the space, he spied his captive, still sitting beside the sleeping mat, her dark eyes lowered, her manner quiet and sullen.

As Two Shadows took in her attire, he began to feel an unreasonable anger. All that covered her still were the small vest of fur about her breasts, and the breechcloth that did little to distract a male eye from her smooth, trim form. "Why have you not put on the clothes that Sky Eyes brought for you?" he demanded, his voice booming as he advanced on her.

At the sound of his voice, Kalina's gaze rose to meet his. Seeing the anger on his handsome features, she inwardly drew back, bracing herself for the ordeal to come.

"The clothes!" Two Shadows now stood over the slender frame of the woman on the floor and pointed to the dress that was neatly folded on the sleeping couch. The Indian woman's dark gaze moved from his face to the object he was pointing at, and then rose again to the stormy face without any form of response. Two Shadows grabbed the clothes in one hand and took her upper arm with the other. "You will wear these clothes! Now!"

Trying to pull back from his harshness, Kalina felt her own anger coming quickly to the surface. She refused him, shaking her head.

Unable to believe her stubbornness, Two Shadows held tighter to her arm. She tried with all her strength to get away from his grasp, but he jerked her up to his chest, more roughly than he would usually have treated a woman—but then, he reasoned, this woman provoked in him wild anger at one moment and then tender fury the next. After his long day of riding and hunting and trying to put this woman's lovely face from his mind, he now wished only for some form of release to the raging feelings that were running rampant through him. He stilled her with his strength, his large arms wrapped around her body, her face a breath away from his own. "You will change into this dress!" he hissed between clenched teeth.

With one last ounce of defiance, Kalina shook her head in the negative, her dark eyes glaring into his steely silver ones.

Cursing, Two Shadows dropped the dress to the floor. He held her two hands with one of his own behind her back, while the other came up between their tightly clenched bodies. His large fingers slowly began to unlace the leather strap holding the fur vest together. When Kalina understood his intentions, she began to fight with a vengeance. She kicked out, trying to pull her arms free, her body bucking and writhing in his grasp. But all that she accomplished was to help the fur vest to open, leaving her firm, heaving bosom free from confinement.

With a gasp the girl looked down at her flesh, so exposed and so close to Two Shadows's chest, and she watched in horror as the rosebud tips began to harden.

With a strong effort of will Two Shadows kept a hold on his emotions as he, too, witnessed the beautifully molded breasts heaving with her exertion. The tips were but a few inches from his own body, and he longed to press her tighter, but he restrained himself, determined that he would press home his mastery over this woman once and for all.

Kalina had all but stilled now in his arms, her breathing labored as her dark eyes looked with fear into the face before her. Now she knew her time had come. Her abductor would at any moment throw her to the sleeping mat and fall upon her with a savage appetite that would totally overpower her. So it was with surprise that she felt one of his hands leave her body as he bent and retrieved the dress.

Pulling the vest all the way off her tempting body, Two Shadows began to pull the dress over her, his eyes beholding her perfection but swiftly covering her from his eyes. Swiftly he laced the front of the dress. As she stood, still now in confusion and wonder at his actions, Two Shadows bent before her and gently eased the breechcloth from her hips, his long fingers lightly brushing the creamy flesh of her buttock and sending a chill down her spine. Quickly he settled the dress around her hips and tied the thin leather belt at her waist. Finally, standing back at arm's length, he let his eyes travel over her form, a small smile now playing about his lips as he admired the woman standing before him.

Kalina filled out the clothing a bit more than Sky Eyes would, her breasts full and pressing tightly against the soft deerhide. Her hips, though slim, were womanly. For a few moments the girl stood with her hands clasped tightly together, feeling strange in these clothes. Even stranger were the feelings that were stirring in her body. She had expected this man to ravish her, indeed to fall upon her, but all he had done was force her to change into the clothing that his sister had brought. Now, with his hands still upon her, she felt her body trembling. Never had a man been so bold with her, never had any other dared to touch her, nor had any other caused her to desire to know what lay ahead.

Two Shadows took everything in as he tried to slow his ragged breathing. She was even more tempting in his sister's clothes. Her feminine allure seemed to sing out to him. Her long, shimmering black hair fell down her back like a cascading waterfall that seemed to beckon to his hands.

Neither seemed to dare breathe for a moment as their eyes met. Two Shadows's hands buried deep into the silky folds of her dark tresses as his silver eyes probed deeply into her features, as though seeking out a part of her very soul. Kalina, also, was held immobile in the trance of feelings that seemed to encircle the couple. Her dark, warm eyes looked up into his, and written in their depths was the desire to face the unknown in his arms. At this moment her feelings betrayed her, and she would have gladly done whatever this tall, handsome Indian warrior told her to do.

Slowly, as though time stood still, Two Shadows's head began to lower, his thoughts only on tasting the sweetness of those berry-red lips before him. And he would have fulfilled his desire, had not voices pulled him upright as Sky Eyes and Nicholas entered the tepee. Their laughter was loud and animated as they put the waterskins away, but as they looked toward the couple in the lodge, their voices quieted. It was obvious that they had walked in at an inopportune moment.

Two Shadows came to his senses and quickly pulled away from the warrior woman when he felt the eyes of his sister and friend upon him. As he looked at the confused expression of the woman standing in front of him, his anger began to overtake him once again—directed now at himself, though. He stepped away from her. He had totally lost his grip on his emotions, which he had cautioned himself not to do so many times since meeting her. He had wanted this woman with every fiber of his being, and in truth, such was his right, for she was his slave. But he had not wanted her as a master would take his property. He had desired her warm and pliant under his hand. He had imagined in his mind the sound of her voice whispering love words in his ear, the feeling of her silken arms twined about his neck. And for a moment he had almost succumbed to losing himself to her charms, losing all his memories, forgetting that her people were the enemy, the killers of his wife and child. With a dark scowl at the woman, he spoke harshly, trying to cover his emotions. "Prepare the evening meal." Turning around, he stomped out of the lodge.

Both Sky Eyes and Nicholas watched his retreating back, and then both pairs of eyes went to the warrior woman, taking in that she was now clothed in the garment that Sky Eyes had brought for her, and noticing the deep flush on her cheeks.

Sky Eyes did not understand the mood of her brother. He was always kind and gentle with her and with other women she had seen him with. Shaking her head, she gave the woman across from her another glance. She had showed her where the food-stuffs were kept and had tried to explain to her what she should prepare for the lodge's meal. She could only hope that the girl would not remain stubborn and defy her brother's command to fix their meal. She did not enjoy the side of her brother that his slave was arousing. If the girl were more docile, Sky Eyes was sure that Two Shadows would look upon her more kindly. After all, she was but a woman. She could not help that her people were the enemy. "I must go to my father's lodge. My mother will need help with the meal," Sky Eyes said to Nicholas, her eyes warm as they looked into his.

"And I must see to the deer that I killed." Nicholas smiled at her, his heart beating wildly. She seemed even more lovely to him today than she had the evening before. He hoped to find more time to be with her. The walk to the river had only seemed to whet his appetite for her company.

When the pair left the lodge, Kalina was at last able to let out her breath. Her knees seemed to tremble under her, and she had to sit down on the sleeping couch to keep from falling. Her hands absently felt the deerhide dress and again she could feel the touch of her captor's hands. She could envision herself as she had been only moments ago, waiting for his mouth to cover her own, her heart racing with the expectation of the unknown. Kalina had never before allowed a man to come so close to her, and never had she come so close to falling under another's spell. Those silver eyes had seemed to see deeply into her soul, and his breath had been warm

83

and alive against her flesh, sending shivers of anticipation down her back. And then, quickly, the moment had been broken and again the warrior who
stood before her was dark, vengeful. She had almost
lost her reason. Now, as she shivered on the sleeping
pallet, she was glad that she had been saved by the
entrance of his sister and friend, even if it was from
herself that she had been saved.

Kalina felt a deep, angry flush as she remembered
his heated words, demanding that she prepare his
meal. Now she was the servant again, bending to his
rule. She, who had always given orders, was now
expected to obey them. But as quickly as her anger
came over her it was replaced with reason. She
would do as he ordered her until the time was right
and she could flee. She would not allow his hands
on her again, for she knew now that this strange,
silver-eyed warrior held an extraordinary power over
her. Perhaps he had bewitched her in some evil
fashion. She tried to find an excuse for the feelings,
so alien to her, that this man inspired. Perhaps his
silver eyes were proof that this Two Shadows was
more devil than man. A slight shudder went through
her slim form, and quickly she rose to her feet,
determined now to do as he bid her for the time
being, not giving him an excuse to hold her once
again in his strange power. She would keep to herself
and bide her time until she could flee from these
horrible people.

Angry and frustrated with himself and the warrior

woman, Two Shadows walked through the village. He was in a quandary as he wondered at his need to punish himself. He could easily send the woman away, and put an end to the pain that filled his chest each time he was around her. He could go to another woman and take her to ease his needs. There were women who lived in a tepee at a distance from the village who stayed in isolation for their shame and ease with men. These women would give him all he desired. He need not feel the emotions that were now assaulting him. But with a loud curse at himself, he saw that these thoughts were like the passing wind. He could not banish the warrior woman from his lodge and he could not take another to replace her. There was more here than his need for release. The woman played havoc with his soul, and he could not send her away.

If his father had been in the village, perhaps he could have gone to him and spoken of the things that were tearing him apart inside, but Star Hawk would not return for another two days. Instead, he found that his steps had taken him to the shaman's lodge. Two Shadows called out softly to Medicine Wolf. Receiving a call to enter, he went inside. The smells of herbs and spices were pungent in the air. Seeing the old man sitting before his fire, Two Shadows greeted him in a respectful manner. "It is good to see you looking so well, Medicine Wolf. I pray that the Great Spirit will keep you for many seasons to come."

"My bones are no longer young, my son, but my heart is as ageless as our people. Whatever time the

Great Spirit allows me, I am grateful." For a moment neither spoke, but looked into the flames that were leaping in the center fire pit, a savory, spicy smell wafting through the air with each spark. "You have come to my lodge to seek my wisdom, Two Shadows?" Medicine Wolf asked, seeing that the younger man was deeply troubled.

"The white man's army is near our lands, and the time shall be soon upon us when we have to defend ourselves against their power. I need the wisdom of the Great Spirit. I need to be sure of the direction in which He would lead me, sure that I am not tempted by my own knowledge and decisions." Two Shadows found that he could not bare his soul about the woman in his lodge even to this old medicine man, so he kept his thoughts of the warrior woman hidden in his heart.

Medicine Wolf did not interrupt his words. He felt that the younger man was not telling all that he would wish to share. "How is it that I can help you in this time of need?" His words were softly spoken, his ebony eyes looking with a wise gleam at the younger man's every expression.

"I would join with the others in the sun-dance ceremony, and I would seek a vision that will show me the way. You are a wise teacher, Medicine Wolf, and can direct me to seek out the knowledge that I must have."

Slowly the gray head nodded, the dark eyes seeming ageless as they kept up their study of the young man before them. "One day you will be the leader of your people. One day your decisions will be law, and will mean the life and death of those who depend on you. Your quest for this vision of understanding will entail more than what the sun-dance ceremony can grant."

Two Shadows looked with wonder and interest at the old man. "What is it that I must do?"

For a time that seemed to stretch out into eternity, the lodge was quiet; then, when Two Shadows was almost sure that the old shaman had not heard his question, Medicine Wolf spoke softly. "You will need to go high into the mountains. Take no food or water. Come to me at the first breaking of light and I will have a parfleche prepared with all that you will need. I will tell you then what you must do."

Two Shadows nodded in agreement, feeling some small reassurance that Medicine Wolf would help him. Perhaps with the help of the Great Spirit, he would be able to come to some understanding. For the moment, everything seemed so confused in his heart. Agreeing to come early in the morning, he left the lodge of the shaman, whose prayers and chants filled Two Shadows's ears as he stepped out into the night.

Only somewhat eased in his thoughts, Two Shadows entered his own lodge. Looking about he found Nicholas sitting alone near the fire.

"Come, sit and have some of this delicious stew that your warrior woman has fixed for us." Nicholas pointed to the bubbling pot of savory-smelling stew over the fire.

"Where is she?" Two Shadows ignored the invitation to eat, intent on discovering the whereabouts of his slave.

"I figured that she was going to the river to bathe. After she cooked this stew, I saw her pick up your hairbrush and a blanket. I thought she was in need of some time to herself."

Two Shadows's first thought was that his captive had found her chance to escape. An unreasonable anger, tinged with fear, surfaced in him. Spinning about, he hurried from the lodge, not seeing the small grin that flickered over Nicholas's features.

Making his way quickly to the river, Two Shadows looked about with his keen eyes, but in the darkness he could not make out anyone along the banks. Only the shapes of the trees and shrubs were visible. For a moment he forced himself to stand still, listening to each noise of the night and trying to sense anything that was out of place. Finally he heard it — a soft, lilting, musical sound. As he started on silent feet toward it, he began to make out a woman's voice singing. The language was not that of the Blackfoot, but it was beautiful. For a few moments Two Shadows kept his presence unknown as he enjoyed the sounds coming to his ears. As his eyes made out her figure sitting near the river on a smooth, flat rock and lightly combing long strands of her midnight hair, he allowed himself to share secretly in this stolen moment.

At this moment his warrior woman was not the one that had stood so boldly before his band and fought so bravely. This woman sitting on the rock was all woman, beautiful, with a light caress of moonbeams golden on her skin. Her voice, which he had not heard until this moment, was the most wondrous that he had ever heard. Spellbound, he stood rooted to the spot, hidden from her by a large tree. All thoughts of foe and enemy, hate and destruction, vanished from his mind as he allowed the gentle caress of her voice to steal over him and bring him peace and beauty.

At the end of the song, Two Shadows was at last able to stir himself. Slowly he made his way to the woman sitting on the rock. "You have a beautiful voice," he whispered, his eyes locking with the dark, warm, liquid pools before him.

Kalina did not respond, but neither did she lower her eyes as she had in the past when he addressed her. She seemed not at all surprised to see this tall Indian warrior standing before her, for had she not been singing a love song? It was a song of beckoning and longing. Had he not appeared as the answer to her longings? Her feelings were long dormant, because of her habit of subduing her innermost desires. This man had a strange power over her, and because of him she was here in this strange village. Because of him she was sitting near the river and singing out her soul to the dark of the night. This strange, silver-eyed warrior was the cause of Kalina's not knowing, for the first time in her life, exactly who she was. She was a stranger to herself, no longer her own woman.

As his large hand reached out and lightly caressed the softness of her cheek, Kalina was brought out of her thoughts, but she did not draw away. Instead her breath caught in her throat and she closed her eyes to the tender touch.

Two Shadows seemed somehow to realize that this was the first time this warrior woman had allowed her gentle nature to overthrow her harder self, and gently he eased down next to her.

For a time neither spoke, allowing the cool night air to touch them. The night creatures scampered about and filled the darkness with soft sounds. An owl hooted atop a mighty pine, and a lone dog barked softly in the distance. These were the only sounds to break the quiet.

Two Shadows removed his hand from his captive's cheek, and slowly a small tear slipped from Kalina's eye. She felt desolate without his touch, and desired only that he reach out to her again.

As if Two Shadows could read her feelings he brought up his hand again and touched her tender cheek. He turned her face toward his own, his arm slipping easily over her shoulder as his lips hungrily swept over hers. Thrilling and tantalizing, they were at first light to the touch, then they became insistent and consuming as his tongue filled her mouth with the taste and sensations of his being.

Kalina had never experienced such feelings as those now raging through her. Her encounters with this man had never until now been as powerful as this. She sat pressed tightly against his towering, hard frame. Her fingers slowly wandered up his muscular back, one hand roaming to the ebony hair that reached low on his shoulders, the other roaming over the sleek, smooth surface of his upper torso, feeling for itself the wonderful texture of his bronzed skin. His strength was thrilling. Only Two Shadows had ever kissed her in this manner; only Two Shadows had made her feel these longings that were now storming through her every fiber. As he kissed her deeper, drawing out her sense of caution, she knew that she wanted something more, more than the magnetic feelings that stirred between them when they were together, more than this touch of his mouth that left her burning with a need she knew not how to appease.

Losing his will in the softness of her hands on him and in the hunger of her mouth, Two Shadows worked skillfully and hungrily to arouse her senses to a flaming peak, knowing that she did not wish to draw back any more than he did, and sensing that she did not fear her need of him. But as his tongue drank of the sweet nectar of her mouth, he could think no more. He encircled her tongue with his and laid flaming, soft kisses against her parted lips, then sensuously drifted across her face, lightly kissing and tasting the texture of her skin as his lips roamed across her cheek and her ear, and then back along her jawline and down the slim column of her throat. Tasting and nibbling her body as though she were made of the sweetest ambrosia, he felt the pulsing of her throat as he moved lower to the soft mound of her breast at the neck of her deer-hide dress. Pulling at the thongs that held the dress closed, his strong hands roamed beneath her bodice and gently caressed her full, straining breasts, and he heard the moaning of her desire.

Kalina held her eyes tightly shut as she allowed

herself to be assaulted by the feelings that Two Shadows was arousing in her body. Never had she felt or imagined such longings before, and as his hands and mouth caressed her breasts, her breathing came in hot ragged gasps. Her senses were lost to everything but him. His manly smell assailed her as she reached out and let her fingers roam again through his dark hair, her lips lightly touching his forehead while the scent of horse and leather and wild, sweet herbs flooded her being. She was aflame and throbbing as he moved from one taut breast to the other, leaving her trembling on the verge of a sweet, raging agony.

For a second his loving stimulation stilled as Two Shadows gently eased the belt from around her slim waist and pulled her clothing from her, but quickly the fire stoked anew as he roamed fully over the curves of her body. Again his mouth captured a full breast, while his fingers slowly stole across her flat belly and lightly touched the hidden dark forest of her desire.

With a gasp, Kalina pushed her body more fully against his own, her beckoning desire wanting to feel more, wanting to know all. And as his fingers grew more bold, stroking and kindling, Kalina was lost to all but the power that his body held over hers. He was her only reason at this moment, his embrace her destiny, and that was all that mattered to her. As he lightly drew her down into the lushness of the sweet-smelling grass along the riverbank, she could hear the song of her heart. This moment, stolen here in the arms of her captor, was meant to be. It would live forever in her mind.

With ease Two Shadows drew the strings of his breechcloth and lay naked beside her, his throbbing maleness boldly pushing against her soft, shapely thigh. As his silver eyes locked with her ebony ones they were lost for a time in the feelings they both glimpsed. With a moan of unbridled passion, Two Shadows caught and held her mouth in his own, delving deeply and fully into her mouth. With her response his spirit soared to the towering peaks of the mighty oaks that surrounded them. Once more he assailed her senses, his mouth and fingers roaming at will over her lustrous curves and sweeping her up with him to the clouds of passion's peak. Finally he rose above her, his hot, fiery shaft pressing lightly at first against her womanhood, but then more forcefully as he pushed within, breaking the hidden barrier of her maidenhead and joining them as one being.

Two Shadows paused, not believing the full truth of the moment. As he looked at the beautiful features beneath him and the slight tension that had come over his warrior woman's face with the pain of his entry, he saw that his slave had been untouched until this moment.

Kalina had felt only a small amount of pain, and it had in no way scared her or turned her away from this man atop her. She had always been bold in whatever she set out to do, and had always done it well. She felt no different about these storms of passion that now claimed her. She felt no shame for what she was doing as she looked into Two Shadows's face, for her feelings were too strong. If ever there arose a need to excuse her being here in her enemy's arms, she could always claim that he had taken her by force because she was his slave, and he her master. As Two Shadows gently moved within her she felt the swift claim of passion's caress steal over her again, and slowly she began to move her hips.

Two Shadows was powerless to sort out his thoughts. With the feel of her body moving beneath his own, his mouth caught hers in a sweet, caressing hold, his fingers lightly moving over her cool flesh and setting her trembling within. And as his body began to slowly move in hers, Kalina felt a boundless joy beginning in the very depths of her being and traveling throughout every portion of her body. There was a radiating stirring deep in her belly, a deep, pulsing rapture as his manhood moved in and out of her body, slowly at first, but then more demandingly. She clung to his back, and as he plunged deeply she arched her body to accept all of him.

Their kisses were raging over one another now as they sought out passion's bliss, their bodies moving with a tempo that was inflaming and sensual. They seemed to be swept upward to rapture, as they rode out the mighty tempest of fulfillment. As Kalina arched her body more fully, his name—"Two Shadows"—escaped her lips, and her dark eyes opened wide in wonder. Two Shadows knew that she had crested the consummation of her womanhood, and the realization sent his senses soaring heavenward. This woman belonged to him fully now, only to him. Slave, captive, whatever one would call her, he alone laid claim to her. With the feel of her trembling body beneath his own, his passion burst with a mighty shudder, and the substance of life spilling forth from him into the womb of his beloved captive.

Their bodies were still entwined as they gasped aloud, marveling at the magic they had just experienced. Their bodies remained in the tight embrace of two who belonged together.

As they came slowly back to reality, Two Shadows held on to his captive, his fingers entwined in her long hair and his nostrils filled with her clean scent. He lay still, thinking about their lovemaking, a small smile playing on his lips. His warrior woman had called out his name when she had met her passion. This night was truly one to marvel upon, he thought to himself. First he had caught her singing to the night wind and then he had been blessed with the sound of his own name coming from her sweet lips. Above all he could marvel over what had brought his name from her mouth. Never could he remember having shared such total rapture with another. Even Summer Dawn had not brought such feelings to his body. Though she had loved him and had seen to all his needs, there had always been a shyness about her that had kept a part of her untouched. This woman now in his arms had given all of herself to their passion, and he felt overwhelmed by her giving.

"I wish I could tell you of the feelings in my heart." Two Shadows spoke softly as he looked into the dark eyes next to him. "But perhaps it is better that you do not understand my tongue; at this moment I do not even understand my feelings." He took the soft, yielding lips again, rekindling the consuming fire that stole over him with her nearness.

Kalina did not speak. She, too, was overwhelmed with everything that had happened in the past moments. She did not care to hear words, or to question herself over her true feelings toward this man. She only wanted to feel his hands upon her once again, to taste his mouth over her own, to feel his hard body joined with hers, allowing her to know the feelings of rapture that she had learned at his hands. Nothing seemed to matter except the feeling of his body pressed into her own.

Two Shadows also seemed to sense that words were not needed. With the touch of her lips against his own, their arms wrapped about one another, they pressed their bodies tightly together. There was a hungry assault that seemed to overcome them, and both felt a need to taste once again the full wonder of the experience they had shared only moments ago.

His hands were everywhere, on her full, straining breasts, across her belly, and sliding lower to touch the heat of her womanhood. With that touch, Kalina shook with renewed desire.

Two Shadows bent over her golden, luscious form, and as his hands worked their magic his mouth covered the spots that his hands missed, his teeth taking small nipping bites of her flesh that left her moaning with pleasure.

"Two Shadows . . ." she murmured. His mouth had left her body and was now devouring her own, and the taste of his probing tongue and the feel of his large hands on her swelling breasts left her incapable of further words.

Drawing his mouth from hers, Two Shadows slowly kissed a path down her slim throat and fastened upon one breast with a hot wetness that made her cry out and clutch his head closer. He reduced her to a kind of mindless ecstasy that left her writhing and gasping beneath him, as his mouth moved over to torment the other soft peak. His hands were stroking her thighs and then touching within the dampness of her craving. He had meant to feast now in leisure upon her wondrous body, but her moaning and gasping beckoned him to quench her inner thirst, and he could no longer resist. Parting her thighs, his mouth fastening on hers, his silver eyes locked on her dark ones, he slid inside of her.

Kalina gasped aloud as he filled her, arching and trembling as she once again called out his name, the words circling and floating on the soft night breeze. The sensations aroused by their joining were exquisite, setting Kalina aquiver from head to toe, stopping her breath and slowing the beating of her raging heart and spiraling her away. Whatever tomorrow offered her, at least this night she had touched and tasted the joy of love.

Her hands clutched him close to her. Two Shadows plunged inside her with a fiery urgency that drove her quickly over the edge of reality and into her climax. As Two Shadows felt the assault of her ecstasy he, too, was swept away with the consuming pull of a searing climax.

As the earth settled, Two Shadows held the warrior woman close against his naked chest, for the moment content to breathe in the smell of her sweet, honeyed body. Briefly he thought that his would be all he would ever need. This stolen captive chased away all his thoughts of war and the enemy while he lay in her arms. She offered sanctuary, and he gladly accepted.

Without a word, Two Shadows rose to his feet. Gathering the warrior woman into his arms, he retrieved their clothing and made his way toward his lodge. It was dark, and no one was about to see the mighty Two Shadows carrying his naked captive so lovingly in his arms. Her head pressed tightly against his chest, her sleek arms wrapped about his neck, the fierce warrior woman gave no resistance to her abductor as they silently disappeared through the entrance flap of his lodge.

Chapter Five

The long trek into the mountains on foot took Two Shadows two days. As the old shaman had instructed him, he ran most of the first day, only slowing when his body could endure no more. When he had caught his wind, he again set out in a sprint. The next day, his body much wearied, with neither food nor drink and the exertion of the day before, he forced himself to go higher, ever higher into the mountains, until with the onset of dusk he came finally to the sacred place that Medicine Wolf had described.

That first evening he crouched upon a flat span of smooth rock, hundreds of feet up, that over-looked the valley, the valley that belonged to his people. With a grudging pride, he reflected that the first part of his journey was now behind him. Sitting there upon the rock, while he waited for the evening to pass, his thoughts were filled with the image of the warrior woman. The night they had spent together was the most incredible he had ever known in the arms of a woman. She had asked nothing of him, in fact the only words he had ever heard her say were when, in the throes of passion, she had called out his name. He could well remember her sweet voice as she sat singing on the river bank, and with this thought peacefulness settled about him.

He had hated to leave her. Yesterday morning he had stood looking at her while she lay deep in her slumber, sated with his lovemaking. Her beauty had all but hurt his eyes as he allowed his silver gaze to caress her face—the shimmering ebony tresses, the smooth, sun-kissed skin, the high cheekbones, and the delicate winglike brows. She was, indeed, a woman of rare beauty, he mused. As he now had all night to do nothing but think, he thought a lot about her, and he admitted that perhaps her inner self was not as hard and unyielding as he had at first thought. Had she not shown him that she was a woman of deep passions and strength? He did not know anything of her past, nor of the circumstances that had brought her to where he had found her. He wondered for a time about the sort of life she must have had. What would make a virgin-woman take up the disguise of a warrior, wielding bow and war club against the enemy? What kind of family could have shaped such a beauty into the woman he had found in the Crow camp?

Shaking his head slowly, Two Shadows knew that it would do him little good to ponder such questions, and if the warrior woman stayed as close-mouthed as she had been thus far, he doubted that he would ever know the answers. More to the fore in his thoughts now, after he had sampled her desirable charms, was the question of what he was going to do with her. This thought had plagued him all the day before as he had made his way up the mountain, but he had pushed it from his mind, trying not to think of anything but the words the old shaman had spoken. The woman was his slave; but would he be content to let her remain thus? In truth, what other choice was there? The warriors of his village did not take slaves, especially from the enemy, as their own. They remained slaves of the tribe until they either died or were traded to another. With this thought Two Shadows felt uncomfortable, for deep within, he knew that when he returned to his village the matter would have to be resolved. How would he be able to face the woman he had tested such wondrous pleasure with, and still have the word *slave* between them? In such a quandary, he fell into an exhausted sleep.

With the first rays of bright sunlight filtering down between the tops of the tall pines, Two Shadows awoke. Shivering, he opened the parfleche that Medicine Wolf had given him. Raising his face toward the sun, he began to chant and sing the prayer that had been given him by the old shaman. Taking a small pouch of dust from the parfleche, he threw portions of it high into the air in four directions on the morning breeze, beseeching the Great

Spirit to be with him and to bless him with a mighty vision. Then, taking some small sticks and tinderbox from the parfleche, he placed the sticks in a circle, set them afire, then slowly raised the gourd of herb water above his head, offering this to the mother earth in the four directions of the wind. Lowering the gourd, he slowly allowed the water to hiss and simmer over the flames until naught was left but wifts of steam. His hands directed the steam toward his body, and he inhaled deeply of the wood and herbs as he chanted out the prayers of his ancestors.

The day passed slowly, Two Shadows feeling the coldness of the mountain air chilling his body. He sat cross-legged upon the smooth foundation, his leather shirt and leggings and a little heat from the small fire his only warmth, his prayers the only sound coming to his ears.

For two more days, Two Shadows remained upon the rock, denying himself sustenance and sleep, constantly directing his thoughts to remain upon the mumbled prayers he spoke aloud.

On the fourth day he thought surely that all strength had left him; but slowly a feeling of calm spread throughout his body and spirit as the brightness of the warming sun shone down upon him.

"Oh Great Father, what trick are you playing upon my mind?" he called softly, as he began to feel his body warming and his head spinning. Slowly he rose up from the smooth surface of the rock, and with the wind he was lifted high into the

102

sky. "Grandfather, hear me!" he excitedly called aloud, holding in his heart not fear, but joy that filled his entire being as the peaceful haze of unreality circled about him. "I am Two Shadows, son of Star Hawk, and grandson of the mighty Golden Eagle. I seek a vision that will help me to lead and protect my people. I call upon the wisdom of the Grandfathers and the courage of a people long past. Show me what you would have me know. Teach me what you will."

Having uttered this plea, Two Shadows looked about the clouds where he now seemed to be standing, and in an instant was surrounded by a group of fierce-looking warriors. Their war bonnets of dyed eagle feathers hung long down their backs, and the warriors' faces were painted with the sacred color. They held war shields and lances and their bronzed skin and ebony hair glistened beneath the sunlight as they seemed to stand encircled in a brilliant sheen.

"We have come to you in your hour of need and want, my son." The largest warrior of the group stepped forward, his voice ringing with authority, the sound vibrating as his words touched Two Shadows's ears. As the young brave stood in awe, and his silver gaze roamed over the mighty warrior, he beheld the design of a large golden eagle in flight upon his war shield. "Our people will one day hold you in great honor for your wisdom and bravery. You will lead the people with a mighty hand that will surely rival that of my own great, great, great grandfather Soaring Eagle."

Another of the group stepped forward and spoke. "The time draws near when the people will prove their strength. This valley below us and this mountain have been the land of our people since the motion of time began. Those that would intrude for their own greed and desires shall be stopped."

Another stepped to this last one's side and added, "Be strong and brave, for the Grandfathers shall be at your hand in your time of need. You shall be guided to victory by the hands of those long past. Fear not, for when you reach out to smite the enemy, you shall be victorious."

Two Shadows watched, then, as the group of mighty warriors vanished, each turning and stepping into the haze of the clouds. Staring after them, he found himself again on the rock, but instead of sitting in the position he had maintained in these past days, he found himself standing upon the very edge of the smooth surface, which jutted out over the valley from the side of the mountain. His hands were stretched high above his head, and he humbly called out his thanks to the Great Spirit.

A noise pulled Two Shadows from his thanksgivings, and slowly his hands lowered to his sides as he looked for whatever had disturbed him. There, bold and beautiful, its head thrown back, its tail stuck straight out, stood the most incredible horse Two Shadows had ever seen. Its body was snow white, its height imposing; each muscle seemed to be throbbing with vitality. But after as little time as

104

Two Shadows's vision of the Grandfathers had lasted, the horse reared up on its hind legs, and with a loud snort of nervousness it turned and vanished on the path that had led Two Shadows to this place.

For a few moments Two Shadows stood, weak and trembling, his silver gaze held upon the path where the horse had disappeared. Shaking his head, he tried to convince himself that this mighty stallion must have also been a part of his vision, for surely there could not really be such a beast.

Slowly he slumped to the coolness of the rock, his body weak and his head light. Even his breathing was barely discernible—he felt his breath lightly touch his hand as he held it near his face. For a moment he shut his eyes in exhaustion, but he felt a soft touch upon his forehead and, looking up, he saw standing before him, with the sunlight forming a halo above her, his wife, Summer Dawn. She bent and lightly caressed his cheek with her lips.

"Summer Dawn," he softly gasped aloud, still unable to move his body.

"Lie still, my husband, and let me tend you this last time." Her voice seemed a part of the whispering of the wind in the tree tops. And as he did as she told him, she brought water to his lips to quench his thirst, and meat for his hunger.

Two Shadows had not been so content for the last two years, but so quickly it was at an end. As he watched, Summer Dawn seemed to lift up on the clouds. "No!" he shouted, and pulled himself to his feet, his arms outstretched as though he could keep her at his side.

"Do not be sad any longer, my husband." Her soft words filled his ears. "When you allowed yourself to forget and join with another, you allowed your son and myself to travel the star path and gain eternity. Live, my husband. Allow the new one to fill your heart. I will await you with the ones of the past." And with this she vanished into the clouds.

Two Shadows felt tears stinging within his eyes. His heart felt once again the agony of her loss. But as he took a deep breath, he knew something was different this time. It was as though he knew that the future would be faced without Summer Dawn, but it would not be faced alone. Then, near total exhaustion, and with the image of his warrior woman filling his mind, he slept.

The morning Two Shadows had left the village, he had awakened Nicholas and asked him to watch over his slave. His serious look told his friend of the importance of his request.

Nicholas had assured Two Shadows that he would indeed watch out for the warrior woman, though he was still unsure of the true feelings his friend held for her. He had been sleeping when the couple had come into the lodge the night before, and he had not witnessed the sight of Two Shadows and his captive climbing naked beneath the soft furs of his sleeping couch.

That first morning Nicholas awaited the warrior woman's awakening with some dread. If, upon finding that Two Shadows had left the Blackfoot village, she were to try and escape, he was not sure that he would be able to honor his friend's wish of watching over her. Deep in his soul, each time he looked into the woman's dark gaze, he felt deeply sensitive to her plight. He glimpsed a fragile, inner beauty in the woman that he had not seen in many others, and he did not like to see her endure the labeling of slave, even if her master was his closest friend. But the fact still remained that Two Shadows *was* his friend, and that he had asked him to watch over the woman. He felt duty bound to make an effort, but he knew that if the moment presented itself, he would be torn between his duty and his heart.

With the stirring of the warrior woman upon the sleeping couch across the lodge, Nicholas turned from the fire where he was making a pot of coffee. He smiled at the girl and called out a morning greeting, and for a moment he saw a warmth fill her features. Then her dark eyes looked about the lodge as though searching for someone, and Nicholas knew that the moment had come when he would have to explain Two Shadows's disappearance.

"Two Shadows has gone into the mountains to seek out the Great Spirit. He asked me to watch out for you while he is away," he signed in the hand language of the Indians. Two Shadows had been teaching him how to sign, and he hoped the girl could understand him.

For a moment she sat staring, a fur clutched to her chest, her eyes following the movement of his hands. Then slowly her eyes lowered to the sleeping couch, and one hand reached out and lightly smoothed the side Two Shadows had slept upon the night before. With this action her mind filled with the happenings of the past night. She was instantly flooded with a warm, tingling thrill as she remembered Two Shadows's strong hands gliding over her smooth flesh, his hungry, searching lips overtaking her own. And as she felt a blush staining her cheeks, she hurriedly pulled her dress modestly over herself, and bent over the couch to straighten out the furs.

Not knowing if she fully understood what he had said, and puzzled at her actions, Nicholas spoke to her again as he filled a tin cup with the fragrant coffee, made from the ground beans he had brought along in his saddle bags. "You do understand me?" And as the warrior woman lifted her eyes to meet his, she slowly nodded her head.

This was the first sign of response he had seen the girl give anyone, and with a grin, Nicholas saluted her with his cup. "Good girl," he said aloud.

A soft call was heard from the front of the lodge and the entrance flap was pulled aside as Sky Eyes interrupted the small truce the pair had established. "I thought that perhaps the warrior woman would care to come with me to the river for a swim to

108

start the day, and then perhaps she could join me this morning visiting some of the elderly of the village." Two Shadows had gone by his parents' lodge early that morning and beseeched his sister to take his slave in hand. Sky Eyes had agreed gladly, not only because it was her brother making this request of her, but also because she saw the opportunity to see Nicholas once again.

Nicholas greeted Sky Eyes, his green eyes coming alight as she entered the tepee. He seemed never to be able to see enough of her. She filled his heart with a special light that radiated throughout his entire being. "Some of the braves have invited me to go on a hunt this morning with them," he told her. "There is sign of a herd of buffalo not far from camp. If you two are occupied together, I shall feel free to go along."

Sky Eyes smiled warmly at this tall man who filled her soul. He was so handsome and strong. When she was in his presence nothing else seemed to matter. "Then we shall leave you to the ways of the braves, and we shall go and greet the mother sun as she rises and warms the day." Sky Eyes held out her slim hand to the warrior woman, her heart warming with its own sunshine as Nicholas's green eyes rested so hungrily upon her.

Without drawing back, Kalina took the hand offered her, for this morning her own spirits were rising to the heavens. She did not feel any hurt with Two Shadows's departure, for she knew that he was a great warrior. If he had gone to the mountains in

109

search of some special wisdom given by the Great Spirit, then surely he did not do so to be away from her side, but rather to aid his strength. She knew much of the ways of men, for she had been raised with many, and she knew that the man she had lain with the night before had not left his lodge and village because of her. His quest must surely be important to him, she thought, as she went along to the river with his sister. And surely he would be granted all that he sought.

As Sky Eyes pulled off her dress and raised her hands up toward the first bright rays of sunlight filtering through the tree tops, she began to chant her morning prayer. Kalina did the same, though her prayers were spoken silently within her soul, as she requested that the Great Spirit watch over the one who had touched her heart. She prayed that he would keep Two Shadows from the danger of evil spirits and wild beasts that could set upon him, and also that the Great Spirit would lead him back to his people quickly, for already she felt her loss.

After greeting the mother sun with their morning prayers, the two girls dove into the chilled, crystal water, splashing and swimming, as carefree as the children of the village who, a short time later, made their way with their mothers to the river's bank.

Drying their bodies in the chilled morning air with the soft deerhide that Sky Eyes had brought, the two women went back to Two Shadows's lodge to set about straightening up the interior.

Sky Eyes quickly noticed a difference in the other

girl, seeing her smile often during the morning and go swiftly about cleaning the lodge. When Sky Eyes hand-signed to the other young woman this morning, she eagerly nodded her head in agreement.

It was not long before the two women were making their way through the village, Sky Eyes's lilting voice calling out to children and mothers alike in greeting as they made their way to different lodges to see to the elderly and those who were ill.

Usually this task was left to Silver Star, who was now revered throughout the Blackfoot village as a mighty healing woman, but this day Sky Eyes's mother had asked her to attend those in need while she helped Medicine Wolf prepare special herbs and medicines.

Sky Eyes had often gone with her mother, and loved visiting the older people of their tribe. It was late afternoon when the two young Indian women stepped into a dimly lit lodge, the last they were to visit. Sky Eyes went quickly across to the sleeping pallet and, bending down, placed a kiss upon the wrinkled, leathery cheek of an old woman.

Kalina stood in the entrance of the lodge, the afternoon sunlight starting to light the interior. The old woman on the sleeping pallet near the pit fire, after accepting the kiss from Sky Eyes, turned in the other's direction. "Bright Lily!" she gasped aloud, and fumbled to raise herself on her elbows, her features coming alight with the vision of the woman standing in her lodge. "Come, come, child! It has been so long, so long."

Sky Eyes sighed softly, and going to get the warrior woman, she led her to the old woman's side. "Grandmother," she said, in respect of her age and wisdom, "this is my brother's slave. She is not the one you think. She is of the Crow village. She is not your daughter."

With these gentle words, the features of the woman upon the pallet seemed to shrivel, as once again memory came to the old woman. Slowly a tear slipped down the leathered cheek. "Yes, yes; you are right, daughter. This one is not my Bright Lily. My daughter and her child, Morning Star, have long been gone to the Great Spirit." With this the old woman fell back against her pallet, and for a moment held her eyes tightly shut as though she could not face the truth of her own words.

"Yes, Grandmother." Sky Eyes spoke softly, and lightly she caressed the trembling chin. "I have brought my brother's slave to help me today. She does not speak our tongue but she will soon learn." Sky Eyes set about pulling out herbs and plants from her parfleche and, after stoking up the fire, she set some water to boil and placed the leaves and herbs in the heated water. She and Kalina set about straightening up the lodge. Falling Leaves's husband had died the winter before, and her family were all long gone, so now all that remained in the large lodge was the old woman herself. Many here in the village helped the kindly old woman. The women of the tribe stopped by often to make sure that there was food and that Falling Leaves's lodge was warm and she was not in need. Kalina herself, as she worked about the tepee and listened to the old woman talking to Sky Eyes, found herself quickly softening toward her. She was so kind and concerned for everyone in her village. She gently questioned Sky Eyes about those who had been ill and asked about the new babies that had been born.

"Your brother's slave is very beautiful." She smiled at Sky Eyes as the young woman brought the herbed tea to her lips for her to drink. "It is strange that she, being of the Crow tribe, would be so lovely. And it is also strange that she reminds me so much of my own lost daughter." The old woman sighed as she finished the drink.

Sky Eyes smiled patiently at the older woman, thinking that her age was playing strange tricks upon her mind. "Grandmother, I have brought a drawing salve to place upon your chest. It will ease the cough that has been plaguing you."

Again the elder woman smiled her thanks, but now her gaze seemed fixed on the warrior woman as she finished folding some of the clothing that was heaped in a corner.

"Perhaps my brother's slave would help place the healing salve on your chest, while I go and fetch some fresh water and some more wood for your fire." Sky Eyes did not give the warrior woman a choice, but rose to her feet and placed the container of the yellowish, thick concoction in the other girl's hand. Quickly she signed what Kalina needed to do, and then without another word Sky Eyes left the

113

lodge. Her hope was that perhaps she could make the warrior woman feel needed. Perhaps this would help to make her open up with her feelings.

Kalina nervously bent down next to the small old woman upon the pallet. She had been given little training in the art of healing in her own village, because the other women of the Crow tribe had always tended to those who were sick. She had always been far too busy practicing with her brothers and Pointed Arrow on the lessons of war.

The dark eyes watched the younger woman as she silently began to unlace the front of her blouse. There was something so familiar about this young woman, Falling Leaves thought. And as the girl applied the healing salve with a light hand, a tender smile lingered about her features.

When Kalina slowly tied the leather lacings back up and tucked the furs about the small, frail body, she also smiled, her hand reaching out and lightly touching the wrinkled cheek.

Falling Leaves patted the girl's arm. As she rested back on the pallet, she sighed aloud.

Wondering what else she could do, Kalina went to the corner where she had folded away the old woman's clothing and picked up the horsehair brush that she had seen earlier. Approaching the woman once again, she bent, and as Falling Leaves looked inquiringly at her, she showed her the object in her hand and what she wished to do with it. The gray head nodded, and Kalina sat back and eased the woman's head into her lap. With a gentle hand

Kalina unbraided the long gray tresses, and with light strokes she combed out the snarls and began the rebraiding.

This was how Sky Eyes found the warrior woman when she reentered the lodge of Falling Leaves. Not saying a word, she placed the wood near the fire and set the water skin to one side. As she waited for the younger woman to finish dressing Falling Leaves's hair, she said, "Grandmother, I will see that you are brought some dinner. My mother will return this evening to change the salve on your chest and bring you more herb tea."

"I will welcome Silver Star. It has been a few days since she has visited me. She always speaks to me of the old days." For a moment the older woman seemed to lose herself in the past, her eyes closed as she imagined once again that her loved ones were all about her. And as the warrior woman started to rise, she took hold of Kalina's hands. "Thank you, child, for coming with Sky Eyes. You have brought happiness to these old eyes and pleasure to this heart. I hope that you will come again."

Kalina slowly nodded her answer, surprising Sky Eyes with her response to the older woman.

For the next two days Sky Eyes came early to her brother's lodge and kept the warrior woman busy the whole day, helping her with her meal in the evenings and always finding a few minutes to be able to speak with Nicholas.

It was on the third day that Star Hawk returned with his band of braves. That evening the village gave a feast as the council met, and talk circulated through the tribe of the war against the white man that was close at hand.

A score of drums throbbed with a steady pulse at the finish of the council meeting. Long into the night the men sat about the fire that had been built up in the center of the village, and at the completion of the talks the shouting and feasting began. Word spread like wild fire that the tribes had banded together and Star Hawk himself would lead the people against the white army. Dancing began, with bodies swaying and feet stamping, faces painted and bodies glistening before the leaping flames, as the men shouted and proclaimed the victories they would have over their enemies.

Nicholas sat back after the council meeting had ended, and watched as everyone in the village rejoiced at the words that had been shouted for all to hear. Hundreds of people sat about the large fire and watched as the dancers preformed. And as Nicholas sat near Star Hawk and the higher chiefs, he gazed across the fire and upon Sky Eyes.

Star Hawk had requested that Nicholas speak to the council and tell them all that his friends in Washington wished him to impart. Nicholas had spoken of peace, and had tried to persuade his new friends to hold off making war on the bluecoats, but his words were like fine-sifting sand in an hour glass, he quickly found, as the council spoke of all the injustices that the white man had inflicted upon the Indian in past years. And now, with an army

116

fort so close to their own village, and after hearing Star Hawk relate what his son Two Shadows had reported when he returned from the army fort, it was an overall decision that the tribes would no longer wait for the white man to attack them. They would join forces with the other four tribes, and attack the bluecoats before the white man could strike first.

It was a kind of mad hysteria that swept through the village. All seemed to be caught up in the throes of their spiritual communion and dancing, but Nicholas, despite his anxieties, was preoccupied with only one thing, and that was the lovely Indian maiden who now sat across the fire from him.

Sky Eyes was dressed in a white hide skirt and jacket, blue beads and quills decorating the outfit with a delicate edging. Her leggings were decorated with the same pattern. As she sat near the large fire, she had listened carefully as each brave of the council rose and spoke his mind. When it came to Nicholas's turn, Sky Eyes's pale glance watched with an admiring fascination. He was dressed in fringed buckskin shirt and leather pants, his clothing fitting his large frame like a second skin. The sight of him brought a tremendous beating to her heart. His golden hair glistened in the firelight, and as he spoke his green eyes seemed to sparkle with a rich intensity. His voice was strongly masculine as he told of Senator Willis and the men in Washington who were trying to help the Indians. He spoke of his uncle, Major Thatcher, and the deep misunderstandings between the white man and the red. He asked that the tribes wait a while longer so that Senator Willis could have more time to pressure the army into removing the fort. But even as his words were translated to those who could not speak English, it was easy to know by the loud murmurings of the crowd that the Indians would no longer be patient. They could not afford to sit and wait any longer. They felt that his uncle, the major, did not like the red man and had singled out Star Hawk's tribe to be the brunt of his dislike. By the time Nicholas took his seat again, the rumbling of the crowd had become a roar. The people wanted victory over this enemy that had trespassed across their lands. They would not sit back and endure any longer that which was being done to them.

Sky Eyes had felt a deep pride in her chest while this large white man spoke from his heart. And as he sat back down amongst those at the head of the council, her eyes remained upon him. She felt the heat of his gaze through the leaping flames. Not distracted by, nor even hearing, the shouts and cries of her people any longer, ignoring those who were stamping and dancing, she seemed drawn to the white man.

For a never-ending moment, their gazes locked. Surely she was a sorceress, Nicholas thought. She was enveloped in a sphere of strange magic. How else could he explain the force that at this very moment seemed to hold him prisoner? His entire being ached for her, and he didn't see how he could endure the pain of looking upon her much longer. And as though she also felt the fierceness that their gazes held, she silently rose to her feet and started to make her way from the large inner fire and the celebrating people.

The most serious part of the ceremony was now at a close. As the chatter and laughter rose to a high pitch and the beating of the drums began to keep a rhythm with the dancers, Nicholas also rose and started toward the darkness of the outer village. None seemed to notice as he disappeared from the crowd. He watched her retreating back as Sky Eyes made her way toward the river and stood at the bank. He approached silently.

Sky Eyes had known that he would follow. With every step she had taken, she had prayed to the Great Spirit that the one of her heart would find her, and now, as she heard a twig break, she turned to face him.

The golden moonlight seemed to encase Sky Eyes in its shimmering light, and as Nicholas looked at her, he felt stunned for a moment. "My beloved," he breathed aloud, but he dared not take a step toward her, fearing that the spell she had cast upon him would somehow be broken.

Sky Eyes felt the pounding of her heart, her ears hearing his words and a fine prickling tingling over her skin. "You will leave us soon." Her words were spoken softly, not as a question but as a statement of fact.

"Aye," came his quiet answer. "I had hoped that I

could help your people somehow. But now I see that I can do little good. I could do more if I were in Washington trying to help Senator Willis. I only hope that I will not be too late to do some kind of good." Still, Nicholas kept his distance, afraid of his own reactions to this woman if he drew closer.

"It will all be over before you ever reach this far-off place called Washington. You know this?"

"I know, Mary Jean." He called her by her white name as he always did, but this night it came as a light caress upon the evening's breeze.

"Why do you leave, then?" Sky Eyes felt the biting sting of her tears.

The moonlight glistened off the silver eyes and crystal droplets. Seeing the full pain of his leavetaking written plainly upon her lovely features, Nicholas could no longer keep his distance. Without regard for his will or his thoughts, he pulled Sky Eyes into his embrace. "I do not know what else I can do." The words pulled from deep within him, as though from his very soul.

"Stay here with my people, Nicholas." She looked into his handsome face, not caring that her feelings were evident upon her own face.

Over the past days Nicholas had dared to hope that this woman felt somewhat as he himself did. Now, with her soft words of pleading filling his ears, he was powerless to withstand the tremendous feelings roiling deep within his chest. "You truly care if I leave?" He seemed to hold his breath as he awaited her answer.

Slowly the shimmering, dark tresses moved as Sky Eyes nodded her head. "I care very much, Nicholas, and I would miss you terribly." Another small tear gently slipped from her silver eyes as she looked into his face.

As the moonlight enhanced the iridescent tear, Nicholas reached out a finger and gently wiped it from her cheek. His head descending, his lips gently covered hers.

Time ceased to exist as slowly the kiss developed into a sweet, sensual coming together of hearts and souls. This was destiny's rapture, a joining that was meant to be from the beginning of time, and a joining of two from totally different worlds. This was all that would ever be right!

Pulling his mouth from hers, Nicholas looked deeply into the face of the woman before him. "I love you, my beloved Mary Jean. With all of my heart and soul I love you."

"And I love you, Nicholas. I have loved you for so long. At times it seems like forever." Her joy knew no bounds as he again pulled her tightly against his chest and kissed her as no other had ever done before.

Daring to believe that she felt the same about him, Nicholas said, "I want you as my wife. I want you as my own, to remain at my side from this day forth. I will take you away from this war. We will go to England, to Rosebriar. My home is much the same as you, my sweet—gentle and serene." Again he kissed her long and hard, and as he did he felt the heat of his body begin to boil, his response to her womanly curves stoking the fires of his desire.

Sky Eyes knew that her fate was now interlocked with this man's, and she could only agree with whatever he asked of her. "I will willingly go wherever you lead."

This final admission of her feelings for him drove Nicholas onward. She was his, his soul cried out. Though he hardly dared to believe all that she had said, his mind kept repeating that this woman loved him. She was all that he would ever desire.

Somehow the pair found themselves lying on the grassy bank of the river. Their coming together was like the first gentle rays of the sun touching the earth on a cool winter's morning, so gentle and loving were their touches upon one another, their kisses seeking and sharing as they quickly divested each other of their clothing.

They clung together naked upon the cool, damp grass, their bodies a-tingle with arousal as their lips merged. And as Nicholas looked upon the perfection of the woman in his arms, his heart hammered fiercely in his chest. "I will love you forever, my beloved. Nothing shall ever come between us." His hands gently reached out and caressed the fullness of her heaving breasts, his mouth raining kisses over her face and throat, his tongue tasting of her sweetness.

Sky Eyes lost all reason as she lay within Nicholas's arms, his hands and lips playing a sensual melody upon her body that left her gasping aloud and calling his name to the stirring winds high atop the trees. Her arms encircled his shoulders, drawing him closer to her, and as she felt his maleness hot and throbbing against her inner thigh, she felt her passions soaring.

Gently and lovingly, Nicholas awakened Sky Eyes to the wonders of love. As he slowly eased her thighs wider and settled his body between them, his mouth sought hers again, his tongue filling her with a heated flame of need, as he sought out the substance of this woman.

Sensing her need was as towering as his own, Nicholas gently eased his body upon her, his searing member pushing its way forcefully but lovingly into the tightly molded sheath of her womanhood. The obstruction was broken. For a moment he stilled.

As the veil of her maidenhead was broken away, Sky Eyes winced with the sharpness of the pain, but as Nicholas stilled and she adjusted herself to the feel of his body and his manhood filling her, she slowly began to undulate her body against his own.

Nicholas kissed the small tears near the silver eyes, and then kissed the lips of rose-petal pink until the pair became breathless, his body slowly moving, his hands gently massaging her and seeking the hidden valleys of her flesh, as he awakened new heights in her desires.

Sky Eyes found her arms closed around Nicholas's body, her fingers digging into his muscular back as they became lost in their oneness. Her body and heart clung to him, and he began to move faster, and still deeper, his tender love words filling her ears as he spoke to her of his love, of her beauty, and of his need of her.

With one desire, which was to please this woman, Nicholas brought Sky Eyes to the highest realm of womanhood, and gently and caringly he swept her over the brink of reality. And as the moment reached them, Sky Eyes's head rolled back and forth upon the sweet smelling grass, her body growing taut as she reached the pinnacle of fulfillment. And in that searing moment of explosive joy when reality slipped away and only the shattering feeling from deep within penetrated, her body shuddered, her arms tightening about his shoulders as a gasp came from her throat. And with the sound of her fulfillment, Nicholas also peaked, his long, hard body trembling and shuddering with his towering climax.

Sweet, loving words filled her ears as Nicholas held on to this woman and, kissing every inch of her face and throat, he told her again of his feelings. Never had he felt this way about any other woman. His Mary Jean was the true woman of his heart, and he would never allow anything to stand in the way of his claiming her.

As they slowly began to face reality once again, and to gather and put on their clothing, Nicholas ventured, "I shall go to your father at once and ask for permission for us to wed."

Throughout her declarations of love and all her dreams of this man, Sky Eyes had not once thought ahead to this moment when her father would have to be approached. And as Nicholas looked at her, he saw fear on her beautiful face. He gently kissed her still-swollen lips. "It will be fine. I must go to your father as soon as possible, for I cannot risk losing what we have discovered. Whatever bride price he asks, I will give. You are worth all I own."

"But what if he refuses?" Now that their passions had been sated, Sky Eyes was thinking fearfully of all the reasons her father could present to keep them apart.

Nicholas, in his contemplations of this woman, had never dared to consider that she would be denied him. "Of course he cannot refuse us. Do not think this, my love. There will be a way for us. If I have to join your tribe and fight every brave your father can bring before me, I will have you." His words were bravely spoken; but upon reflection Nicholas wondered what the reaction of the fearless Star Hawk would be, when he went before him and requested the hand of his only daughter. Though it was true that the chief's own wife was a white woman, it was known that the Blackfoot had reason to hate those of the white race. In fact, at this very moment, these people were celebrating the coming war with his own kind. But still, he stubbornly refused to admit that they could be denied their love. "I will speak with him first thing in the morning."

"I think you should wait until after the sun-dance ceremony. My father will be very busy in the next few days and I would not wish him to hastily reject your request." Sky Eyes tied her leather belt about her waist as she said this.

Nicholas drew her once again into his arms. "You are very wise, besides being beautiful, my love. I shall wait until after the sun-dance ceremony, but no longer. I would wish to claim you as my own this very night if possible. I fear that I shall not be able to wait too much longer to know his answer."

Melting against his sturdy chest, Sky Eyes agreed with him. She also could not wait for him to claim her. With this first taste of love, she feared that she would die without feeling his body next to hers again.

The pair left the river, and Nicholas soon stood outside the lodge of Star Hawk and gently kissed Sky Eyes. As he left her side, a dark shadow stood nearby, the warrior's face contorting with rage at what he had just witnessed. With a muttered oath, he swore his revenge.

Early next morning Two Shadows returned to his village, but before going to his own lodge, he made his way to the tepee of Medicine Wolf.

The old shaman listened to all that Two Shadows told him of his days in the mountains. He patiently let the younger man tell all before he responded. "You have indeed received a mighty vision, Two Shadows. This eve you will begin to prepare yourself to participate in the sacred sun-dance ceremony.

126

You will purify yourself and your vision will be stronger. Then we will speak again."

Two Shadows looked upon the wise old man, not believing his ears. Was this all that he was going to say about his mountain vision? What of the mighty white stallion? Was it also a part of the vision, or had it indeed been real? Not wishing to offend the elder, but having to know these answers, he said, "Medicine Wolf, you are very wise. What can you tell me of this strange white horse that came to me high upon the rock? If it is truly real, perhaps I can capture it." A strange excitement filled Two Shadows as he thought of the wild beast. He felt exhilarated at the thought of sitting atop its mighty body.

For a full moment the black, ageless eyes peered into the young warrior's, and then softly Medicine Wolf spoke. "The sacred sun-dance ceremony will lead you where you will go. Prepare yourself, young warrior, for there is still much that you will learn."

Chapter Six

The steady pounding of the ancient medicine drum now beat with an incessant purpose. Evil spirits were being driven away and good spirits brought forth to be made welcome in the purification lodge. Medicine Wolf himself chanted as his frail hands tapped a rapid tattoo upon the stretched hide of the drum. Every now and then he would rise from his sitting position and pour a gourd of water over the heated rocks, causing warm steam to rise about the small tepee.

Two Shadows was with several other young men who were to perform in the sacred sun-dance ceremony. They were sitting or lying stretched out about the lodge, their own chants and prayers filling the small space as they beseeched the Great Spirit or a special spirit to help them in the ordeal that lay ahead for them.

Whenever Medicine Wolf poured the gourd of water over the rocks he would go to each of the young men and pray over them, making sure that the small piece of peyote button that he had given them was still held between their teeth and their lips. This piece of dream cactus helped induce a hazy state that allowed the spirits to enter into the minds and souls of the warriors.

Two Shadows lay upon the pallet nearest the heated stones. As his body sweated great droplets of water, and his insight became sharper with the help of the vision cactus, he felt almost as though he were floating. The colors of the lodge seemed the same shades as a rainbow. As his lips mumbled his prayers, each prayer seemed to hold a clearer meaning, coming to life with the utterance upon his tongue.

Prayers that his father, Star Hawk, had taught him as a child now seemed to come from deep in his being. His inner vision now was able to conjure up glimpses of the many faces of the people of his tribe, and his prayers were called out for each one. He saw the ragged, dirty hides of the herds of buffalo that his people hunted to survive, the thunder of their mighty hooves coming to his ears and the smell of their dung filling his nostrils; and with this vision, he prayed for his people to be fed. And as he prayed for their shelter, he could envision himself helping the meekest of the tribe with the building of a lodge. His insides were wrenched with a charity and a love for his people that he had never before known. It was as though he were being reborn, created over again, with the express purpose of caring for his tribe, these people he called his own.

Throughout the long day and night, Medicine Wolf poured water upon the coals beneath the heated stones, and often he would replace the vision cactus inside Two Shadows's lips, sensing the inner sweeping of this young warrior's soul.

The sun was streaming brightly down upon the land. A cooling breeze of mother winter forced those who were standing about to pull their blankets tighter about their frames. Medicine Wolf led Two Shadows and the other young warriors toward the open area that had been prepared for the sacred sun-dance ceremony. All the people of the village were sitting and standing about as they watched the young men who had prepared themselves for the ordeal of this most sacred ceremony.

Two Shadows was led toward the sacred poles, and as he stood, weak from his purification and fasting, Medicine Wolf called upon the Great Spirit to guide him as he slowly cut the flesh upon the young man's chest with a long-bladed hunting knife. Making two incisions and chanting a prayer, he drew the claws of the sacred eagle within the incisions and beneath the tendons of Two Shadows's chest.

Two Shadows stood straight, in no way indicating that he had felt the pain of the knife, and as the ropes tied to the two claws were slowly pulled, Two

Shadows was slowly raised off his feet and was held in the air upon the sacred sun-dance pole. His features were contorted now with tormented pain.

Only a few of the others were raised in a like manner. Most accepted the lesser torture of the eagle claws, but they were left on the ground and walked about the sun-dance poles in a state of exhaustion until the ropes attached to the pole and tied to the claws were strained enough to pull the tendons of the chest apart. The greater test was to hang in the air upon the sun-dance pole, but no matter what the method of the ordeal, all endured the ritual with the strength of their forebears.

The family of Two Shadows sat in the forefront of those watching, their own features bearing the pain that they knew he must be feeling. Star Hawk himself remembered the feel of the talons in his chest and the way the ropes would sway and pull the flesh with the slightest breeze, as he had hung in a like manner when he was much younger. He felt his insides turn with empathy for his son. Stoically he watched on. He knew that the pain was great, but the reward that his son would gain for these moments of torture would far override all that he had endured.

As Silver Star watched her son hanging in the air, she felt tears in her eyes, but she forbade herself to shed them. Such torture of the body was one of the hardest things for her to accept as a part of this tribe. The whites knew no such communion with their God. There was no need for such a test of strength. But as she loved these people, she also accepted their ways. And silently she bore the pain that her son was now enduring.

Sky Eyes, Nicholas, and the warrior woman sat behind Two Shadows's parents, all deep in their own thoughts as they looked at those hanging in the air or upon the ground and pulling against their tethers.

Kalina had not seen Two Shadows since the night they had made love, and as she watched him being led with the other braves, her heart began to beat rapidly. He was taller and broader than the others about him, his body stripped except for the brief loincloth about his hips. His arms, legs, chest, and face were painted with his own design. He looked invincible as he stood waiting for the medicine man to make the cuts upon his body; and when the knife had touched his flesh, it had been Kalina who had flinched, tears coming to her dark eyes as she watched the instant crimson flood of blood run down to his loincloth. Pulling her eyes from his chest, Kalina looked upon the bronzed face, and in his handsome features she could see no recognition of anything about him. His lips were moving in a chanting rhythm, his silver eyes were glazed as though he were in another world. Clasping her hands tightly in her lap, Kalina forced herself to sit still with the others and watch. She was called this man's slave, and she would not dishonor him by giving vent to the pain that was searing her heart. If he could capture the pain in his body and not show it, she could endure it from this distance.

As the heat of the sun bore down upon those swaying in the sky, their calls to the Great Spirits could be heard loudly above the sound of the ceremonial drums and the old shaman's voice calling to the spirits for strength and endurance.

For Two Shadows, time seemed nonexistent as his own voice mingled with the others. His pain now seemed only a throbbing numbness deep in his soul as he sought out the hand of the Great Spirit. He cried aloud over and over for the strength to tolerate the pain and to be worthy. And as, one by one, the other young warriors were answered by the Great Spirit, their bodies broke through the restraining ropes and they either fell to the earth or were freed upon the ground. Still, Two Shadows swung high in the air, his prayers now barely heard by those still sitting about as the afternoon slowly passed and the dusk from the evening skies deepened.

There came a time when the pain in Two Shadows's body seemed to become a solid part of his being, and for a moment he smiled as though welcoming this torture. He was absorbing the many plights of his people that would one day come, absorbing within himself all that they could be offered of grief and hardship. He was their buffer, the pain that would be inflicted upon them, he would bear as his own. And with this thought, the pain slowly seemed to slip away and he rose up beyond himself. High into the clouds he floated, as he had

133

that day in the mountains, only now he could see his body hanging by the eagle claws, he could hear the chanting of Medicine Wolf and see the faces of his family and friends. He was standing upon the clouds and watching the scene below, and as he looked about again he was circled by the fierce warriors of the days long past.

"You have done well, my son. Your heart is with your people, your strength, their shield." It was again the one with the golden eagle painted upon his war shield who was the first to speak to Two Shadows.

"Your might shall be beyond compare throughout the nations," another pronounced.

"We give the promise that we shall ever be at your side," still another voiced.

"Look up, for one day your name shall be shouted across the enemies' camp fires with great reverence. The legend of the Sacred Eagle and his Eagle's Wing shall be spoken upon the tongue of our people and all people alike. Your enemies shall fall at your feet in defeat. You shall raise up the people and bestow upon them the victory of many coups."

And as Two Shadows looked in the direction where the last warrior pointed, he saw himself sitting proudly upon the prancing back of the mighty white stallion, his body draped with a splendid cloak of white eagle feathers, and the war bonnet of a mighty chief upon his head. The stallion reared up on its long, muscular legs as it had that day in the mountains, but the warrior upon its back held easily to his seat, as one with the splendid beast. Two Shadows was in awe as he watched the scene that the Grandfathers were showing him, and at that moment, with a mighty cry of triumph, he pulled down upon the eagle claws wrapped through the tendons of his chest.

His vision was at an end. Two Shadows fell to the ground, his father swiftly going to his side as did Medicine Wolf himself. Picking him up, Star Hawk bore him to the shaman's lodge so the old man could tend him and hear of his vision. The rest of the family followed and awaited word of his condition outside Medicine Wolf's lodge.

Two Shadows had lost consciousness. His recent days seeking a vision in the mountains, and now his endurance of the sun-dance ceremony had taken their toll. But Star Hawk and Medicine Wolf made him comfortable in the old shaman's lodge, and as the elder man mixed some herbs in a small gourd of water, held this to his lips, and gently poured the mixture down Two Shadows's throat, he slowly began to revive, his breathing shallow and his pulse erratic as he remembered all that he had seen a short time ago.

Medicine Wolf sat down next to Two Shadows's pallet, as was the custom. After one had endured the sun dance and desired to know fully what the vision meant, the shaman was the one that helped sometimes to make sense of things that at first seemed incomprehensible.

135

Star Hawk sat off to the side, not wishing to interfere between his son and the wise man, but desiring with all his heart to hear the words that Two Shadows would say, for he felt that the vision that had come to his son was monumental.

"The Grandfathers came again, Medicine Wolf. And as in the mountains, the one with the golden eagle painted upon his war shield called me his son, and told me that I had done well and that my heart is with our people and that my strength would be their shield."

The shaman now spoke softly. "This one that called you his son was your grandfather, Golden Eagle."

Two Shadows had thought as much, and was not surprised by the wise man's words. But Star Hawk felt his heart race at this news that his son had spoken with his own father.

"Go on, Two Shadows; tell me all," Medicine Wolf prodded gently.

"Another then spoke aloud, and said that my might shall be beyond compare throughout the nations. What could the Grandfathers mean by this, Medicine Wolf?" Two Shadows asked the shaman, for he knew that at times things were not as easily explained as they appeared.

"What else was told to you?" Medicine Wolf ignored his questions until he had heard all and could better explain what he was being told.

"As in the mountains, another said that the Grandfathers would always be at my side. The last pointed to the heavens and told me to look up, for one day my name would be shouted across the camp fires with great reverence. Then he said something very strange." Medicine Wolf and Star Hawk both seemed to hold their breath in anticipation, and he added, "He said that the legend of the Sacred Eagle and his Eagle's Wing shall be known upon the tongues of all the people."

Two Shadows looked inquiringly into the wise eyes of the man sitting next to him, but Medicine Wolf waved his questions away. "And did you do as he said? Did you look where he pointed?"

Slowly Two Shadows nodded his ebony head. "I looked to where he pointed, and I saw again the mighty white stallion, only this time I was sitting upon its back and about my shoulders was draped a cape of white eagle feathers. A war bonnet of the same feathers was upon my head. The great beast reared up on its hind legs, as it did that day in the mountains, but with ease I controlled it. And then the vision was gone." He let out a long breath.

Medicine Wolf stared hard at the young warrior lying upon the sleeping couch. Then, taking his medicine pouch, he began to smear a soothing ointment on the open wounds on his chest. "You have been given a mighty sacred vision. Many years ago, Chief Soaring Eagle wore the cape that you saw in your vision. The cape was revered as sacred, and held mighty powers that aided our chief to be invincible. The cape was placed in the care of the shaman of our tribe in those days, and upon the death

137

of Soaring Eagle it was placed in a special hiding place. The secret of the cape and its place of rest has been handed down to me. Your vision tells me that it is now time to bring the sacred cape out of rest."

Two Shadows was surprised by the old man's words, but he did not speak, lest he break the spell that was about the lodge and he learn no more of the meaning of his vision.

"The Grandfathers have assured you that they will help you to be a mighty leader of your people one day. They have also given you a new name — a name that will be heralded about the camp fires of the people in the new dawns to come. That name is Sacred Eagle. You are no longer Two Shadows. Your shadows have been joined, and the Grandfathers have willed that you be known no more as a part of another, but as a great war chief in days to come. The mighty stallion shall be known as Eagle's Wing, and it shall be a beast sent from the Grandfathers themselves to aid you in your quest to help your people."

For a time the lodge remained quiet, almost in reverence of the words that had been spoken. But when Medicine Wolf added, "It was wise that your father, our chief, sent you to the white man's world, for this will help you in the days to come, and will help our people know victory."

"My father has always been a wise man." Two Shadows, now called Sacred Eagle, looked to where his father was sitting and saw the gleam of new respect in the dark gaze held upon his son. There was love and pride between father and son that with this vision would be strengthened. "But how will it all come about, Medicine Wolf?" Sacred Eagle questioned. "What of the sacred eagle cape and the white stallion? How will I come by them?"

"If the Grandfathers showed you them, then have patience and all will come to you at their will."

Star Hawk nodded his dark head at his son, confirming the wise man's words. These were spiritual people, led by their visions and dreams, and there was no doubt in the minds of the three men in the lodge that all would come to pass as Sacred Eagle had seen.

The sky was just turning the pearl-gray of early dawn when Sacred Eagle roused himself from the sleeping couch in Medicine Wolf's lodge. With a glance to see that the shaman still slept, he rose to his feet in slow, halting movements. His body was sore from yesterday's experience, and looking down at his chest and the yellowish salve still over his wounds, he smiled slowly as his vision once again filled his mind. He felt rather well considering all he had endured in the past days, and with the sunlight slowly coming through the edges of the old shaman's tepee, he was anxious to greet this new day.

He stood at the entrance of Medicine Wolf's lodge and, raising his face toward the sun, he greeted the day, his hands raised in supplication to the heavens. He began to chant his morning prayers as he had been taught at an early age. This morning, though, he felt a new vibrance in his being. He had been reborn, and now he wished to thank the Great Spirit for all that He had bestowed on him. His broad, bronzed body stood straight and bold as he called aloud to the Grandfathers, and as Medicine Wolf slowly roused himself on his sleeping mat and his dark gaze beheld the young, near-naked man standing in his entrance with the sunlight shining on his body, he knew in his heart that Sacred Eagle would be a fierce and worthy leader of his people.

After his prayers, Sacred Eagle made his way slowly to his own lodge. As he entered the flap, his silver eyes were instantly drawn across the space to his sleeping couch. The furs were pulled back and his slave was deep in slumber. Her long, silky, dark tresses were fanned out about the furs, and her face in sleep seemed peaceful. He remembered yesterday, as he had hung upon the sun-dance pole and had been given the sight by the Grandfathers to look down upon his family. He could see her now as he saw her then. The worry and concern for him etched upon her beautiful features had told him much of her inner feelings. And as he now looked down upon her, the night they had spent together came boldly into his mind.

Without a second thought, he climbed beneath the furs, pulled her slim form up tightly, and molding his own body about hers, he sighed with contentment, his silver eyes closing as her sweet scent circled about him.

Kalina awoke the instant Sacred Eagle touched the sleeping couch, but as he settled his large body about hers she tried to remain as still as though she still slept. These past few days she had thought of nothing else but this man and what had taken place between them. Now, as she felt his breath along the nape of her neck and his hands lightly touching her flesh, with a thrill and a racing heart she forced herself to stay relaxed. She knew that he still must be exhausted and in pain from all he had gone through. There would be plenty of time for her to show him her feelings.

Sacred Eagle, though, was of a different mind. With the feel of her satin skin against him and his memory kindling the pleasures he had enjoyed while lying next to this woman the night before he left to go into the mountains, his flesh tingled. At the simple feel of her, his manhood quickly rose and boldly pushed against her thigh.

Sacred Eagle shifted his body so that he was lying half atop her. His seeking mouth came down on hers, tasting and exploring the sweet desire within her. His embrace was so tight and fierce that for a second Kalina feared she would not be able to breathe, but in that second, she did not care. Sacred Eagle hungrily took her lips with passionate skill and resolve.

Easily slipping her arms about him to encircle his

141

waist, Kalina allowed her hands to slip over his back. He was a potent drug that dazed and intoxicated her senses. The feel of flesh tightly molded to flesh left not a spot upon her body that was not tingling with his tantalizing presence. Sacred Eagle's warm breath caused her to tremble as he lightly murmured words of passion in her ear. His large but gentle hands roved over her sensitive body and brought each inch to life and full awareness.

As his hands became bolder, her entire body molded against his, urging him to conquer and claim her, to possess her, to explore, and to declare her flesh his own, to mark her thoroughly with his ownership. Wild and shattering sensations assaulted her, enslaving her more fully than the words of master and slave. Wanting to fully savor his touch and caress, Kalina tried to prolong her fiery want, but alas, her need was far too great.

With a slow, seductive movement her hand twined within his long, dark tresses, drawing his mouth fully against her own. As one of his hands provocatively eased down and across her flat stomach, seeking out the hidden place that called out to his touch and stoked his desires, Kalina moaned deep within the back of her throat and writhed beneath him in unleashed rapture. For a time he let his hands explore her most enticing hidden treasures. He roamed, charted, invaded, sought out, conquered, and claimed as his fingers branded her womanhood with a fiery invasion. His heated tongue caressed her lips and he tasted the full eagerness of her sweet mouth.

Feeling only his transcendent need for this woman beneath him, Sacred Eagle rose and shifted between her parted thighs. His body smoldering with passion, he swiftly and urgently filled her. The contact of his manhood with her warm, pulsing sheath staggered his senses. He moved deliberately, holding himself in check so as not to allow his self-control to vanish too soon.

Lightly moaning with each exit of his manhood and arching fully to meet him with each entry, Kalina more than responded to his every touch. Her slim hands lightly wandered over his strong back, feeling for herself the large muscles rippling with his every movement. And as her body moved faster and faster, as she rose up to meet the cascading pleasure that showered about her, Sacred Eagle increased his pace and stormed her body with a savage gentleness that left her gasping and trembling in his arms.

A bursting cry of victory was pulled from Kalina's depths as the towering release claimed her. And as if it was a signal to claim his own passions, Sacred Eagle quickly and eagerly followed her blissful journey. His large body shook with the full force of an equally staggering release. His lips sought hers again, blending them together as one until their bodies had ceased their spasms of trembling, and his body was fully as conquered as hers.

They lay entwined as their senses floated back to them, and a peaceful contentment settled about them, lulling them into a light slumber as though no words of shared tomorrows were necessary.

Sacred Eagle's last thoughts were of the words that Summer Dawn had spoken as she departed from him, high in the mountains: "Live, my husband. Allow the new one to fill your heart. I will await you with the ones of the past."

Chapter Seven

Nicholas washed himself at the water's edge. He had risen early after a fretful night of little sleep, his mind filled constantly with the image of Mary Jean. His heart hammered each time he thought of the night before last, when he had lain with her and claimed her. All day yesterday he had been near her during the sun-dance ceremony, but he had been unable to reach out and touch her. Today he had determined that he would approach her father on the matter of taking his daughter for his wife.

He had already thought about the bride price that might be asked, and though he held much wealth in England, here in the wilderness he knew that wealth would do him little good. He could purchase blankets and other supplies that the Blackfoot people could need, but he would value the prize more if he was not able so easily to gather the bride price. He would offer horses, as the other braves of this village did. This was the usual gift offered to a father for the hand of an Indian maiden. He would offer Star Hawk as many horses as he wished, a whole herd, if that would gain him the woman of his heart. And he would come by them as her own people did. This, he knew, would earn the respect of Star Hawk himself and of the other braves of the tribe. Nicholas was sure that Sacred Eagle would help him capture the horses. His only real doubt was the fact that he was a white man, and he knew that for this reason alone Star Hawk might reject his suit.

This thought brought more worries to his mind as he secured a loincloth about his hips and tied his leggings in place. His friend had given him these when he had arrived at the village, and Nicholas thought now would be a good time to wear them. He wished to present himself as one with these people, and worthy in Star Hawk's eyes to claim his only daughter.

As he nervously gathered his clothing from the riverbank and went back to Sacred Eagle's lodge, Nicholas noticed that his friend had returned. Across the tepee, he saw the warrior woman nestled tightly against Sacred Eagle's chest. With a small grin, he poured himself a cup of coffee from the pot he had set upon the fire earlier. He had wondered how long it would take for the beautiful Indian woman to capture the heart of the mighty eagle. He knew that it would not be smooth going for the couple. There would be many obstacles to overcome before they would truly find happiness, for the warrior woman, like himself, was of a different people and would have to prove herself. The smile returned as Nicholas again looked at the pair. He had seen much in the warrior woman to assure him that she could easily conquer any adversity that would come before her. This thought inspired him as he started from the lodge. The sun was rising and he, too, would begin the day with no thought of defeat.

Star Hawk and his family had just finished the morning meal when Nicholas made his entrance into their lodge. Silver Star smiled with pleasure at the young man who had befriended her son when he had been away at school. In a pleasant tone, she offered him a seat in the center, across the fire from her husband. She did wonder at the young man's appearance so early in the day, and when Sky Eyes looked upon Nicholas and then quickly lowered her eyes and flushed lightly, Silver Star studied the couple, looking carefully from one young person to the other.

There was definitely a tension in the air of the lodge; it seemed to pass between Nicholas and Sky Eyes as the white man softly greeted the Indian girl. Even Star Hawk himself noticed the expectation in the atmosphere.

"I am pleased, friend, that you have come to visit this day." Star Hawk smiled at the white man, his dark gaze taking in the native attire, which looked well upon his tall, muscular frame. "Your words at the council two nights ago were wisely spoken. I thank you for speaking your heart to my people."

Nicholas sat cross-legged across from Star Hawk. "I wish there could truly be peace between your people and my own, Star Hawk. Your son is like a brother to me, and my heart is saddened by the fighting and bloodshed that has occurred between the white man and the red."

"Will you be leaving our village soon?" Star Hawk asked, wondering if this was the reason for the white man's visit. "I would not wish to force you to choose sides against your own people if you were still among us when we face the bluecoats. And I would not expect you to raise your knife against your own blood." He was conscious that the leader of the bluecoats was Nicholas's uncle.

"This is one of the reasons why I have come here this morning to speak with you, Star Hawk. I would ask that you hear me out before you answer what I ask you to consider. I have brought this to you as a small token of my respect." Nicholas drew from his leather shirt a pouch of tobacco and handed it to Star Hawk.

Inhaling the fine aroma of the tobacco, Star Hawk grinned widely. He spoke a word to Silver Star who was across the tepee with Sky Eyes, working quietly on a pair of moccasins; she rose and brought her husband his pipe.

"You are a guest here in my village, and a close friend of my son. I will hear your words and consider them fully before I venture to answer." Star Hawk filled the pipe with the rich tobacco and lit the bowl with an ember from the glowing coals.

Nicholas let out a long sigh as he went over again in his mind all he had rehearsed during the night and on his way to Star Hawk's lodge. He knew that he had to present his suit in a competent manner if this wise chief were to even consider allowing his daughter to wed him. And though Nicholas felt his chest tighten with fear as he looked into the strong face across from him, he took a deep breath and began. "First, I would like to say again that your son, who is now called Sacred Eagle, is indeed a brother to me. We have fought and hunted, laughed and learned together over the years, and nothing could ever sever the tie between us."

Star Hawk drew upon the pipe and savored the fine taste of the tobacco. Slowly his dark head nodded in agreement. "Your words strike sharply in my heart, friend. My son has also told me of this friendship, and how you offered him your hand in a time when he had no other to call friend."

"I do not mean to presume upon this friendship, Star Hawk," Nicholas responded as he took another deep breath and went on. "In my youth I longed to see your way of life, to hunt the buffalo, to ride with a group of young braves, to know that I can fight for my very life if necessary. In days past, Sacred Eagle drew pictures of all this in my mind when he told me of this life, so far from civilization and also so different from anything I had ever known. He also told me of the hearts of his people, of their tender and caring ways, how they helped

149

each other and depended upon one another for their survival. Since coming to your village, I have found all that he told me to be true."

Star Hawk only nodded his head. He passed the pipe to Nicholas and then quietly sat back as he drew upon it and returned it to him.

"I have also found, since being here in your village, that I care a great deal for your people." Clearing his throat, Nicholas tried to come to the point. "You see, sir, the thing is, I have fallen in love with your daughter. I have come today to ask for her hand."

Though he did not say anything and his face did not in any way show his surprise, Star Hawk was indeed taken back by the young man's frank words. But as he sat and smoked his pipe and watched the younger man, he remembered the tension between the two young people when Nicholas had first entered the lodge. "Has my daughter made known her feelings on how she would accept such an offer?" Star Hawk did not look across the tepee, but he could feel the eyes of both women upon him from across the room. They had halted their sewing and both sat watching the men.

"Perhaps you would care to ask her yourself, sir. But I confess that Mary Jean does know how deeply I care for her."

"You call by her white name? In your heart, then, you see her white blood? You wish to take her from her village to the white man's land, to live in your home across the sea, in England?" Star

150

Hawk asked this but did not give him time to answer his questions. "What of her family here?" Now he did wait for an answer, for already he feared that his daughter felt strongly about this young white man. And he did not know if he would be able to deny them the desires of their hearts; but before he could agree he would have to hear all.

"Yes, sir, I would take Mary Jean as my wife back to my home in England, for I have many responsibilities there. And yes, sir, it is a long way from her own people. But I promise that we would return to visit. I would never want her to forget or to set aside the ways of her people or her life here. I love her for what she is now, not what she will be one day. And also, sir, I would want to stay here until all is settled between the army and your tribe. I would fight with my brother Sacred Eagle, for those who would harm the family of the woman I love are also my enemies." As the dark eyes seemed to stare through to his very soul, Nicholas quickly began to fear that he was losing ground. All he could envision was this man saying no to his request. "Sir, if you think that because of my white blood I am not worthy of your daughter, I would be the first to agree. But I am unworthy not because of my blood, but because I cannot think of any man who could be worthy of such a treasure. I will love her forever if you agree. Never have I felt for any other as I do for Mary Jean. I would move heaven and earth to see that she remains happy. If she desires to remain with her people, I would agree

151

to make her happy. I would become one of your tribe. I would do anything that is demanded of me. Only, sir," — Nicholas was pouring out his heart, for he saw no other way in which to explain how he felt for Sky Eyes — "please think upon the matter and do not refuse out of hand just because of my white blood."

For a moment the lodge was quiet. Sky Eyes, having heard the words of her beloved, felt the sting of tears behind her eyes. Slowly Star Hawk lowered the pipe and emptied the bowl into the ashes. "In my youth, I knew many worthy white men, men whom I trusted with my very life and whose lives were entrusted to me. I also traveled the vast waters years ago, and went to this place called England. It was not of my choosing, but my most valuable treasure had been stolen from me and I had no choice." He stopped, and his dark eyes went across the lodge and fixed upon his wife. For a second her shimmering eyes locked with his ebony ones and they both seemed to be pulled backward in time.

"I went into the white man's land, as you are now in mine, and I joined my strength with a small band, for it seemed the only way to regain that which had been taken from me. I can hear much of my own heart in your words, friend. My own story had a happy ending, and I cherish now the memories of those who befriended me. I will consider your words, and shall give you an answer before the women and children are moved back into the mountains."

152

As Star Hawk sat back against his couch and looked quietly at Nicholas, the younger man knew that their talk was finished, but as he rose to his full height, he ventured one last thing. "The bride price, sir?"

A slow, wide grin settled over Star Hawk's features. "My daughter is a Blackfoot princess. Her price shall not be small; but you shall also have my answer to this before the move to the mountains."

Nodding his head once again, Nicholas turned to leave the lodge, his green eyes looking to Sky Eyes and his heart melting as she blessed him with a beautiful smile that spoke fully of her love. It would be at least a week, he knew, before he would be given an answer. The council had spoken the night before of moving the women, children, and elderly, with a small band of warriors to guard them, back into the mountains near their summer camp. This precaution was to be taken in case the fighting came too close to the village or the army attacked sooner than they expected. A week, Nicholas thought. At least he had not been told no, as he had truly feared.

For the rest of the day Nicholas's mind went over and over the interview with Star Hawk. At times he feared that he had not said the right things; then he would sense that he had said too much. His insides rumbled with the fear that he would not be granted his heart's desire, and with this thought he was filled with a dark, desperate ache. What would he do if he could not have Mary Jean? How could he leave this place, knowing that he was turning his back on her and riding away from the woman he loved? As he set his dinner bowl off to the side, he sighed aloud. If only Star Hawk had told him his answer today, he would not be in this torment. He would at least know, one way or another.

Sacred Eagle looked at his friend and then at the warrior woman, who gazed back at him with a worried frown.

Rising to his full height, Nicholas muttered under his breath about needing some air, and left the lodge, leaving Sacred Eagle and Kalina to stare at his retreating back.

Nicholas had not told even Sacred Eagle about his approaching Star Hawk that morning. It was as though he thought that if he kept his request to himself he would have a better chance of Star Hawk agreeing. Kicking at a rock as he walked along the riverbank, he thought how foolish this was. More than likely, half the village knew by now of his visit to their chief's tepee. News traveled quickly in this tribe.

The moon was just beginning to shine golden moonbeams through the scudding clouds as Nicholas, his mind in turmoil, sat down, his back against a large pine tree. He had not even been able to see Mary Jean during the rest of the day. He had hoped that she would come to her brother's lodge and they could talk for a small time. Perhaps she would offer him some hope. But all day she had remained in Star Hawk's lodge and Nicholas had wandered about the village without a clue as to what had been said after he had left the chief's lodge that morning.

Then, as though his turmoil was sufficient to conjure forth the image of the one he so desperately desired, Mary Jean suddenly appeared out of the shadows of the forest.

Time seemed to flee as the pair found themselves in one another's arms, their bodies molded, their lips sealed. For an eternity they stayed thus, not able to feel and taste enough of each other. All their worries and problems were gone. This moment, this feeling of belonging and oneness, was all that mattered.

"I thought I would not see you again today. I thought I was dreaming when I saw you walking toward me," Nicholas breathed next to her cheek, loath to release her from his arms.

Sky Eyes sighed with contentment as she relaxed in his arms, her heart pounding in her ears. "I went to my brother's lodge and he told me you had gone for a walk. I had hoped to find you here near the river."

Again Nicholas's lips descended to hers in a gentle clasp of love. "I have done nothing today but think about you," he sighed, as his mouth roamed from her lips to her cheek and then tasted the tender skin of her forehead. "My body seems to ache for the slightest glimpse of you."

"My mother has kept me busy all day at her side." Sky Eyes smiled into the glittering emerald

155

eyes that were shining their devotion.

"And did your father say anything about my visit to your lodge this morning?" Nicholas was anxious to hear the reaction of Star Hawk.

Still smiling, Sky Eyes slowly nodded her head, and as his hands gently tightened about her forearms to prod her further, she answered. "He said that the white man has the courage of our people. He was impressed that you came to him in the manner of our tribe."

"Was that all he said?" Nicholas was incredulous. Was he truly going to consider his request?

Sky Eyes saw the fear upon his face and with a small laugh she caressed his furrowed brow. "Do not worry so, my love. My father knows my feelings for you, and he has never denied me my heart's desire. He has wished me to find the one I would spend the rest of my life with; and now that I have, he will not lightly turn his back upon the one I choose."

Feeling his chest swell with the unbearable fullness of love for this woman, Nicholas pulled her tightly against his chest. "I love you so much. At times it hurts when I think of how slim the chance is that you will be mine."

"I have always been yours," Sky Eyes murmured as her lips sought his.

Slowly they slipped to the grassy banks of the river, their bodies clasped tightly as their lips and tongues sought out the inner depths of each other. Their fevered hands roamed over clothing and flesh until all that lay between them was their raging needs.

His lips devoured hers like the most potent wine, bringing his senses to a heady peak and inflaming his body beyond the boundaries of rational feeling. He felt a throbbing wantonness deep in his very soul. Sky Eyes was all he would ever need. She was Woman, spellbinding and beautiful, her touch as soft as satin, her voice a lilting song. She was his, only his.

Strong, probing, plundering fingers roamed freely over Sky Eyes's body, bringing her passions to a flaming peak. Nicholas's mouth seemed to be in all places at one time: opening to take a full, ripe breast, his demanding tongue making delicious patterns across her engorged, rose-tipped breasts; his lips going lower and his tongue now covering her skin, bringing soft moans from her as he tasted of the sweet ambrosia of her body.

As his head went even lower to the triangle of her passion, Sky Eyes felt herself slipping from the sane world. Her body was a throbbing, volcanic storm, aching for something beyond her reach, but knowing fully that this man, this towering warrior now mounting her, could guide her to fulfillment.

His mouth and tongue seemed to plunder her very core of existence, to drain her of substance and then to raise her once again to the very pinnacle of pleasure. She was swiftly taken up hills and plunged into valleys of feeling that she had never known before, then swept into a world where only she and he existed.

As he rose once more above her and lay at her side, prolonging the sweet fulfillment that was to come, Sky Eyes reached out a slim hand and boldly ran it over his body. She felt the corded muscles of his chest and belly, and when her hand roamed farther down and gently held on to his throbbing member, she heard and felt the quick catch in his breath.

"Oh, no more, my love," he moaned, taking her hand and bringing it to his lips. He had no desire to waste himself; he wished only to lose himself in the sweet folds of her body.

Sky Eyes was passion-filled as he rose above her, spreading her thighs gently, his manhood probing her innermost recesses. And as his throbbing organ pushed its way within, her moans of pleasure filled his ears.

Nicholas slowly developed a sensuous, luring rhythm, each movement tender and gentle, his lips kissing her throat and face. From deep within him came sweet love words, praising her beauty and expressing his love.

The soft music of the moonlit night seemed to settle about the pair and enhance this secret interlude. The chirping of the cricket, an owl hooting off in the distance, the gentle lapping of the river against the grassy banks, and off in the night the activity of the Indian camp—all seemed to heighten the sacredness of this magic moment.

With a deep moan of unbearable pleasure Nicholas wrapped Sky Eyes's satin legs about his waist, plunging deeper and deeper inside her, making her body one large unquenchable force that strove for fulfillment. Pulsating, sweating, she strove for the earth-shattering pleasure that she knew was so near.

And when it came, she gloried in the towering feeling, losing her senses in sheer, pulsating pleasure that left her gasping and clinging to his broad back as though he were her only link with a spiraling world.

When she reached fulfillment, Nicholas felt his whole being swell with an unreasoning pride. For a few short moments longer, his large body drank of hers and then he, too, felt that sheer, brilliant delight begin at the center of his being and radiate in a mighty, plunging storm of rapture.

Finally his body stilled. His breathing was ragged, but his lips roamed over Sky Eyes's face and throat, still unable to get enough of her passion-drenched body. "You inflame my senses beyond reason, my little Mary Jean." He finally managed to say.

Lightly, Sky Eyes's hand came up and caressed his jaw. "It is like heaven here in your arms," she said, her face against his chest, hearing the turbulent beating of his heart.

For a short time they were encircled in quiet as they lay clutched together, their bodies naked and intertwined, their breath mingling, their hearts sealed in the love that lay between them.

* * *

The large Crow village lay deep in the forest by a fast-flowing stream whose life-giving water sustained the encampment. Nicholas, Sacred Eagle, and Night Rider lay flat upon their bellies and watched the activity of the camp from a small rocky cliff. As they spied the herd of horses near the stream they grinned largely at each other.

It had been three days since Nicholas had approached Star Hawk to request Sky Eyes as his wife, and Sacred Eagle was now fully rested after the ordeal of his vision quest and the ritual of the sacred sun-dance ceremony. When Nicholas had awakened this morning, Sacred Eagle and Night Rider had urged him to accompany them. Their mission had been a secret until this very moment when Nicholas saw where their eyes rested.

"It will be much easier than we expected, Sacred Eagle." Night Rider spoke softly. "There are no guards in the village. Our enemies go about their days without a care. Their men are lazy and play games, and their women gossip and visit with one another. We will await the darkness of the night, steal into their village, and capture the prize of their fat horses for your brother."

Nicholas looked with unbelieving eyes at the two men at his side. They had brought him to this Crow village to steal the horses! And if he had heard Night Rider correctly, the horses would be for him. They must have planned this escapade to try and help him win Mary Jean! "If you mean to help me

160

gain the bride price I will be needing, I am grateful, but do not wish you to risk your lives on my problems. Anyway, Star Hawk has not as yet made his decision."

Sacred Eagle grinned widely. "You would do the same for me or Night Rider. And my father will have to look upon you with much favor when you come riding into the village with this large herd of horses. Besides, I need some excitement, and nothing excites me more than to torment the Crow." Sacred Eagle turned his gaze back to the village. The thrill of their venture started all the old familiar feelings stirring once again in his chest, as always happened when he was so close to his enemy. "We will not await the cover of darkness as our cowardly enemies, the Crow, do," he said. "We shall go up stream, to there." He pointed toward the stream and disclosed to his friends how if they moved quietly upstream, since there were no guards to warn the village of their approach, they could easily steal away with the horses.

Nicholas listened to Sacred Eagle with fear in his heart. This was surely the most daring exploit he had ever attempted with this friend he called brother, and he knew, as he looked upon Sacred Eagle and saw the flush of excitement high upon his cheeks, that there would be no dissuading him.

Even though he, too, knew that the plan was very daring and dangerous, Night Rider nodded his head in agreement with Sacred Eagle's words. Sacred Eagle had always been the leader of the two and this situation was no different.

Silently, the three mounted their horses and slowly led them down to the water where they could venture upstream along the shallow side, which lay nearest the village. They bent over their mounts' backs in case they were seen, but as they neared their destination and no alarm was given, they sat upright and slowly walked their horses toward the bounty they sought.

It was Sacred Eagle who went in the lead and approached the large herd of horses. Without dismounting he entered the enclosure, his own horse like one of the herd as he slowly went to the rear of the animals.

It all seemed to happen in the blink of an eye. With a loud shout and then a mighty war cry that carried harshly in the early afternoon air, Sacred Eagle kicked at his horse's sides. With a start, the group of horses responded, their ears turned back as they crowded toward the entrance of the enclosure. Then, as one, they were out and racing toward the stream.

Night Rider's and Nicholas's voices could be heard along with Sacred Eagle's. They followed him as he herded the horses back downstream, in the direction they had come.

The village came alive when the Crow heard the war cries of their enemies, the Blackfoot, and the mighty noise of galloping horses. The braves came from their tepees, their hands grasping their weapons as they ran toward the corral. But they were too late: all that could be seen was the Blackfoot warriors riding fast, herding their horses downstream.

Curses and shouts of retribution were shouted toward the retreating backs as the enraged Crow Indians watched their horses being stolen from them. With mighty oaths they swore that they would have their revenge.

The threesome hurried their pace as they herded the horses away from the Crow village, fully alert now to the danger of the Crow braves gaining in pursuit; but as they got further away they realized that this herd must have included all the horses of the village. And by the time the sun had lowered and there had been no sign of retaliation, the three were in jovial moods.

"Your bride price will be higher than any my father could ever expect," Sacred Eagle laughed aloud as they made camp and secured the horses for the night.

"I do not know how to thank you both for your help." Nicholas was amazed that they had managed this theft and that he had now got the bride price he would need to claim Mary Jean. "But I still have a couple of days before Star Hawk will give me his answer."

Sacred Eagle heard the note of fear in the white man's voice. "Do not worry, my friend. When my father is presented with this herd of fine horses in front of the whole village, he will be filled with pride that you value his daughter so highly."

Night Rider nodded his head in agreement, understanding the white man better, after this day. He, too, had heard the fear in Nicholas's voice of the possibility of Star Hawk rejecting his suit, and he realized how much the man cared for Sky Eyes. Though he was somewhat younger than Sacred Eagle and his sister, Night Rider himself had pursued the lovely Sky Eyes in the past, and he had even considered trying once again to win her attentions; but now he knew that he would have little chance. Sacred Eagle had already told him that his sister looked with favor upon his white brother. Now he would have to be content with another. There were several young, beautiful maidens in their village, and many had lately cast their eyes upon him. Still, Sky Eyes had seemed to stand out among all the others, her beauty and innocence rare. But he told himself he would never think these thoughts again. He would be satisfied to one day find a maiden who would touch his heart as Sky Eyes had surely touched this white warrior's.

Chapter Eight

It was not until the afternoon of the following day that the three men, with Nicholas sitting tall upon his horse and riding at their head, rode down from the forest into the valley where the Blackfoot village was encamped. Their shrill war cries and shouts of victory brought the villagers from their lodges to witness the herd of horses being led through the village.

Nicholas led the horses to the lodge of chief Star Hawk and, from astride his horse, he spoke in the Indian tongue that Sacred Eagle had been teaching him. "I have brought you these horses as a gift, Star Hawk. I know that you have not yet given me your answer, but if you refuse me, this gift is still for you." Nicholas knew that Star Hawk would be pleased with his generosity, for this was the way of his people. And his words could only help his cause.

Sky Eyes stepped from her father's lodge, and as

Star Hawk stepped forward to admire the finest of the herd, she gazed with glittering silver eyes at the man she loved. He looked striking on his horse, his wheat-colored hair carelessly held away from his face by a pale yellow headband, his upper torso naked even in the coolness of the afternoon, and tanned to a golden hue that greatly enhanced his muscular form. With his loincloth about his hips and his leggings strapped his calves, he resembled her brother and his friend completely except for his white features. As she devoured him with her heated gaze, her brother called her attention.

"Sister, you should have seen my brother Nicholas as we captured the horses from under our enemies' noses. He is truly a warrior of great valor, and his coup shall be shouted about the village this evening for all to hear." Sacred Eagle hoped this boasting would increase Nicholas's value in the people's eyes.

Those standing nearby began to shout aloud as they heard Sacred Eagle's words, and Sky Eyes's grin was wide as she looked at Nicholas and felt the rapid beating of her heart.

But there was one man standing about with the villagers who did not look with favor upon the white man and the herd of horses. Thunder Spirit glared his dark hatred at the golden-haired warrior. As he witnessed the longing upon the features of the woman he wanted—Sky Eyes's face was tilted up and glowed with a special admiration that

Thunder Spirit had never received—his anger boiled to the surface. He had heard a rumor that the white man had asked Star Hawk for the hand of his daughter, but Thunder Spirit had discounted the story. Even if it were true, Star Hawk would never agree, and he, Thunder Spirit, still had plenty of time to make his own suit known. But at this moment he realized that it was true: this white man had dared to ask for the woman that *he* desired! And as he looked about and saw Star Hawk fondly stroking one of the large beasts and the rest of the village murmuring the praises of the white man, he knew that he had waited too long. For a moment he had to restrain himself. His fists were clenched at his sides and he felt the heat of his fury surface. He would not allow any other to claim Sky Eyes. And as he heard Sacred Eagle's words of praise for the white man's courageous actions, he could not quell his rage any longer. *"I* claim this woman, white man!" The angry words burst forth as Thunder Spirit stepped before Nicholas's horse.

The entire village hushed as the group about Star Hawk's lodge looked in the direction of the one who had made such a bold claim. Even Sky Eyes seemed held immobile by the shouted words.

Star Hawk was quick to react. He took in the two young men and his daughter with a glance. "What is this?" he asked as he stepped between Thunder Spirit and Nicholas, his ebony eyes fastened upon the tall warrior who had so abruptly made his presence known.

"All in this village have known of my intentions toward Sky Eyes. She also knows that I want her as my wife. I have only put off approaching you, Star Hawk, because of the sacred sun-dance ceremony and the trouble with the bluecoats."

"You should have come forth sooner and made your desires known, Thunder Spirit. My son's friend has come to me and offered for my daughter already." Star Hawk did not want trouble between this young warrior and the white man, and he wished to ease the tension crackling between them.

"Sky Eyes is a Blackfoot princess, and he is nothing but a white man." Thunder Spirit spat upon the ground at his feet as though the very words "white man" rankled in him. "This one cannot claim her!" He stood glaring at the man on horseback.

Nicholas quickly slipped from his saddle and stood looking at the one who disputed his claim for the woman of his heart. "She will be *my* wife," he said between clenched teeth. He did not wish to fight in Star Hawk's village over the chief's daughter, with one from his own tribe, but he could not stand by and allow her to be taken from him. If it cost his very life, he had to try and claim her as his own.

"You are unworthy, white man." Thunder Spirit

spat out more of his contempt for the one who tried to claim Sky Eyes.

His face flaming with his quickly mounting fury, Nicholas took a step toward the fierce Indian brave. But before either could strike a blow, Star Hawk stepped between them.

Often in the past, Star Hawk had had to make decisions in this village, but now, as he looked at the group standing about him, he felt uncomfortable. For a second his obsidian eyes remained fixed upon his daughter, seeing easily in her lovely face where her choice lay. Her eyes were upon the white man, full of her love and her fear for him. With an inward sigh, he spoke as he looked upon Thunder Spirit. "The white man has proven that he will provide well for my daughter by winning this fine herd of horses for her bride price."

Thunder Spirit's features were contorted with rage. "This means nothing. His blood is as weak as all the palefaces'."

Star Hawk had guessed that Thunder Spirit would give such an answer, and now he had little choice. "Then he will have to prove to all that he is worthy of my people and my daughter. You two shall face each other with war ax and knife. The victor shall have the hand of my daughter, Sky Eyes."

A loud gasp issued from those standing around. Quickly Sacred Eagle jumped from his horse and stood before his father. "I ask that I be allowed to

169

take my friend's place in this battle of honor. I will face Thunder Spirit."

Nicholas knew what this had cost Sacred Eagle, for with this request he was standing against one of his own and for him, a white man. "Nay, Sacred Eagle; this is my fight, and no other can take my place."

For a full moment Sacred Eagle looked into his friend's features and glimpsed his strength of character—and his sorrow that he had brought this event about.

It was Star Hawk who spoke aloud, nodding his dark head in agreement with the white man's words. "He is right, my son. If he cannot win Sky Eyes's hand with honor, he cannot claim her as his own. Our way of life teaches us that our strength is all that stands for our survival. The strength must prevail."

Feeling tears streaming down her face, Sky Eyes quickly turned and fled into her father's lodge. Was it meant to be that she was only to know those stolen nights of love? Were these small tastes of passion all that she would be allowed? Her father's words were law. Whoever won this contest of strength would also win her. And with fear she wondered how Nicholas would be able to defeat such a warrior as Thunder Spirit, who had been raised and trained by his people to be strong and invincible. She threw herself on the furs on her pallet and her sobs filled the large lodge. She thought of her visions. Never had she dreamed of herself with Thunder Spirit; she had always been in the arms of Nicholas. Had her visions been only a passing thing, like the love she had known with Nicholas? Had her visions been a gift of such small meaning? Was her true destiny to be lived as Thunder Spirit's wife?

With her heart aching, Silver Star stood over her daughter. She, too, had heard her husband's words, and she felt as heartsick for her husband as she did for her only daughter. She knew that Star Hawk loved Sky Eyes very much and did not wish to force her into joining with one she did not love. But if Thunder Spirit were to win the contest, that was exactly what would happen. "There, there, my love." She sat down next to the young girl and wrapped her arms about her, her hand lightly stroking the silky, dark tresses that fell down her slender back.

With her mother so near, Sky Eyes threw her arms about her, greatly needing her support. "What am I to do?" She gulped back a racking sob.

"You will do what you must, my love." Silver Star held her tightly to her chest, taking her daughter's pain as her own. "You are a brave girl and the daughter of a great chief. You will not shame your father, but will do what is required of you." As they left her lips, the words sounded harsh even to Silver Star, but she knew that her daughter knew the truth of what she was saying.

"Sometimes I wish I was just one of the people, like my friends Running Deer and Singing Waters. They would never have to watch the one they love fight against another, or fear that they would be forced to join with one they do not desire."

"Daughter, do not blame who you are for what has taken place. Your father loves you dearly and has never thought to force you to wed. The decision has been taken out of his hands. And would you have Nicholas shamed in front of the whole tribe? Would you desire a man who would not stand against any for you?"

"I do not blame Father. It is only that I thought that all would go smoothly. I thought that father would agree to allow Nicholas and me to join, and then after the trouble with the bluecoats we could begin our life together. Now everything sems to be falling apart around me. When I see Thunder Spirit, I feel fear. I have denied him over and over and still he will not leave me alone. Even my visions have not showed me this day and what the outcome will be. I am so afraid!"

"If your visions have not allowed you to glimpse the outcome, perhaps all is not yet lost. Nicholas is a strong young man. He will not easily be defeated. You must dry your tears now, and wash your face. The village will be watching the two men fight, and you must watch with them, and not shame your father nor the one of your heart. The

Great Spirit will help you in this time of need. You have only to call upon him. He alone knows our destiny. Come, it is time for us to go and join the others." Silver Star hated to appear callous, but there was no way out for her daughter. Star Hawk had already spoken, and at this very moment the two men were preparing to do battle. Every-one would wonder at the absence of Sky Eyes, for she would be expected to greet the victor, whoever he would be.

Forcing herself to halt the flow of tears and control her emotions, Sky Eyes slowly nodded her head in agreement. She had always obeyed her parents. Her duty to her people had been instilled in her since before she could remember. Going to the water pouch she wiped her face, combed out her hair and rebraided it, and changed her dress.

Silver Star smiled at her daughter as she stood before her, and together they stepped out of the lodge. Sky Eyes had changed into her best dress and had placed the new headband she had been working on about her forehead. She looked very beautiful, despite the tragic cast to her features. "You make your mother very proud, daughter," her mother said. She clutched her hand as they left the lodge and made their way to the area where the entire village had turned out to watch the white man stand against Thunder Spirit with war ax and knife.

As the two men stood in the center of the ring

173

of villagers and waited for the word to begin, Star Hawk stepped toward them with a long piece of leather thong. Nicholas wondered at his actions as the chief began to tie Thunder Spirit's wrist. Sacred Eagle, who was standing at his friend's side, quickly told him what was happening. "You shall be tied together. The only way to sever the leather binding is with the death of the one at the other end."

Green eyes met pale silver ones, and slowly Nicholas nodded his head as the full realization hit him. He had not thought that he would ever intentionally kill a man, but at this moment, as he thought of all he might lose, he could think of no other way except to try and be the victor in this vicious game of life and death.

As each man was handed a war ax and a large, sharp-bladed hunting knife, Nicholas looked up, his eyes drawn by something. And there before his gaze, in the center of the onlookers, was Mary Jean. She looked enchanting even under these circumstances, and for a moment he seemed lost to what was taking place around him. She was his soulmate; he could not lose her. For a moment he glimpsed a small, trembling smile on her soft lips as she looked back at him. And in this small moment of time he saw all her fears and heartache. Pulling himself together, Nicholas forced his gaze from her and concentrated on what he was being told. He could not afford to make a mistake, he cautioned himself sternly. He would not dare another look at this woman for whom he felt so much. He could not afford to lose a second's concentration, for that second could well decide his life or death.

Both men wore nothing but the breechcloth of the red man, and though the afternoon was cool, the sweat upon both men's bodies glistened in the sunlight. The two circled each other for a moment, Nicholas seeing quickly the feral glint of hatred and blood-lust in the tall, muscular Indian's features. Thunder Spirit's right arm was raised overhead, his hand clutching the war ax, and he held the hunting knife lightly in the other hand.

Thunder Spirit also took in the features of the white man, as he circled him. Though he appeared strong and his body rippled with muscles, the Indian discounted any real strength or endurance. In his eyes, all white men were weak and ignorant. He had little doubt of the outcome of this battle, and with this thought an ugly smile stretched his lips. He would win Sky Eyes this very day, and he would quickly set about teaching her who would be her master. By Star Hawk's own word, she would be his when he stilled the heartbeat of this white man. At this, he charged at the one he hated. His war ax struck out as he pulled upon the leather thong about his wrist and tried to force the white man closer.

Nicholas had been waiting for the Indian to

make the first move, and when he did, he deflected the blow with one of his own, and with apparent ease bent his body low. Then, with a swift movement, he flipped Thunder Spirit over his broad back.

With a large whoop of rage, Thunder Spirit was once again on his feet and charging at his opponent. His blind anger now lent him strength, but hindered his ability to fight with any reason. His ax and knife flashed in the sunlight as Nicholas forcefully tried to defend himself.

Their labored breathing was the only sound as the villagers stood with bated breath and watched the pair fight. They circled and attacked, circled and attacked, until finally, with a lunge, Thunder Spirit struck out with his war ax and hit Nicholas upon the shoulder. With this first taste of metal touching flesh, he gave a war cry and slashed with his knife, drawing another streak of blood across Nicholas's belly.

The wound was not deep but the blood seemed to incite Thunder Spirit with a taste of premature victory, for he seemed to gloat for a moment, standing back and grinning. "You shall die slowly, white man, by my hand. You shall know fully of my anger, and perhaps as I am killing you, I shall tell you of the many different ways I shall pleasure my wife this very night." He chuckled loudly, and for a moment let his gaze circle about the villagers until it rested upon Sky Eyes. The taste of victory was sweet in his mouth.

Nicholas felt an absolute and total rage sweeping over him. The wounds on his shoulder and belly were nothing. With a loud yell of his own, he charged like an enraged bull, knocking Thunder Spirit to the ground and sending his war ax flying through the air. Without hesitation, he straddled the large Indian and held the large hunting knife to his throat.

Thunder Spirit's smile of victory turned instantly to monumental fear as the towering white man held the knife tightly to his throat. Thunder Spirit barely dared to breathe.

It seemed as though the villagers made not a single sound as Nicholas bore down upon Thunder Spirit, his rage warring with his humanity as he looked into eyes full of hatred. For a moment Nicholas's hand pressed the knife of its own volition more fully against the throat of the red man. And with an effort of will he restrained himself, and with a curse spewing from his lips, he jumped to his feet, cutting the leather thong that bound them and throwing the knife to the dust at his feet.

Thunder Spirit could not believe the white man's action. His soul seemed to burn with an even fiercer hatred for this enemy. He had spared his life. He had shamed him in front of his whole village. He had defeated him, and now he shamed him, taking his woman and laughing in his face. Slowly Thunder Spirit rose to his feet, his head hung as he cursed the white man and again swore vengeance.

Sacred Eagle was the first to reach Nicholas. Wrapping his arm about his shoulder, he lent him his full support, feeling the weakness of his body from loss of blood and the strain of the fight. "You should have taken his life, my friend. Now you will always be watching your back. You have shamed him in front of his people. He would be better off dead."

"I could not just kill him as though he were an animal. I proved what I had to, and I will be the only man to claim Mary Jean," Nicholas said. The villagers were surrounding him, none going to the losing warrior.

"You have fought well, white friend," Star Hawk grinned as he stood before Nicholas. "You have won the hand of my only daughter and none can deny you."

At this Nicholas also grinned, his green eyes traveling about the crowd in search of Sky Eyes.

Sky Eyes held back within the crowd, still not able to believe what her eyes had seen. She had frozen, with bated breath, as Thunder Spirit had struck Nicholas with his war ax and had drawn the red line of blood across his stomach. She had known with a surety then that her very soul would be forever doomed. In only seconds the one of her heart would be lying still and quiet upon the mother earth. And as Nicholas had somehow miraculously retaliated and attacked Thunder Spirit, she had stood as though totally witless. Even now, watching the one she loved standing before her father and next to her brother, she could not believe that he was still alive. He had won her!

Kalina had also been standing watching the fight, her own feelings much the same as Sky Eyes's. She had hoped that the white man would win. There was a cruelty about Thunder Spirit that made her ill at ease when she was around him. The way he looked at her when she was near him made her wish that she had her knife strapped to her side. When he had drawn the white man's blood she, as all the others, had thought that Nicholas would lose his life. She sighed now as she released her pent-up breath. Slowly she stepped around those who were crowding around Nicholas and made her way to Sky Eyes. She touched her elbow lightly to draw her attention, and nodded toward Nicholas and smiled.

Slowly Sky Eyes nodded her head, but she did not go yet to Nicholas and her father. Instead, she smiled fondly at the other young woman. She had learned to truly like this warrior woman in the past days. Even though the girl never spoke, since that first day when she had gone about the village with Sky Eyes and helped tend the sick, Sky Eyes had found her a dear friend. Often, now, the warrior woman went on her own to Falling Leaves's lodge and saw to her needs, spending time with the old

179

woman and brightening her day. She held high hopes that the girl would begin to learn their tongue soon and would one day truly fit in with her people. The only blight upon this image in her mind was the fact that the girl would always have to remain a slave.

Meanwhile, Star Hawk concluded his praise of the white man and turned to see his daughter. As his ebony eyes rested upon her and he read the relief upon her features, he smiled fully. "I would only ask that you wait for the trouble with the bluecoats to be finished before you join with my daughter," he told Nicholas. "We shall need your strength soon, and I would not wish to hurry the days that you will enjoy in your joining lodge." For a second Star Hawk glanced toward his wife, and the full remembrance of their own joining came to his mind. He had built a cabin at the foot of the mountains for his copper-haired beauty, and there they had shared blissful days of love and serenity. He wished the same for his daughter and this man who had won her heart.

Nicholas felt some disappointment at these words, but he could not disagree. He could not easily tell this imposing war chief that he was in too much of a hurry to wait for his bride. He would simply have to restrain his desire for her for a time longer. But despite the knowledge that she would soon be his, he knew that the waiting would be much harder than he could ever imagine.

All the village heard Star Hawk's words, including Sky Eyes. Taking the warrior woman's hand, she turned from the group and started to her brother's lodge. She would heat some water to wash away the blood and dirt from Nicholas's wounds. There would be nothing that she or any other could say to change her father's mind, so she would have to force herself to keep a strong hand over her emotions. She could be happy for now with the fact that Nicholas would soon be only hers.

Chapter Nine

Silver Star, Nicholas, and Sacred Eagle made their way to Sacred Eagle's lodge to take care of Nicholas's wounds. As they entered the tepee, Silver Star smiled to herself as she noticed her daughter anxiously moving about the lodge.

The two young women had started a savory-smelling stew and had built up the pit fire, so that everything was warm and inviting. Sky Eyes looked at Nicholas as the small group entered the lodge, and then without hesitation she ran to him, her arms held out to him, as she at last expressed her relief that he had not been killed—and that it was with him and not Thunder Spirit that she would join.

Nicholas inhaled the sweet, delicate scent of the woman in his arms, and for a second he felt the full force of all that he had done this day and all that he had won. Tenderly he placed a kiss upon her brow, just below her headband. "Were there any doubts, sweet?" he jested, his tone low so that only she could hear his words.

"Never." Her silver eyes sparkled with joy. Taking his hand tightly in her own, she led him to his sleeping mat. "Lie down now, and allow my mother to tend your wounds."

"Only if you will sit here at my side." Nicholas was loath to let her out of his sight, now that she was truly to be his. He had been willing to give his very life for this woman, and at this moment he knew just how truly precious she was.

Silver Star washed the wound on Nicholas's belly and then sprinkled a powdered mixture over the cut, noticing with a practiced eye that the injury was not deep and would heal quickly. Wrapping a bandage about his middle, she sat back upon her knees and looked into the grass-green eyes of the smiling man. "Does your shoulder pain you much?" she asked, her gaze going to the already discoloring wound.

"Only if I move it." Nicholas grinned; even his pain could not dampen his happiness.

Silver Star mixed a light sleeping potion in a cup of heated water. After seeing that he drank the entire mixture, she felt the shoulder to make sure that nothing was broken, and placed a heated cloth over the injury. "You should rest for a time. It will only be a day or so before you are once again your old self."

"Thank you for your kindness," Nicholas told

Silver Star. He appreciated the kindness of the beautiful mother of the woman he loved. Even though she was no longer young, he could easily see what had attracted and captured the heart of the fierce and mighty Star Hawk. Her copper hair, gleaming and curling about her slim shoulders, was held back only by her thin red headband. Her features were tanned, free of wrinkles, and glowed with life and vitality. But what truly held one to her face were her silver-blue eyes. They were much like her twin children's, except that hers seemed to flash with a wisdom and sensitivity that she had gained with the years.

"My daughter will stay a while longer, and then she must return to her father's lodge. There is much that must be done before the move to the mountains, and we must also begin the preparations for the day of your joining." Silver Star rose to her feet, once again letting her eyes roam over the man her daughter had chosen. Perhaps all her worries over this white man and her daughter were for nothing. He had proven his courage and his love for her. Could there be any doubt that he would always provide and care for her? Still, there was a small ache of loss in her heart. She and her daughter had always been close, sharing everything. How could she bear Sky Eyes leaving with this man and going far away? Would not her heart be longing day and night for her daughter? With a small sigh she turned from the young couple. Destiny would lead where it chose.

As she reached the entrance flap she turned and looked for a moment toward her son, who was sitting relaxed near the fire. It seemed that he had changed since the sacred sun-dance ceremony. He no longer looked on the verge of the fury that had held him for so long. He now seemed more at peace with himself and those about him. For a second her gaze traveled past him to the young woman sitting toward the rear of the lodge, her hands busy as she worked on a pair of moccasins. She, too, had changed since Silver Star had first set eyes upon the sullen girl. For a second, she wondered if her son and his slave had reached some sort of agreement. With this thought a small pang touched her heart. Her son had already felt so much pain and suffering. She hoped that he would not have to endure any more but in truth she could not see how a relationship between him and a Crow slave could offer much of a future. "Will you be going with the band to the mountains to check the passages?" she finally asked Sacred Eagle.

"Yes, and when I return I will go back again with Night Rider to the Army fort to see if I can find out what the white major's plans are."

At these words Kalina's hands stilled in their work and her dark eyes rose up to his back. He would be leaving once again, and as close as they had been in the past few days, he had not even spoken to her of his plans. She did not think that she had never spoken aloud to him. She assumed that he would consider it a waste of time to voice his plans to her. All she could conclude was that she was truly nothing more than a slave, to be used and set aside at his will. As tears began to sting her eyes, she knew that she should have tried to escape before now, but instead here she was, sitting and sewing a moccasin for him, her abductor. Her world seemed desolate at this moment, because she knew full well that she would not be able to break free of her imprisonment. She was more of a slave to this man than anyone knew. Her heart was bound with the heavy chains of desire. The thought of not being able to have Sacred Eagle next to her at night, bringing her to the wondrous delights of passionate fulfillment, filled her with dread. What would be worse—being treated callously by him, or not being with him at all?

Silver Star glanced thoughtfully at the girl, catching the look of dejection and hurt in the warrior woman's eyes. "You will come by your father's lodge before you leave with the rising of the sun, then, my son?" Sacred Eagle agreed, and his mother rose. She would ponder over the girl's strange reaction later, Silver Star thought, as she left the lodge and made her way through the village to her husband's lodge.

Sacred Eagle was indeed content. He relaxed

near the fire, allowing the heat of the flames to settle over his body. It had been a long time since he had felt such a sense of well-being. His friend had won the fight with Thunder Spirit and would make his sister a good husband. He had a warm lodge, and good food to fill his belly, and a more than desirable woman to fill his arms at night. The only blight on his outlook was the fact that the bluecoats would still have to be dealt with. He had little fear that his people would not be the victors. His tribe was not like others. All the Blackfoot tribe would band together as one and make a strong front. They would not let themselves be attacked and surprised, but would themselves be the attackers. He was sure that the Blackfoot would be victorious over the foolish white men, and felt little need to worry over the war now. Again his thoughts went to the warrior woman, and he thought about the last night they had lain together. She had proven once again that she was all that any man could possibly desire. Their raging passions had lasted well into the night, sated only as exhaustion had overcome them. Just thinking of her, he felt his loins surge with hot, raging desire. She was indeed a temptress, a seductive wanton who fulfilled all his deepest desires. Again, the fact that she was a slave surfaced to his mind, but as in the past, he pushed these thoughts from him. He would deal with them at another date. For now he wished to enjoy the peace and pleasure he had found at last.

His peace and pleasure were not fated to last long. For as Sacred Eagle turned around to see what Kalina was doing, he was stunned to see fury and contempt in her features. What could have sparked her wrath, he wondered. Had someone said or done something to offend her?

Looking about the lodge, Sacred Eagle noticed that her look of anger was directed only toward him. He searched his mind for a reason. He had been gone with Nicholas and Night Rider these past two days, capturing the herd of horses for his friend's bride price. Could this be the reason for her anger? Was she angry with him for stealing the horses from her people? Slowly he realized that this must be the answer, for he had come to his lodge before Nicholas and Thunder Spirit had fought and had been met warmly with her sweet lips and warm embrace. He had had only a small time to take with her freely given gifts of passion, and then he had quickly gone back to his friend. She must have realized that he had attacked her people — more than likely her own village. With a sigh, he turned back to the fire with the resolve that later this evening he would have to sway her from her anger. After all, he would be leaving early in the morning and would be gone until the following day and then, shortly after his return, he would have to leave again with Night Rider. For the first time, this thought of leaving his lodge and village did not excite him. The thought of sleeping upon the cold ground and having only the company of his warriors was not as appealing as it once had been. He looked about the lodge and felt the warmth of its interior settle him once again. Yes, he would turn his warrior woman's fury into heated sighs of rapture as soon as they settled upon his soft sleeping mat.

Sky Eyes lightly rubbed a damp cloth across Nicholas's forehead, wiping some of the day's dirt and sweat away. And as she did, her pale eyes seemed to devour his every feature.

With a small, shallow groan Nicholas reached up and grasped the small hand on his forehead. "I beg you to stop looking at me in such a manner, my love. Have mercy upon an ailing man."

With an innocent tilt of her chin, her eyes now sparkling with mischief, Sky Eyes queried, "Whatever do you mean? I only wish to make you a bit more comfortable."

Raising her hand to his lips, Nicholas kissed each delicate fingertip. "Mary Jean, you would drive any man to distraction with your beauty. I fear that if your hands are upon me much longer, the restraint I have placed upon my longings because of our lack of privacy may soon come to an end. Do not tempt me, my love, for it is torture to glimpse your love and desire and feel the softness of your touch, to be unable to quench my need to hold you as my own."

Not caring if the others in the lodge were watching her, Sky Eyes bent over Nicholas and kissed his mouth. "I did not mean to stir needs that cannot be appeased, my darling. But truly, I cannot control the love glowing in my eyes when I look upon you. I can still hardly believe the outcome of this day. Now nothing can stand in the way of your belonging to me."

Nicholas chuckled deeply. "You minx, you are as eager as I to share the pleasures that lie in wait for us as man and wife."

Sky Eyes fully agreed with him, for indeed she was eager, more than eager, to belong in every way to this man. She had already tasted his tender touch, his searing lips and heated flesh. What heaven to be able to lie with him each night! To hear forever his husky voice next to her ear, speaking of his love for her!

As though reading her mind, he whispered softly, "I love you, Mary Jean. I would have willingly stood and fought every brave of your village to prove my worthiness of you."

Conscious that they were not alone and that her brother sat across the lodge, Sky Eyes tried to lighten the moment. "You proved that you are all that any warrior should be. What other man had brought before a maiden's father such a large herd of fine horses? I only hope that you do not come to regret such a gift after we have been joined for a time." Her smile never left her soft lips.

190

"Never!" Nicholas declared adamantly. "When we are both old and gray I will still think the price small for such a treasure."

Again Sky Eyes bent and placed her lips upon the sensual mouth of her love, but this time the kiss was met, and the pair lost themselves in sweet togetherness.

At length Nicholas placed his hands lightly upon her shoulders and drew her away. "You had best return to your mother, my sweet, for I fear that your temptations are too much for a mortal man to bear."

Slowly nodding her dark head, still quivering from the encounter of their joined lips, Sky Eyes agreed. Without another word she rose to her feet, but before she could step away from the sleeping couch, Nicholas grabbed her hand.

"You will return as soon as possible? Perhaps in time I shall be able to build up my strength to resist your charms." His grin enhanced his handsome features and caught at Sky Eyes' heart.

Fearing that her words would come out in a muddle as she felt the turmoil of her feelings, she could but nod her head as she fled the tepee, her heart rejoicing with each step she took through the village.

Kalina was not as easy to handle as Sacred Eagle had hoped she would be. As the pair readied for bed that night, she shed her clothing but presented her stiff back to him as she pulled the furs up about her chin.

Sacred Eagle grinned at the challenge, dropping his breechcloth and settling his large frame down next to her. As he let his gaze glide over her smooth, golden back, he felt his body draw tight. His long fingers lightly trailed across her flesh, feeling for himself her body's slight trembling.

Determined that she would not allow herself to be overcome by her need for this man, Kalina forced herself to remain rigid. The erotic sensations he was stirring were almost more than she could bear.

Taking a lock of her silky ebony hair and rubbing it between his fingers, Sacred Eagle huskily whispered, "If I have angered you, my sweet, I am sorry." He knew that she could not understand his words, but he could sense that his actions were having the desired effect as she wriggled her tempting body under the furs.

"Do not try and pull away from me." Sacred Eagle caressed her nape and with one finger tantalized her backbone.

It was against her will that Kalina found herself lying on her back, her dark gaze locking with his. For a time she was lost, swept into his domain.

Sacred Eagle became breathless, his large form visibly shuddering with his need. As if mesmerized, he went over every inch of her delicate face—

the lips beckoning to be kissed, the fragile but determined jawline, and the soft sable eyes surrounded with sooty, long lashes that rested softly upon the creamy-rose high cheekbones. His gaze slowly roamed down her slim neckline and settled upon the slowly heaving breasts, bare now to his gaze, the furs pulled back, leaving nothing to his imagination. As though caught up in a powerful spell, his lips descended with a tantalizing softness to the areas his gaze had just traveled over. He placed a light kiss upon her forehead and slowly stole down her nose to her petal-soft lips. There he lingered for a time as he explored and tempted, his heated tongue circling and tasting within. Breaking this contact, he began his explorations once again, his fiery lips devouring the creamy texture of her throat, raining kisses and building passion as he reached the pulsing of her heart.

With a deep indrawn breath, Kalina fought for sanity as Sacred Eagle's moist tongue delightfully circled and teased each rose-hued point until she fairly writhed upon the fur of their bed. His mouth captured each passion-firm breast, driving its peak to tautness. He sucked upon one and then the other in turn as if pulling a lifegiving substance from within.

It seemed that time stood still. His kisses were hungrily compelling, urgent and intense, but still he kept his body from joining with hers as he forced her with him along the trail of rapture.

Kalina's fingers played wildly in his raven hair, which hung loose across his shoulders and down his back. There was a heady, intoxicating scent about him, fully manly, which teased her senses and filled her head with sensual images. As his long fingers played slowly over her body, she tensed and then relaxed as he went lower to the dark triangle at the junction of her thighs. Shifting her body, she made room for his loving skill, delighting in his touch. Her entire being seemed to radiate with a shining glow from the heat of his actions. This man, this abductor, captor, master, was all man, enticing and stimulating. No other could compare with him. Though she would try with all of her might to shun him, she could not resist his touch. He was everything to her, she realized in this moment of heady delight. He was her life, her honor, her reason. How could she hold anything from him? Her body had its own reaction to each simple touch of his hand, each tender kiss from his heated lips, and with no shame she pleaded for more.

Sacred Eagle could feel the heat blazing from her womanhood as though it radiated from a roaring fire. Smoldering rapture filled his entire body, for he desired her with a savage need; but still he forced himself to be gentle, to be leisurely. He called on all he knew to bring her to an almost unbearable height of arousal. His fingers made a skillful attack upon her hidden jewel, causing her to moan aloud with her passion and writhe and push toward him as his mouth added further delightful torment to her lips and breasts. He diligently and greedily worked upon her body to prepare her to accept his passionate member, but Kalina had been ready for him from the moment of his first touch.

Loving his fiery ministrations and desiring to lie here forever upon this soft fur-matted bed with him, Kalina's body and thoughts were totally ensnared by each touch, each kiss. She wanted to relax, to savor, but she was starving for all that he could give her. Each time his fingers touched a new, hidden valley, a soft peak, a hidden crevice, she felt a deep fiery torment, a deep-seated need for appeasement.

Lightly parting her soft thighs, Sacred Eagle pressed down and entered her, the contact staggering both of them with rapturous sensations. As his large body rocked back and forth, he set the pattern, and she joined him. Their bodies clasped and pulled apart, moving to and fro, back and forth in a wondrous assault of love. His slow and gentle strokes became stronger and swifter as his need grew with each stroke. They soared urgently toward the promise of fulfillment, until there was no holding back or halting the esctasy. For a moment they labored lovingly as though there were no beginning or end to the dynamic spinning of their senses. But soon their bodies could contain their striving

hunger no longer and each demanded the passionate climax that was lying in wait. They strove in
unison as they irresistibly sought the ultimate
peaks of pleasure's victory, and with a last long
stroke they found it together. Finally each spasm
and tremble had ceased and they were languidly
drained. But still they clung together, their lips
lightly touching, Sacred Eagle whispering the words
of love that easily sprang to his lips.

The only promise of tomorrow was this hold
over their senses, and each was loath to be released
as they fully savored the contact of heated flesh
against flesh. They treasured this moment upon
this bed of furs. This moment was all that mattered. With light kisses and caresses, their bodies
at last cooled and relaxed as the aftermath of their
fierce union held them sated and content, until
sleepily they fell into slumber, still wrapped in each
other's arms.

The band of warriors that left the village the
next morning, led by Sacred Eagle, was going to
the mountains to ensure that there would be no
enemies or any other hazards lying in wait when
the women, children, and elders of the tribe
started the trek back up into the mountains in a
few days.

None of the band seriously thought that they
would find anything to hinder the move, but still

196

the need for more meat was always important too, with winter fast approaching. Each kept an eye out for any kind of game.

The trail to the winter camp of the Blackfoot tribe was still passable, not yet snow-covered, and with any luck the move would not be a permanent one. The other tribes would start arriving any day, and soon they would be ready to stand and fight off the bluecoats. Star Hawk planned that most of the population of his village would be in the mountains and out of the valley for only a few days. His own wife would be making the move, and he hated to be parted from Silver Star. This fact helped Sacred Eagle, too, to feel more at ease about the move that the women would be making. Already he dreaded the separation from his slave that this move would cause him.

He had not allowed himself to fully examine his feelings for this woman since he had had his vision in the mountains and upon the sun-dance pole. He knew in his heart that the day would soon come when he could not postpone facing what this woman truly meant to him. As he rode his buckskin pony near the end of the band of warriors, he again went over in his mind the night just past. His warrior woman flashed in his mind night and day, always stirring his senses and seeming to stoke his ardor even when she was not near at hand. She seemed to have cast a potent spell over his senses, leaving him powerless not to desire her, to crave

197

her more than meat and drink, than his very breath. He felt alive only while in her presence, his vision seeming dim until she stood before him. He needed to hear her words, to know her inmost thoughts. With a sigh, he wondered what the outcome of this folly would be. How could a mere slave have such a hold upon him? He had seen her fight as well as any warrior, and she could love more fully than any woman he had ever known. She was a beautiful, fleeting gossamer strand within his thoughts, and for a moment he wondered why she had not fled. He had been so sure that she would escape the first chance she got! But to his surprise she had seemed to adjust to his lodge and his people. His mother and his sister seemed to like her, and she them. He reminded himself once again that it was time she began to learn his language. There were so many things he would like to share with her. Forgotten now was the fact that she was of the Crow tribe, one of his hated foe.

The rest of the band had gone on ahead while Sacred Eagle lingered behind with his thoughts. A small noise caught his ear and he quickly rode his mount off the trail. They were in a thick forest of pines that grew high in the mountains, and Sacred Eagle knew that much game was to be found in this area. Looking about for some sign of the noise he had heard, he glimpsed a large buck and a doe. Slipping quietly off his pony and readying his bow, he slowly approached the pair. The buck was standing rigid now, his ears flickering with unease as he lifted his nose for a scent of strangeness in the breeze.

Sacred Eagle circled his quarry so as not to be upwind, for a slight breeze was blowing. As he kept his body low, his leather shirt and leggings blended in with the foliage about him. He bent on one knee, drew an arrow from the quiver strapped across his back, and aimed at the large buck.

As he drew back, aimed and was about to let the arrow fly, he stopped, scarcely daring to breathe. Sacred Eagle saw a sight that left his heart hammering wildly in his chest. There, appearing before his eyes, was the mighty white stallion of his vision. It stood still, as though sensing the fear of the deer near it, and cocked back its ears and listened to the noises of the forest, its eyes looking about for anything amiss.

Keeping as still as possible, Sacred Eagle watched with apprehensive amazement, his mind going over all the possibilities. He had only his bow and quiver of arrows with him; his horsehair rope was with his pony. Sacred Eagle dared not move as he watched the stallion; and as the great horse seemed to settle down and began to eat the sparse grass growing beneath the pines, Sacred Eagle slowly began to make his way back around the trees toward his pony.

Fearing that the slightest noise would set the

stallion fleeing, Sacred Eagle took twice as long to return to his pony as he had taken to stalk the deer. Finally reaching the buckskin's side, he put down his bow and quiver, took the long horsehair rope, and slowly made his way back along the arc he had followed before.

The stallion stood as though unaware of any human presence, its head lowered as it nibbled at the grass. Sacred Eagle drew as close as he could to the mighty beast, his breath stilled in his lungs, his body atremble as he watched his vision come to life. He drew as close as he dared. The animal's full attention was on its search to fill its stomach. Holding the rope in a lasso, he drew his arm back and let the rope fly high overhead, the loop circling about the stallion's neck and drawing tight. As it felt this, its forelegs rose in the air.

Quickly Sacred Eagle drew the end of the rope tightly around a tree and tied it fast. The stallion was now running back and forth as it pulled at the rope about its neck, the sound of its hooves striking the ground filling the forest as it tried to gain its freedom.

Sacred Eagle spared only one more fleeting glance at the large beast before he started to run to his buckskin pony. Jumping on its back, he quickly went back to the tree and the stallion, knowing that he had to act quickly before the stallion broke free. The Grandfathers had sent him this gift and he had to use all his cunning to hold it.

Slowly he began to approach the stallion from the back of his pony, crooning soothingly as he let his hand easily run down the length of the rope. The white horse halted its frantic attempts at freedom, its ears pinned back against its head, its eyes wide and panicky. It waited, trembling, for the other horse to draw near.

"Come to me, Eagle's Wing. You belong to me now. The Great Spirit wills that you bend to me." His voice was gentle, the words floating upon the cool breeze. Sacred Eagle locked his silver gaze upon the horse's eyes, and slowly drew closer, the rope in his hand brought up short as he reached his quarry. As he came within a few short steps of the stallion, the beast drew back once again, rearing up on its muscular haunches and pawing high in the air with its front legs. But this only lasted for a moment. Sacred Eagle began again to call out to it and that seemed to settle it once again.

"Come, my friend; you and I shall be as one. Sacred Eagle and Eagle's Wing shall be known about the enemies' camp fires throughout the Indian nations. Do not fight me; there is much that we shall have to learn of one another." Sacred Eagle's hand reached out slowly in the air, and as it did, the horse settled down.

Slowly he drew the rope up tighter in his hand, until he could feel the very breath of the large animal in the cool air. As he drew his pony abreast of the white stallion, he softly crooned to it, telling it of all that they would discover together, and of the victories that would be laid at their feet.

With disbelief and a racing heart, Sacred Eagle slowly began to lead the white stallion from the pine forest and onto the trail that the rest of his band had taken. It was much later that afternoon when he met up with the others. They had all heard of his mighty vision, and now they looked in amazement at the white stallion he was leading into their midst.

As one of the warriors went to get a closer look at the incredible animal, the horse reared up on its hind legs, its teeth bared as though in attack, and its forelegs striking out in the air.

Only Sacred Eagle could calm it with his soothing words as he led the stallion away from the rest of the band. The animal seemed as wild and untamable as the fiercest bronco until it heard Sacred Eagle's voice; his soothing tone seemed to settle the wildness in the fierce stallion.

With the agreement of Night Rider, Sacred Eagle left the band and started back down the trail to the village, the stallion claiming all his attention.

It was dusk when Sacred Eagle rode through the village leading his mighty stallion, Eagle's Wing, closely behind his buckskin pony. And as the shouts of amazement raised about the village, everyone stepped from their tepees to witness the sight of a vision come true.

Chapter Ten

Sacred Eagle rode straight to his lodge. Once there, he called to the warrior woman, wanting her to come and take his buckskin pony to the corral where the village horses were kept. When she appeared he dismounted and signed his wishes to her.

Kalina hurried to the entrance flap the moment she heard the voice of Sacred Eagle, thrilled at the sound of his voice. And when she stood outside and saw the large, white stallion, she gazed with full appreciation at the man and the beast. Taking the buckskin's halter rope, she stared after Sacred Eagle as he walked toward the river with the white horse following.

Quickly she secured the buckskin with the village horses, not lingering but hurrying toward the river. She wanted to see what Sacred Eagle would do with the great white horse.

Sacred Eagle had kept a blanket from the back

of his buckskin pony. Leading the stallion slowly into the river, he began to talk softly to it, his hands stroking the animal with the wet blanket, allowing it to smell the scent of him that lingered upon the blanket, and getting it used to the touch of a man's hand.

The beast seemed docile enough; as long as Sacred Eagle spoke in his soothing tone, it stood still, trembling slightly under the pressure of Sacred Eagle's hands as he touched every part of his body, lightly caressing its head, roaming over its ears and down its face, letting Eagle's Wing smell his hand as well as the blanket. He touched its long, thick neck, and tenderly, slowly, he went over its taut, muscular flanks.

Kalina watched from the riverbank, feeling her own body quivering as she watched the intimate actions of her lover. She could well remember his hands upon her own body, his husky voice whispering words into her own ear. She felt her body grow hot with longing.

Sacred Eagle spent a long time with his horse, going over and over its body until he felt the animal completely relax under his hands. Then he led the horse to shore, walked it to a copse of trees, and tied it, his hands still touching and caressing it so as not to let it become frightened or panicked again.

Catching sight of Kalina, Sacred Eagle sighed softly. All morning he had thought of nothing but her and his need to get back to his lodge and to feel her soft body held tightly against him. Now, with a pang of regret, he knew he would not be able to fulfill these dreams. He would have to stay with Eagle's Wing this night. The animal would have to fully understand that he was its friend and it could trust him. He could not leave it tied or in the corral with the other horses, for he could not risk its running away from him now that he had captured it. "I will have to sleep here tonight," he called to the warrior woman as she slowly drew closer. And once again, he signed his words to her.

Kalina's eyes devoured him when he stripped his leather shirt and leggings and breechcloth from his body, as they were soaked through. She gathered up the articles of clothing, keeping her distance from the wild animal. Then, without a word, or any indication that she had understood him, she returned in the direction of Sacred Eagle's lodge, coming back shortly with her arms laden. She had brought a large bowl of the venison stew she had cooked and kept warm on the coals for his return, and over her other arm she carried a pile of furs for his bedding.

Sighing aloud with pleasure, Sacred Eagle sat down upon the furs. "How did I ever survive without you, my little warrior woman?" He quickly started the bowl of savory stew, not expecting any answer and not receiving one.

After eating and warming his body in the furs,

Sacred Eagle went once again to the horse, his voice and hands seeming to work wonders upon the beast.

Kalina set about building a small fire near the furs, and as she sat back and watched Sacred Eagle, she allowed her gaze to feast upon his masculine perfection. His long, glistening ebony hair hung unbraided down the length of his back and over his shoulders. His legs were smooth and glowed with a golden hue cast by the flickering firelight, his back broad and tapering to a narrow waist. Firm buttocks sat well upon the muscular, long legs.

As though sensing her gaze upon him, Sacred Eagle turned, and also admired her as she sat upon the furs. Her beauty seemed incomparable as he took her in. Her long hair was streaming out about her and lying loosely over the furs, her deer hide dress molded tightly about her form and bringing his senses to full alertness. His body, with a will of its own, responded.

Kalina gasped aloud as he turned in her direction, entranced now with the full, frontal view of his body. She sat spellbound. He was magnificent, formidable, beautiful to her eyes. She looked from his handsome face which was looking back upon her, to his broad chest, hairless and tanned and tapering to a firm stomach, lean hips, and long legs. But what drew her heated gaze above all was the length of his pulsing manhood.

With a slow tread, Sacred Eagle came and stood before the sitting Kalina. She saw the naked hunger in his pale eyes, and felt her heart begin to hammer wildly as he lowered his body to the furs and looked deeply into her shimmering onyx eyes.

Without a word Sacred Eagle reached out and tenderly traced her heart-shaped face. His fingers lingered on the soft, creamy skin of her neck as he undid the leather thong that held her blouse together.

Kalina's dark eyes glazed in wonderment. He held such a strange and compelling power over her senses! Tentatively, almost as though they held a life of their own, her hands reached out to his handsome face, touching his cool lips, the straight bridge of his nose, lightly brushing the silky dark hair that lay about his face and shoulders. And then, quickly, her fingers went back to his lips, the tips brushing them like a butterfly's caress.

Kissing the delicate fingertips hungrily, Sacred Eagle untied the belt to her skirt and pulled the clothing aside, his mouth covering hers in a deep, penetrating kiss. And with the joining of their mouths, he knew that this was what he had desired all day long. She was in his blood and he was powerless to do anything but claim her.

As the kiss deepened, Sacred Eagle entwined himself about his warrior woman, clasping her tightly, molding her soft coolness to his hot, hard body. As his broad, smooth chest covered her taut, firm breasts, he felt the rapid tattooing of her heart, which told him far better than words of her flaming need for him.

Secluded in the copse of trees, the young couple lay upon the softness of the thick furs, the soft glow of the moon and the now dim firelight encasing them in a golden light, the autumn breeze cooling their naked bodies, the rich smells of dark earth and forest filling their senses. As the lapping of the river and the sound of the night creatures played a wistful tune under the trees canopied overhead, their passions exploded.

Instincts as old as time itself overcame Kalina, and she reached out to caress Sacred Eagle's powerful chest. Then, boldly, her lips slowly explored his strongly chiseled chin and made a delightful path along his strongly corded neck. Her entire body was a searing flame, the towering storm of her desire overwhelming her being.

Sacred Eagle's senses soared toward rapture as his hands caressed her shapely form, cupping her small waist and firm buttocks. Her rich earthy scent, her yielding, soft touch upon his flesh, and her luscious softness beneath him sent him ever onward until he burned to give her all that he possessed. And so they were joined, losing all power of reason as they gave in to their passions, and Kalina cried out aloud, *"Sacred Eagle!"* She loved his body atop hers, his hardness, his searing strength, and she clasped him more fully as she was whirled into a vortex of pleasure.

Sacred Eagle looked down at the woman beneath him, her thickly lashed eyes tightly shut. Her passion-bruised lips were parted and soft, throaty moans of pleasure escaped her. With her velvet softness wrapped tightly about his throbbing manhood as her body arched toward his, he was lost to the sweet savage pull upon his insides, slowly lifting him toward his climax. With fiery thrust after thrust he carried Kalina with him to completion.

As she approached this peak of raging ecstasy Kalina's senses were burning. Sacred Eagle's entire being was suffusing throughout her and sending her towering upward until she was carried upon the sweet wings of bliss.

The couple hung for a time together on the very edge of existence, the searing white heat of their passions encircling and inflaming them. And as they were swept over the pinnacle of pleasure's domain, they clung to one another, their bodies quivering. Slowly they returned to earth, their bodies still joined, bound to one another in a hold that would surely last throughout all eternity.

After a time, when Sacred Eagle had caught his breath, he said softly, "I love it when you call out my name. Even though it is only your cry of passion, I love to hear the sound coming from your lips." He lightly caressed her hair, pushing the dark tendrils away from her face, as he rose

209

up on an elbow and gazed into her warm velvet eyes. He knew that she did not understand his words, but he felt the need to speak them aloud.

Kalina wished she could speak to him, but she cautioned herself not to. Not yet. She was still so unsure of his true feelings for her. He no longer spoke of their relationship as slave and master, but she was loath to give him any weapon that could be used against her. The longer she could keep her knowledge of his language a secret, the more advantage she had over him. So all she offered him now was a soft smile and her hand lightly touching his cheek.

"There is much I would share with you, my warrior woman, but there is so little time now and so much has to be done. The time will come soon, though, when decisions must be made." He seemed to be talking absently now as he lay curled about her body.

Decisions made? What could he mean, Kalina wondered. Did he mean that he would soon be letting her return to her people? Did he care so little for her then? She felt her heart sink. Did she wish to leave him? Would she cry aloud and beg him not to send her from him, if that was what he desired? Did she wish to return to her people? It seemed that she had not lived until she had met this man. Was she willing to go back again to her old existence? Was she still Kalina of the Crow? She no longer knew. And as a small tear slowly slipped from her eye and rolled down her cheek, she admitted only that she knew lying within Sacred Eagle's arms had brought her to life. She felt alive and desirable, a woman of heated desires and wants. Could she ignore all that he had taught her? Her soul seemed to fill with misery as she lay within his arms, until sleep finally overcame her senses and she was lost to her dreams of Sacred Eagle, loving her at last. Only in her dreams was she free to allow her feelings to surface and her desires to become reality.

As the pair slept peacefully within the small copse of trees, the army fort was beginning to settle down after the long day's activity. Major Benjamin Thatcher looked about at the four officers, studying each in turn before speaking. "Sergeant Hadely." His piercing gaze rested upon the one he spoke to, and then, leaning forward on his desk, he continued. "Have you gathered the Crow scouts together and explained to them what they are to do? I want nothing to go wrong with this plan. The name of the game is surprise and destroy."

"Yes, sir," the sergeant replied, his long, bony fingers nervously scratching through his long, unevenly cut sandy hair. "I only hope sir, that old Conroy won't be letting them get to that whiskey before they finish the job. I ain't never seen no

Injuns take to liquor like these Crows. They seem to be an unruly bunch, sir. Liquor and women seem to be all they got on their heathen minds."

"You did tell them that the woman is not to be harmed in any way when they find her? I'll not allow any white woman to be handled by savages while under my care. No matter that she lives with one of these devils as his wife."

"Yes, sir, I told that big buck that seems to be their leader and he agreed that they would bring the woman straight to you. The Injun be saying that they've all heard of this woman of Star Hawk's, the one with the silver eyes. They claim that she's big medicine for her tribe, and they think that if they bring her to you, Star Hawk and his people will lose some of their strength and give the Crow a better advantage over their enemies."

"Big medicine, indeed!" Benjamin Thatcher grinned at the sergeant's words and sat back in his chair. "The bitch will serve her purpose and will be the key we have been needing to bring this Star Hawk under control. Once he knows that we have his woman, he will do whatever he is told. We will have him and his people right where we want them, and this will be the time to attack. When we are finished there won't be much for the Crows to worry about." Turning away from Sergeant Hadely, he now fixed his gaze upon one of the other men sitting in the small office. "Are all the supplies ready and the men alerted to move out at

212

a moment's notice, Corporal Patterson?" The major studied the tall, thin-featured man sitting upright in a straight-backed cane chair.

"Aye, sir. The men have all been put on notice. Their packs are ready and sitting by their bedsides, their rifles primed and loaded. We only await the word to move out. A great many of these men are chafing at the bit to be on the trail. Most of them have only joined the army to get their hides out here in this wilderness and skin themselves an Injun or two. The small division you requested to stay put here at the fort were complaining, and I had to assure them that they would get themselves some souvenirs."

Benjamin Thatcher relaxed back in his chair, a wide grin upon his features. He felt the same as his men—he was restless to be gone from here. This waiting and biding his time was wearing on his nerves—he had not come this far to sit out his time on his backside in this godforsaken place.

"Tell the scouts to leave at dawn. It should only take them a couple of days to reach the camp and to find the woman. Once she is in our hands we will have all the leverage we need."

"Yes, sir," Sergeant Hadely responded. The other three men rose to their feet, knowing that the meeting was at a close.

"Once those scouts leave the fort, have more men posted about the barracks as lookouts until the full detachment leaves the fort. I want no mistakes. Washington will be watching our every move and we cannot afford to let our guard down." The major dismissed the men and they quietly left his presence, then he turned his attention to an unfinished letter upon his desk.

Yes, all seemed to be going as planned, he wrote in response to some correspondence from Washington. Within the month it should all be cleaned up and the pass through the valley should be open for the first settlers to make their way to the mountains. And as Benjamin Thatcher laid his pen aside, his thoughts turned to himself. Within the month he should be making his own plans to leave this wilderness. This would be his last campaign. He should make a hefty profit from his backers in Washington, and his plans were to take it easy from then on. He would travel, see the world, and live a life of ease. He had only to deal with the Blackfoot tribe and this Star Hawk.

That morning, before daylight, when the sky was just turning the pearl-gray of dawn, Sacred Eagle awoke to the feel of a cold, damp nose pressed upon the back of his neck.

Eagle's Wing had broken free of his rope and now snorted lightly as he smelled the familiar scent of the Indian warrior. His nose also filled with the scent of Kalina's long hair, which was not known to him, but as she was so close to Sacred

Eagle, he felt no fear or distrust.

Slowly Sacred Eagle brought a hand out from the furs and rubbed the soft nose. He felt an almost unbearable pride as he admired the smooth flanks of the large beast above him. Never had he seen such a magnificent animal. No other had ever possessed such a horse as Eagle's Wing.

Kalina wriggled under the furs and against Sacred Eagle's side when she felt the cool nose upon her head. As she heard Eagle's Wing's soft neighing, she stirred awake.

Sacred Eagle smiled down upon her as he rose up on an elbow, his lips slowly descending and gently taking hers in a morning greeting. It seemed so peaceful here near the river, under the canopy of trees. For a long moment Sacred Eagle wished that he and his warrior woman were far away from it all, away from the worries of a chief's son, not having to act in a certain way in front of people, but able to live and hunt without anyone to censure their movements. He would even delight once again in seeing his slave in her breechcloth and fur vest. But he knew all these dreams were impossible here in his village. He could not tolerate any of the other Blackfoot braves looking upon the perfection of his warrior woman; nor could he live and act as he would please. But in a secret corner of his mind, he still longed for the unreachable. He heaved a sigh and his lips pulled away from Kalina's, but as her warm, dark eyes

215

beckoned to him, he lovingly allowed his fingers to outline her beautiful face.

All her worries of the night before were now forgotten as she was held within the warm embrace of this strong brave. Kalina lost herself to the feel of his hard flesh next to her soft form to his searching gaze that seemed to devour her.

"The sun will be up soon, my beauty, and there is much work to be done today. I must train Eagle's Wing to accept my weight upon his body before I leave again with Night Rider to go to the bluecoats' fort." Again he gathered her soft lips beneath his own, loving the feel of her mouth and her body next to him. He had begun lately to speak to her as though she understood his words. It was as though a part of him wished to share with her, to bring about a union that would be more binding than that of slave and master.

Not receiving any more attention, Eagle's Wing made his way back down to the river and began to breakfast upon the lush, tall grass growing there. Meanwhile, the couple snuggled deeply beneath the furs and allowed their peaceful interlude to stretch out for a while longer. Their lovemaking could not be kept within the bounds that reality imposed upon them. Here, within this small glade, they were alone, their bodies, minds and souls entwined. Languidly they discovered and rekindled the flames of the night just past.

The early hours of the morning passed magically and as the morning sunlight began to filter through the treetops, with a sigh of regret, Sacred Eagle climbed from within the warmth of the furs. "Come and bathe with me." He reached out his hands, gathered his warrior woman tightly against his chest, and started toward the river.

Making their seclusion last as long as possible, the pair swam and played the morning away, their laughter breaking the silence of the area and their hearts delighting in the chilled water and the sleekness of their wet bodies.

At last Sacred Eagle carried his slave to the bank, his hands and lips atremble as he took in the full magnificence of her enticing curves. And as his eyes slowly passed over her face, the full force of her being here at the riverside hit him. He had made himself stay apart from women for so long, but this woman, this daughter of his enemy, had found her way into his heart, where only one other had ever been. In wonder he gently kissed her pink lips, knowing that no one else's could taste so sweet and cool. He thought fleetingly about those things he had forced from his mind so often of late. This warrior woman, with her incredible beauty, had somehow insinuated herself into his soul, and he could not push her away.

His strong hands, admiring and loving at the same time, slowly roamed over her. His whole being wanted nothing more than to worship her; to adore her for being herself; for being the one

217

that had brought him back to life.

Kalina sensed something of Sacred Eagle's mood, and the small crystal tears came easily to her eyes. She could read his tenderness and caring clearly upon his handsome features, and in them she glimpsed a side of Sacred Eagle that he had not revealed before. He was vulnerable, as other men were. His fear of loss and deprivation were not concealed as they had been in the past. He was only a man, she thought, and as she saw and understood that, her heart went out to him. She had heard about his wife and child being taken from him by her own people, and now she wished only to give him her love.

"You cannot know what you have given me this morning, my beauty," he whispered softly.

As Kalina opened her mouth to speak, Sacred Eagle pressed his lips over hers, and then with a small chuckle he withdrew them. "We shall have to begin your lessons in my language this very day, my sweet, for there is much that we have to speak about, much that my heart needs to share with you."

With his words Kalina was brought back to her senses. For the first time she felt he thought of her as more than a slave. She could hear in his tone a softening lilt that could only be meant for her ears. And in fear of losing what she had just gained, she kept her mouth shut. If she revealed that she knew his tongue, would it not lay mistrust

218

at his feet? Would he not be reminded of the trickery of an enemy? A small glistening droplet squeezed from her eye as she realized the lengths she would go to to make this man care for her. She would deny herself and all that she had ever known or been to win his heart.

Sacred Eagle's smile slowly faded as he viewed her distress. Slowly he kissed each of the sable eyes closed, and with a husky whisper he said softly, "You shall always remain at my side, my little warrior woman. Nothing shall ever part us." And this said, his mouth covered hers, his tongue silkily circling within and branding his words in her mind.

Kalina would have welcomed joining his body with her own, as her feelings for this man overwhelmed her, but Sacred Eagle pulled reluctantly away. "Come, my little passion flower." He rose to his knees and pulled her up into his grasp. "We have lingered here all morning, and there is much that still needs to be done."

Smiling now, Kalina allowed her feet to be set upon the cool damp grass, and before she could turn to dress and gather up their bed of furs, Sacred Eagle halted her with a gentle hand.

"I am hungry, my sweet." He rubbed his belly and pointed to his mouth. She nodded her head in understanding. And as she looked in question, he said the words slowly for her to understand. "Food," he said, over and over, in his own tongue.

She could see by his look that she was expected to say the same.

Softly she repeated the word, and Sacred Eagle grunted in praise and swung her about in the air. As she was once more set on her feet, he said again, with a grin, "Food." And nodding his head toward the village, he left her with little doubt as to his instructions.

Nodding her head eagerly to please this large, handsome brave, Kalina got dressed and then made her way back to his lodge, her face breaking into a large grin as she thought over the wonderful morning just spent.

For the rest of the day Sacred Eagle worked with the mighty white stallion, Eagle's Wing. The horse seemed not at all nervous of him, as he had the day before, and as the day wore on Sacred Eagle was able to lead him back into the river. Coaxingly he rubbed his flanks and back, and every now and then he eased some of his weight upon the horse and then as quickly he would pull away, all the while talking reassuringly.

It was late afternoon when Sacred Eagle felt that the moment was right. He led the great beast out into the river until the water was just touching the lower portion of his belly. With his hands caressing and his voice crooning, he gently eased his full weight across the stallion's back, his strong hand clasping a handful of the long mane, At a jerk from the stallion, he held on a bit tighter.

Though a gift from the Great Spirit, Eagle's Wing was unused to anyone upon his back, and with a loud snort, he threw back his head and began to buck, his object to throw off the weight.

The water did what Sacred Eagle had hoped, and hindered the stallion from throwing its great body about as it would have liked. With use of some strength, Sacred Eagle kept his position.

For several moments Eagle's Wing snorted, jumped, and bucked, and as Sacred Eagle felt some of the fight go out of his mighty friend, he began again to talk to him, letting him know that it was he upon his back. And after an hour or two more, horse and warrior were racing through the village and out into the open plains of the valley, which stretched out for miles.

The ride was exhilarating for Sacred Eagle, and with the cool wind blowing over his body, his long, black hair streaming out behind his back, and his body held tightly to his mount, he laughed aloud to the heavens. The image of himself and Eagle's Wing came to his mind just as he had seen it when he was raised up on the sun-dance pole. They would be a mighty team, and with the help of the Grandfathers and the Great Spirit, they would be invincible.

Chapter Eleven

Two days later the small band of Blackfoot warriors left the village for the army fort. They had lingered at the village for the extra two days to allow Nicholas to rest and be able to make the ride with them. During this time Sacred Eagle grew even closer to his slave and formed a binding friendship with Eagle's Wing. The women, children, and elders of the tribe would also make the trek up into the mountains later this same day, for chief Star Hawk, feeling the changing of the winds, had declared to the high council that the time to move was at hand. The army would shortly make their first move, and the warriors had to be ready to strike back.

Kalina awoke early. Stretching upon the soft bed of furs, she reflected on the searing passion that had overtaken her and Sacred Eagle the night before. She sighed aloud as her hand roamed over his side of the pallet and she realized that she would not be seeing him for the next few days. He would be at the army fort hoping to get more information, and she was to go the mountains with the rest of the women. At this thought she made a sour face, opened her eyes, and slowly looked around. She could easily dismantle and pack up this lodge, and afterwards she would go to Fallen Leaves and help the old woman get ready to go with the tribe when the time came. And she would go up into the mountains with the rest of the camp, but she would not stay! She was only going to ensure that Falling Leaves was well taken care of. She had been raised to use weapons, not to sit with the women, children, and old men. She would return here to the valley as soon as she was able to and await Sacred Eagle. She would fight at his side and help to defeat his enemies as though they were her own. She had made up her mind about this last evening as Sacred Eagle was falling asleep upon her soft bosom, and she had absently entwined her fingers in his long black hair.

She did not wish to question herself too deeply about her decision, for she feared her answer, so she left it alone now that she had made up her mind. Why should she stay in the mountains when she could be of help here? Kalina rose and quickly began to pack the contents of the tepee. She had often done this same task in the Crow village when they moved from one campsite to another. Although Pointed Arrow had raised her in the manner of his sons, she had still had to learn to cook, sew, and care for their lodge.

By the time she was finished with her packing the sun was just starting to rise and the other villagers were moving about. When she finished placing the packs outside the horses' corral, she went to Falling Leaves's tepee and with the same speed began to dismantle and pack the old woman's possessions.

Falling Leaves smiled fondly at Kalina as she watched her move about the lodge. There was something special about this Crow slave that touched her old heart each time the maiden came to her lodge. And the girl now came often, at least once a day, and sometimes more frequently. After seeing to her needs, the girl would sit and work upon a hide or a pair of moccasins, not saying a word but smiling at the old woman whenever she would look up and find the dark eyes upon her.

From that first day when Falling Leaves had mistaken the girl for her own daughter, she had felt her heart lurch each time the girl came to her tepee. She resembled her dead daughter so much; even her mannerisms reminded her of Bright Lily—the way she stood, and the way she had of tilting her head back when the old lady would speak to her. The old Indian woman had wished more often of late that the girl could speak her tongue. There was much she would like to tell the girl of her own family that was now long gone, and of her own life as a young girl here in the Blackfoot village. She had no one with whom to share her past, but there was something in this slave girl's manner that told her she would listen, and would one day share the old stories with her own daughter.

It was not long before Kalina had all Falling Leaves's possessions strapped onto the back of the horse Star Hawk had brought for the elder woman. Kalina also helped Falling Leaves to lie comfortably upon the travois made from her lodge poles and hides, which were now strapped to another animal. The rest of the village was ready, and waiting for Star Hawk's word to move out.

Kalina mounted her own horse, which was laden with Sacred Eagle's many possessions and her own few. Sky Eyes held a horsehair rope that would lead the horse with Falling Leaves's travois as well as the lead horse carrying the elder woman's possessions.

It was late morning on a pleasant, cool day as the three rode together near the center of the moving camp. Though Kalina remained quiet, this in no way bothered Sky Eyes. She herself was a solitary person, and often sought out isolation. With the warrior woman as a friend she found that she did not have to share everything, but still had her companionship. As the ride continued throughout the long day, she was engrossed in her own thoughts, which lately were upon only one thing: Nicholas Prescott. Last night they had been able to steal away by themselves. His wounds had healed, and he had seemed as anxious to fall into her arms as she into his, while the rest of the village celebrated and prepared the moving of the camp to the mountains.

It had been a cold evening and the wind whistled through the tall pines. Nicholas's first words were, "You are chilled." He had begun to rub her arms and then had gently drawn her to him, a large sigh, as though of relief, escaping from his throat. "I thought I would not get the chance to hold you again before we had to part," he said.

"I, too, have been waiting for this moment," Sky Eyes had breathed against his neck.

"I still cannot believe that soon you will be all mine. If I could I would put a stop to this cruel war between our people. The ugliness of it must not affect the beauty of our love." His lips had slowly caught her in a tender kiss of mutual love, their breath mingling as they lost themselves in a tranquil, spellbinding ardor.

Within moments, not realizing how, they were lying naked in each other's arms, their bodies starved for this moment, their hands devouring as they roamed over each other.

"I can never get enough of you. When I am not next to you, I think and dream of your loveliness, your soft voice, your gentle ways," Nicholas had whispered, his lips lightly wandering over her slim neck, his kisses barely touching her soft flesh until he caught and held between his teeth a hard, straining crest. For a time he lavished his full attention upon the tempting morsel, and then he went to the next, leaving Sky Eyes panting and writhing beneath him. For a while it was as if the world had passed away and the couple were lost in the spell of velvet pleasure. His mouth seared her breasts, and with a will of their own her hands roved over his hard, strong body.

For the first time, Sky Eyes had touched and wrapped her hand about his throbbing manhood, delighting in the straining heat of such an instrument of pleasure.

With her play upon his body, Nicholas's arousal increased, his mouth now roaming over her breasts, enflaming the rose-hued peaks with a desire to be taken. The cool moisture upon her breasts seemed to heighten her erotic passions. Slowly his lips began to trail down her body, raining light kisses across her tight abdomen, his heated tongue languishing about her navel before continuing its titillating journey downward, evoking low moans from deep within Sky Eyes's throat.

As her hands searched and stroked his magnificent body, Nicholas penetrated her hidden forest and, as one finger boldly entered her warm

227

sheath, his lips and tongue teased her heated flesh. With this contact he felt her stiffen and heard her gasp. He lavished kisses upon the delicate bud of her womanhood. Her body responded quickly to his enticing stimulation, and his joy was boundless as he thrilled to her enjoyment. As his lips and tongue feasted upon her, his one finger eased in and out of the moist, dark cavern.

With her head thrown back and her moans loud, her body writhing under his delicious torment, Sky Eyes lost her reason. Never had she felt such exotic feelings. She felt her body turn to heat, to flame, tingles of gooseflesh spreading over her from head to toe and leaving her shaking with passion. She delighted in his attention, but still felt a need for more, for a fulfilling of her entire being.

Nicholas knew exactly the right moment to halt his play. Rising above her, with a sure, leisurely stroke he made them one.

Caught up in a feverish intoxication, Sky Eyes boldly pressed her body against his and greedily ensnared all of his throbbing manhood within her tight sheath. She seductively pulsed beneath him, her body in motion with his, her mouth ravenously seeking his lips, and her hands wrapping about his back trying to clutch him more tightly against her.

Amazed to find in this woman an appetite to match his own, Nicholas labored with pleasure to bring about their mutual victory. With a stroke he burst through his thoughts of holding a tight rein upon his emotions, and eagerly spiraled toward the peak of his passion. They crested together over the ultimate boundary, increasing their tempo and seizing their fulfillment together, their lips sealed as their bodies clutched tightly and their joy showered about them.

The lurching motion of her horse brought Sky Eyes back to reality. She had been so caught up in those moments of intimate joy with Nicholas that she had forgotten where she was. Her face flamed as she looked about as though expecting someone to be watching and reading her thoughts.

Kalina was lost in her own thoughts of Sacred Eagle and did not notice her friend's quietness, but as Falling Leaves spoke out in her friendly tone, she caught the attention of both young women. "I remember as a girl, I would sit upon my own grandmother's travois when we made this same move up into the mountains. Though it never was this cold when we traveled."

"Are you cold, Grandmother?" Sky Eyes halted her pony to make sure that the furs were tightly wrapped about the old woman. She and the slave girl had both nursed Falling Leaves back to health and she did not wish her to take ill once again.

"I am fine, child. With both of you always near, how can I be otherwise?" She blessed both the young women with a wide smile. "I think often of the past and the days when I was younger. I was told long ago that the more one dwells upon one's past days, the more those who have already traveled across the star path tend to beckon."

Sky Eyes smiled at her words, but Kalina frowned as she thought of the elder woman leaving this life and going on to the next. When this happened she would miss her terribly. She had never known a grandmother's loving concern, for Pointed Arrow's mother had passed on before Kalina had reached the age of five summers, and she had never really known her mother. Shortly after she had been adopted into Pointed Arrow's family, his wife had died. She did not wish to think of this old woman leaving her, now that she had grown to care so much for her.

Falling Leaves must have sensed something in Kalina for in a soothing tone she added, as her dark eyes looked into the younger woman's, "There is much I must still do and see before I can peacefully leave this life. I was born in the time of the falling leaves, and my mother always said I would leave this life in the same season as when I entered it."

Kalina relaxed at her words, feeling assured that there would be much more time for her and this grandmotherly woman. The season of the falling leaves had just passed, and winter was now at hand.

During the rest of the afternoon, the main portion of the Blackfoot tribe traveled up the trail through the mountains, and made camp in the late afternoon. Kalina and Sky Eyes joined Silver Star and erected Sacred Eagle's lodge, which was smaller than Star Hawk's, and easier to put up. Together the three women prepared a meal and shared it with Falling Leaves and those of the tribe who were elderly and unable to cook for themselves. Soon the fire began to chase away the chill in the lodge. After the meal the women finally found a few moments to relax. They settled around the small pit fire, next to which they had earlier made up Falling Leaves's pallet.

Silver Star's hands were busy as she sat cross-legged before the fire and worked on the dress she was making for Sky Eyes's wedding day. The beautiful bleached hide was stretched over her lap. "The day my children were born was much as this one just past," she started, as her fingers busily stitched out an intricate design. "Star Hawk and I had traveled a long distance that day, and thought we would find the village still camped in the valley, but they had moved only days before up into the mountains."

Everyone listened attentively as she spoke, each woman working at her task. Kalina was shelling the walnuts that several children had gathered that day and given to Silver Star, and Sky Eyes was sewing the shirt that she was making for Nicholas, which would match the dress her mother was now fashioning. Falling Leaves was the only one whose hands were not busy, but she lay alert, listening to all that the beautiful white woman was saying, loving a story better than anything.

Silver Star continued, "Star Hawk had built a cabin at the foot of the mountains for our joining lodge." She smiled softly in remembrance. Her husband had built the cabin in the fashion of the white man, in the hope of pleasing her. "We had been riding all that day, and my labor had been hard the whole afternoon. I was relieved when Star Hawk led our horses to the cabin. It was not the custom of his people for a warrior to be near a birthing hut, but I had no one else, and my husband would not leave my side. The pains were almost unbearable, and only Star Hawk's gentle voice kept me holding on. He drew within my mind all the beauty I had ever known, and with my inner vision I clutched his words. At last the pain seemed to slacken, and my first child was born." Again a smile lingered on her lips as she thought of that day so long ago when she had first glimpsed the tiny being in her husband's large hands.

"You did not have long, though, to think upon my brother," Sky Eyes interjected with a soft laugh. She had heard this story in the past, told by her father, who always seemed to tell it with great reverence.

232

Smiling upon her daughter, Silver Star nodded, her eyes going back to her sewing. For a moment, as though holding the tension within the lodge, she did not speak. She had learned the ways of the Blackfoot, and they included being a good story teller, so Silver Star kept them waiting for her next words. "It was, indeed, only a small time before I was taken up again with the pains of another child coming from my body. Again, I held on only with the help of my husband's words and direction. After the birth of my daughter, I fell instantly to sleep. When I awoke, my husband brought me my children and told me their names. Star Hawk had pondered long upon the names of his children. His daughter had looked upon him with her silver-blue orbs, and that is why she was called Sky Eyes. His son he named Two Shadows after the two parts of his spirit, himself and his sister, and through prayers he knew that the Great Spirit would guide him throughout his life. And the Great Spirit was the one that changed this name to Sacred Eagle. I also gave my children names, for I could see that the days might come when they would have to step into the world of the white man." Silver Star remained quiet at the end of her story, her fingers working expertly on the soft hide.

Kalina had sat spellbound, and now she allowed herself to breathe deeply, hiding within her heart all that Silver Star had said about her son. She could never hear enough about Sacred Eagle. Hearing this story of his birth allowed her to feel somehow a part of his family, closer to him.

It was Falling Leaves who broke the quiet that had settled about the lodge. "My child was born high in the mountains. As is the way of the people, I went to the birthing hut that had been built close to the outskirts of the village. I remember the old healing woman, Cloud Dreamer, chanting to the Great Spirit to bring my husband a strong son or to bring to me a helper in my husband's lodge. There were herbs that she gave to me to help with the pain, and for a time I seemed to slip away into a dreamy limbo. I thought it was summer and the lilies in the valley were in full bloom. They seemed so bright and light, almost as though I could walk upon them. My daughter was born soon after, and she was called Bright Lily." The old woman wiped away the tears upon her cheek, and Silver Star also felt a tear as she remembered the daughter of Falling Leaves.

When the fierce and powerful Star Hawk brought his beautiful white captive, Jessica Coltin, to the Blackfoot village, another had been in love with him and had desired to be the mate of the chief's only son. Bright Lily was both beautiful and desired by many of the braves of the tribe — but not by Star Hawk. He chose Jessica Coltin for his wife, giving her an Indian name, and his choice had stoked a fierce hatred in the other girl. Bright Lily had followed them to the cabin at the foot of the mountains on the night they were joined, and when Star Hawk had gone out to tend the horses the girl had stolen in and attacked Silver Star with a wicked, long-bladed knife. Jessica could still feel a ripple of goose flesh go over her body as she thought about that evening. If not for Star Hawk's coming back into the cabin at that moment, she would have been left dead and her husband would have never known who her attacker was. As it was, Star Hawk had surprised the girl with her hand held high, the knife ready to do terrible damage. Star Hawk had thrown his full weight upon the girl and had all but choked the life from her body. Indeed, Jessica knew that if she had not stopped him, the girl would have died at his hands. Star Hawk had spoken to Bright Lily's father upon their return to the village, and not long after, the girl had been married to another brave of the village. And though Bright Lily often directed dark looks in Jessica's direction, she had never come too close to Star Hawk's wife again.

"My daughter was all I had, and I missed her terribly when she was joined with White Skies. But she visited her mother often and was still a dutiful daughter. Her happiness was not to last for long, though, for her husband was killed by a Cheyenne brave, and she was left with a small

235

daughter. This, too, was only for a short time, for she and the child were also taken by the Great Spirit. I do long at times to be with my family." The tears now were streaming down the old woman's face, and her words were spoken softly in grief.

"Rest easy, Mother." Jessica set her handiwork aside and went to Falling Leaves. She lightly kissed the leathered cheek and tucked the furs tightly about her. "Your daughter and child have traveled the star path and are now with White Skies. All three are now with your husband Leaping Elk, and are happy."

"I know this, but at times I am so lonely for them."

Kalina could bear no more. Setting aside her bowl of nuts, she also knelt beside the old woman, taking her frail hand in her own. She patted it lightly, trying to impart some of her feelings to her.

Jessica sat back and allowed the warrior woman to tend Falling Leaves. Though the girl never talked, Jessica had found in her a warmth and inner strength that she had glimpsed in very few others. At times she felt sympathy for her plight, but the girl always held her head high, as though she were not the slave and all who stood about her were inferior. Taking up her sewing once again, she marveled at the closeness that had so quickly arisen between the warrior woman and

Falling Leaves. Perhaps it was because they had both lost those they had loved and now had no other to share their hearts. Jessica herself could well remember when she had been taken from everyone she had known. Without the kindness of the old healing woman, Cloud Dreamer, she would have been miserable and lonely, and without Star Hawk's love, she would have been wretched. Again she thought of her son, and wondered about the relationship between this beautiful slave and Sacred Eagle. He had changed since he had brought the girl to their village; she could sense that his heart was not as heavy as in the past. The desire for revenge upon his enemy seemed not as strong. As her thoughts led her in this direction, she pondered the outcome. The girl was a slave, and one of the enemy. Could she truly find a place in her son's heart?

Late that night, when all in the lodge were quiet and settled upon their sleeping couches, Jessica lay awake thinking about her children. It was her maternal wish to see them both happy and content in their choices, and she prayed that their hearts' desires would see them to this end. Snuggling deeper into the furs as the fire faded and the lodge cooled with the night air, she let her mind drift to her husband. She hated each time that they were separated, and longed to be back in his strong arms as quickly as possible. Even after all this time, Star Hawk was her heart, her

237

only love.

The camp awoke early the next morning, and in the cold sting of the frost upon the ground they set to the breaking-up of camp and the packing of the animals. The morning passed much as yesterday morning had: the long line of women, children, and the elderly slowly set out upon the trek up into the mountains. This day their spirits were higher, though for they knew that by late afternoon they would at last be at their journey's end.

Throughout the day Kalina kept watch for any game that might be near. She had fashioned her own bow and several arrows during her free time over the past few weeks, and though she had kept these weapons hidden, today she had strapped them on her horsehair saddle and covered them with a blanket. She longed for a challenge, and the thought of a hunt exhilarated her. She was not sure Sacred Eagle would be pleased to see her with a weapon, but no one would be able to argue with her when she brought back meat for the camp. There was always the need for more food in an Indian village.

A short time later, as the long line of villagers went through a narrow pass and started through a thick pine forest, a flash of brown off to Kalina's right caught her attention. Slowing her mount until she was at the back of the line, Kalina eased her horse to the right and, gently kicking his flanks, directed him into the forest. With her senses fully attuned to her surroundings, she started quickly down a small ravine, her dark eyes watching every tree and shrub for the game she knew was close by.

Ahead of her she glimpsed a slight movement from the corner of her eye. Dismounting slowly and pulling her bow and the arrows from her saddle, she cautiously tied her pony and then upon silent feet climbed to the edge of the ravine and approached the magnificent elk.

He seemed not at all interested in his surroundings. With his head lowered, he nibbled at the winter grass that grew sparsely in the forest. Kalina crept from tree to tree, her body crouched low, her arrow drawn back and at the ready, and her body tense as she all but held her breath.

With a fleeting moment of panic, the large beast threw back his head and snorted the cool air. Too late he discerned his danger, for the moment his head rose from his mid-morning meal, Kalina let fly the arrow. Her aim was true, and the arrow pierced through the heart, hitting just behind the left shoulder. With a whoop she ran toward the staggering prey, the knife that she had kept hidden beneath her skirt now clutched in her hand.

With his lifeblood flowing from the mortal

wound, the elk, his eyes glazed, ran until he finally dropped, his breath coming in ragged gasps and blood foaming from his mouth.

Kalina gave chase, easily trailing the beast from the red blood on the forest floor. They left the higher ground and went back down into the ravine, and it was only moments before Kalina was standing over the animal, her sharp knife swiftly cutting his throat. With a grunt of satisfaction, Kalina turned about and ran back to her pony.

The elk was young but he was still too large for Kalina to lift him by herself onto the back of her pony. So, gutting the beast and removing the larger cuts of meat, she packed what meat she could in leather bags that had been tied to her saddle. She worked hurriedly, knowing that at any moment the shout could be given that she was no longer with the tribe and the braves who were traveling with the women for protection would be scouring the forest for her.

Sweaty, and with blood still on her hands, Kalina finally met up with the encampment. They had halted for the midday meal, and as Kalina rode her pony to where Sky Eyes was resting and helping Falling Leaves to a drink of cool water, the silver-eyed young woman smiled with some relief.

"I feared you would not return." Sky Eyes felt some guilt, for she had not called out the alarm that her brother's slave had disappeared. If Kalina had escaped, Sky Eyes would have had to accept much of the blame. Now, looking at the girl, she glimpsed a vitality about her that she had thus far not seen. And when she saw the blood upon her hands and the spatterings of red upon her dress, she sighed aloud as she realized what the girl had been about. "Whatever did you kill?" She quickly rose to her feet and approached the pony.

With a large grin of satisfaction that she had been able to prove herself at last, Kalina jumped to the ground and quickly pulled open the leather bags tied to the sides of her saddle.

Seeing the large haunches of meat, Sky Eyes gasped aloud. "But how could you possibly have brought down such a beast?" As soon as the words were out, Sky Eyes regretted them. She had no desire to know about any weapons this slave may be concealing. She liked the warrior woman and she did not wish to cause her any more grief than she had already had to endure. And if the girl were to tell her about weapons, Sky Eyes would be bound to at least mention to her mother what she had learned.

But Kalina acted as though she did not understand her words, and stepped past the girl and to the small running spring. Washing her hands of the blood and trying to get some of the stains from her skirt, Kalina smiled with pleasure at her deed. Falling Leaves would have fresh meat for her dinner this eve, and so would many of the other elders of the tribe.

It was late afternoon when the tribe arrived at
their winter camp. Hurriedly the lodges were
erected and everything was put in order. By early
dusk the encampment looked as though it had
always been there. Children were running about,
shouting and laughing, the dogs were barking,
hides were stretched out on drying racks, and at
the far end of the camp a pair of skinny dogs
were fighting over a bone that had been thrown
aside as two warriors skinned and gutted their
kill.

Kalina helped Silver Star and Sky Eyes to set
up Falling Leaves's lodge, and then she erected
Sacred Eagle's lodge. She had little desire to stay
here at the mountain camp. She wished only to
make sure that all was in order before she headed
back to the valley once again. It had been two
days since the tribe had set out for the mountains,
and it would take her another day to get back to
the valley. There was no telling what could take
place in this length of time. Every moment she
was away from Sacred Eagle, she worried over his
safety. What would become of her if something
happened to that mighty warrior? In her heart she
was worried: even the most worthy brave was not
totally invulnerable. But she forced herself to push

242

these thoughts from her mind, warning herself sternly that it did little good to think in such a manner.

On her way to the river to get water and firewood, she noticed that the braves who had escorted the tribe up to the mountains were now splitting up, half staying on to guard the women, children, and elders, and the other half returning to the valley to fight the bluecoats with the rest of the warriors.

Reaching the riverbank, Kalina found that the only other person who had made her way to the water was Sky Eyes. The young woman was filling her water parfleche, and at her feet was a small stack of wood. As Kalina approached, Sky Eyes straightened up and smiled fondly. "I thought to make a stew for our dinner," she signed with her hands. "Would you like to join me and my mother?"

Kalina quickly shook her head in the negative. She did not want anyone to notice that she was no longer here in the mountains. If they all thought she was alone in Sacred Eagle's lodge for the night, perhaps she would not be missed until morning. By then, if the alarm was shouted out, she would already be near the camp in the valley, and it would be too late for anyone to catch her and bring her back. Sacred Eagle would have to allow her to stay at his side.

"Well, if you are sure." Sky Eyes assumed that

the girl was tired from the day's long ride and from all that she had gone through to bring them fresh meat. "At least I can wait and walk you back to camp." She noticed now for the first time that the sun was beginning to lower, and that they were the only ones at the river.

Kalina also looked about her. The trees and brush blocked most of the view of the encampment. Bending, she filled her parfleche with water and, still with a slight feeling of unease as she looked about, she began gathering wood.

Finished with her own tasks, Sky Eyes began to help the warrior woman to gather her wood, and their steps took them slowly down the riverbank. Just as the pair had gathered enough wood for the evening fire, a Crow brave stepped forth from behind a tall pine near Sky Eyes. With a quick movement he pulled Sky Eyes up tightly against his naked chest, and as she opened her mouth to scream, his large hand covered her lips.

Kalina looked with disbelief at the warrior holding Sky Eyes, but before she could rush to the girl to give her aid, she, too, was grabbed from behind. With a grunt of pure fury, she struck out at her assaulter with arms flailing and feet kicking, but arms like bands of steel encircled her tightly, bringing her hard against his body.

Barely able to contain the spirited woman in his grasp, the Indian holding Kalina hissed next to her ear in the Crow language, "Keep still, woman!"

Kalina's mouth had not been covered, as had Sky Eyes's, and without a thought, she exclaimed aloud in the Crow tongue, "Take your hands away from me, and release my friend this moment!" Her words were a command.

"You are a Crow woman?" The warrior spun her about, his dark gaze scanning the area and watching as the other five braves who had come with him on this mission stepped forth. "What does a Crow woman do in this Blackfoot camp? And why does she call this white eyes her friend?" The Crow warriors had been hiding by the river the whole afternoon waiting for just such a chance as had presented itself. They had been told by the sergeant at the fort to bring back the white woman, and she had been easier to abduct than they had dared hope. The only problem now was that this Crow woman was with her.

"I am Kalina, daughter of Pointed Arrow. I was captured by the Blackfoot warrior known as Sacred Eagle. I am his slave." Even as this word left her lips she despised all that it meant. Slave. Was that truly all she was to Sacred Eagle?

The warrior holding onto her brought her back to reality as he snorted with contempt at the name of Sacred Eagle. "The mighty Eagle shall shortly be brought down low. You will come with us, and we will take you back to your father and your own village."

"No!" Kalina had no desire to return to her village yet. There was still much that had to be sorted out between her and Sacred Eagle. And what had this brave meant by saying that Sacred Eagle would soon be brought down? "Why are you here, so close to a Blackfoot village?" For the first time, she took a good look at the warriors grouped about Sky Eyes and herself. They seemed only lightly armed, as though this enabled them to move more swiftly. There was something in their manner that bespoke stealth.

"We are here to take the white woman back to her own people, and now that we have found you we shall also return you to your own. A Crow woman does not belong in the village of her enemy." His arms tightened about her and he squeezed to emphasize his words.

"But she is not—" Kalina was not allowed to finish her sentence, for the warrior clasped his large hand over her mouth. Mumbling that he had heard enough, he motioned for the other warriors to bring Sky Eyes and to follow him to their horses.

The brave that held Sky Eyes had tied a leather strap across her mouth to keep her from calling for help. She tried to pull back, but he easily lifted her into his arms and carried her to the place where they had hidden their mounts.

Kalina was now in much the same position as Sky Eyes, except that her mouth was not covered.

246

Yet, given the opportunity to call out for help, she found that she could not betray her own kind. She would have to go along for the time being, until she could form some kind of plan for their escape. For a time she tried to use her mind to her best advantage. She still had her sharp-bladed hunting knife tied securely upon her upper thigh and hidden beneath her dress. Surely this warrior who now held her captive in his arms would not guard her as closely as he would Sky Eyes. For a time she would act as though she would comply with their demands and try to appear eager to return to her father. Perhaps she would be given the chance to free Sky Eyes and herself if she kept her wits about her and did not let panic override her better judgment.

Seeing some of the terror in Sky Eyes's pale eyes as they reached the horses, Kalina spoke to her in the Blackfoot tongue, daring to reveal her secret in the hope that her words would soothe the frightened young woman. "Do not fear, friend; we will find a way to escape and win our freedom." We *must*, she thought to herself, as the large warrior's words about Sacred Eagle being brought low came again to her mind. She had to free herself and find Sacred Eagle to make sure he was not harmed and to warn him that he was in danger.

Sky Eyes was startled by the warrior woman's words. She had never herd Kalina utter one word until this moment, and the words she had spoken in her own tongue were as clear and well pronounced as those of any of her tribe. Her surprise was clearly visible upon her features, but slowly she nodded her head in agreement. She was pulled onto the back of her captor's horse, and Kalina was taken up behind the leader of the small band. She held little hope of her freedom, except what this warrior woman was offering.

Chapter Twelve

While the scene in the mountains near the edge of the river was being enacted, Sacred Eagle and Nicholas set a fast pace through the forest, their destination the army fort. Eagle's Wing held the lead and the excitement of the men was high, for each had his own thoughts about the outcome of what they would find at the fort.

Sacred Eagle hoped for an end to the threat of the white man against his people, so that he could have the time he needed to sort out his own life. Already, with the passing of two days, he felt a deep loneliness filling his soul for the woman who now shared his lodge. And though he knew her to be safe in the mountains with the rest of the women of his village, still his thoughts were constantly upon her welfare. He had to admit that she was only a slave, albeit a beautiful one, and this fact in itself was one of his greatest fears. He thought it likely that a bold brave would take it upon himself to try and steal her favors. Though she wore his necklace and in his mind this marked her as his own, he knew that few considered a slave worthy of protection, and many men would dare anything for just a few moments to sample her rare beauty. Kicking Eagle's Wings sides, he pushed his mount into a quicker pace.

Nicholas, as he closely followed his friend, also wished for an end to this conflict, since with the finish, he was promised the greatest of treasures. And after sharing a night of wondrous passions in the arms of the woman he loved, each time he thought of Sky Eyes he wished time to fly. He cursed the fates that had placed the red man against the white.

Without the hindrance of the other braves, and making fast time, the pair arrived at the fort late that same afternoon. They were allowed entry without question through the large wooden gates. The officer watching from the lookout recognized the major's nephew and Sacred Eagle attracted no attention as he wore his white man's clothes. As the pair dismounted in front of Major Thatcher's office, there were several officers standing outside and the tension was palpable.

Sacred Eagle stroked Eagle's Wing with a firm hand, his voice soothing as he whispered in his ear, for he sensed the large beast's nervousness in these strange surroundings.

"That be a fine-looking animal ye have there."

One of the men near the major's office stepped closer as he admired the large white stallion. When he reached out to touch the sleek neck, Eagle's Wing bared his teeth, his head jerking back ready for an attack. Quickly the man stepped back and put his hand behind his back.

Taking a few moments to settle Eagle's Wing with his gentle touch and low voice, Sacred Eagle finally looked at the man who had dared to reach out to his horse, and then slowly the crystal gaze surveyed the others standing about the watching. "Sorry, but my horse is a bit skittish. He only tolerates my touch. I would advise you all to keep your distance."

Murmurings of agreement came quickly, and the nodding of the man's head indicated that he would not be so foolish again.

Nicholas grinned widely at the men before him as he tied his horse to a post and started along the wood planking of the sidewalk in front of the major's office. Everyone at the fort remembered the major's nephew, but each man looking at him now was amazed at the change that had taken place in him. Where before they had thought him a rich young man of leisure, used to having everything given to him because of his wealth and standing, and had tolerated him because of his kinship to the head of this fort, now they saw an entirely different Nicholas Prescott. Here was a man who seemed a part of this wild countryside.

He was tall and broad, his buckskin shirt and pants fitting tightly upon his frame and lending him a lithe, athletic appearance. "Is the major in?" Nicholas's strong voice carried over the group standing about, and several heads nodded.

Nicholas and Sacred Eagle started toward the office, but Benjamin Thatcher met them in the doorway. "Why, Nicholas, I am glad to see you, lad." His eyes went to the man at his nephew's side. "And you also, Mr. Coltin. I was about to send out a party to see if you could be found or if anyone had heard of your whereabouts."

"Is there a reason for your wanting to see me?" Nicholas asked. "Heath and I have been trapping, and have brought in a few furs to trade."

"There is trouble brewing with the Indians, and I wanted to make sure you were not in the middle of it. Your mother would never forgive me if something happened to you."

Looking quite unruffled, Nicholas stepped farther into the small office, and Sacred Eagle followed close at his heels. He took a seat, as though expecting his uncle to do the same, crossed his legs at the ankles, and responded. "Take a seat, Heath, it's been a long ride today. What kind of trouble are you talking about, Uncle Benjamin? We didn't hear of anything happening with the Indians while we were up in the mountains trapping."

"I told you about that Blackfoot tribe that has

252

been troubling the army. Their leader is Star Hawk. Well, things are finally coming to a head."

Nicholas sat up a bit straighter at these words, and he noticed something in his uncle's manner that spoke of repressed excitement. The older man paced about the small room. His nephew continued. "I don't understand. We saw other trappers and even some Indians out there, and none of them mentioned anything about Star Hawk's people stirring up trouble."

"Trouble? They are holding a white woman against her will. Would you not call that asking for trouble?" Benjamin Thatcher's face turned bright red as he shouted this across the room. He had built up his own excuses for what he planned to do to these red devils, and he had made himself righteously irate over the fact that a white woman was living with this Indian chief called Star Hawk.

Sacred Eagle felt his own blood boiling with this accusation. His hands grasped the arms of his chair to keep him from jumping to his feet and strangling this white man who thought himself so important that he would start a war and cause loss of life for his own concocted reasons.

Nicholas also felt his anger rise. "Perhaps the woman wishes to be there in this Star Hawk's village." He forced himself to sound calm, and for a moment tried to convince himself that his uncle had not even considered this possibility.

253

"Rubbish! No decent white woman would wish to be kept by a savage. Why, the stories I have heard about the treatment of white women at the hands of these red heathens! It makes me shudder to think of what this woman has been forced to endure."

"Uncle, I think you should reexamine these accusations when you have heard the truth of the matter for yourself. Perhaps you could send an envoy to Star Hawk's village and speak to this woman." Nicholas rose slowly to his feet, knowing that if he did not do something quickly Sacred Eagle would surely explode and give everything away.

"I have found out enough, and have already sent a full report to Washington explaining my reasons for quelling these savages' rebellion. And as far as the woman is concerned, I shall have all the proof I need very shortly."

"And what kind of proof is this?" Sacred Eagle sounded as though he was merely interested in what the major had to say.

Easing his bulk down into the chair behind his desk, Major Thatcher allowed his gaze to rest upon the young man for a few moments. As though feeling assured of his trustworthiness, he began. "My scouts are at this very moment finding the woman we speak of, and are ordered to bring her here to me. If you have reconsidered the offer I made when we met for the first time,

254

perhaps you would care to join us now. I must confess that these Crow savages turn my blood. Can't trust any of these murdering savages."

"You mean you have sent men into the Blackfoot village to capture Star Hawk's wife?" Sacred Eagle felt his blood run cold at the major's words.

"Our reports tell us that most of the tribe has moved back into the mountains. My scouts will find the woman there, and when they do they will bring her to me. We pull out with the first light and will head in the direction of the Blackfoot valley. We intend to establish our presence there while those savages are high in the mountains. My scouts—they are Crow, and hate the Blackfoot— will bring the woman to me on the trail, and we will bring this Star Hawk to his knees with little bloodshed. And then, of course, the woman will be returned to her own kind." Benjamin Thatcher now had a smug, satisfied smirk upon his face, as if to imply that he had everything figured out to the last detail. He stood and walked up and down behind his desk self-importantly. Apparently he had not even considered his own defeat.

Both Sacred Eagle and Nicholas rose to their feet at the same moment, outrage marked clearly upon their faces. It was Nicholas, though, who shouted, "You cannot be serious? Star Hawk will never give in to your demands, nor will he allow you to take his wife from him! He will pour down

255

his wrath upon you and your men, and you will be the cause of a horrible bloodbath."

"What have we here, Nicholas?" Benjamin Thatcher sat back down and stared hard at his nephew. "Have you found yourself a cause to champion? I am afraid you have misplaced your loyalties, lad. You and your friend here will do well to stay here at the fort and keep out of the way. I estimate that within the week I'll have everything under control and all those heathens cleared out of that valley. Once the trails are opened through the valley and the mountains, this part of the country will be civilized."

Nicholas was shocked. "Misplaced loyalties? Do you know what you are saying? Do you have any concept, Uncle, of the strength of these people you think you will so easily chase from the land that they have called their own for hundreds of years? If you think they will leave all that they have loved and called dear, you are mistaken. They are people, not animals to be chased down and slaughtered as you would a herd of wild buffalo. They will fight back. Every last man of them will stand and die for what you want to claim in the name of civilization."

"Then *let* them stand and die!" The major also rose to his full height. "I'll be damned if they will find me coddling their red hides. If they think they can go about the countryside pillaging and murdering helpless people, they are mistaken. And if they think for one moment that I will allow them to hold a helpless woman captive, they will shortly see the extent of my resolve for themselves."

Both Nicholas and Sacred Eagle saw that there would be no way to reason with Benjamin Thatcher. There was just one track to his thoughts, which was also the thought of many white men: the only good Indian was a dead one. "I can only ask you one last time, Uncle, to reconsider your plans." Nicholas thought it worth one last try to plead with this man who was his mother's brother. There was so much at stake. The lives of all the soldiers here at the fort and those of the tribes who had joined forces with Star Hawk's people were infinitely more valuable to him than to this man who, although he was his kin, Nicholas barely knew. And what of this kinship? How would he feel to be opposed to his mother's only brother? Would he be able to fight his own relative for what he truly believed in?

"I don't know what you think you have learned in the short time you have been here in America and in this part of the country, but I can see now that I should not have allowed you to go trapping with Mr. Coltin. Let me assure you, Nicholas; I know what is best in this matter. This whole affair will be over with soon and then you can return home to England. Perhaps in a year or two, I will be able to make a visit to your mother.

I miss my half sister dearly at times."

There was just no reasoning with him. Shaking his head sadly, Nicholas looked at Sacred Eagle, who showed that he understood his feelings and held similar ones of his own.

"Well, now that we have this settled, why don't you two go to the cook and have him fix you something to eat. We are to pull out early, and you should both rest and relax in the next few days. That is, unless you would care to accept my offer to scout for me, Mr. Coltin?"

Sacred Eagle, with a cold, dark glare, glowered at the man who was causing his people so much anguish and would soon cause blood to flow upon the floor of their valley. "No, I will not work for you. And I will not stay here at your fort." Already Sacred Eagle's mind was at work. He would have to travel fast if he was to overtake the Crow scouts the major had sent to his village. If his father or some of the warriors of the tribe had not already found them and halted their mission, he had to ensure that his mother and his sister were safe. Again thoughts of his slave passed fleetingly through his mind, but quickly he pushed them aside. He had enough to worry about without thinking once again about the warrior woman.

"If you decide to go back out there and go trapping, then I can't stop you, but I would warn you to be careful. The Indians are roaming about in the mountains and will soon be looking for the scalp of any white man they come across."

"I will be safe, Major. You had best look to yourself and your men." Sacred Eagle gave this one last warning before turning and walking through the door.

"I will go with my friend, Uncle Benjamin. I do ask you to reconsider what you are doing this one last time." Nicholas felt torn, but his loyalties were definitely not here at this army fort. His best friend and the woman he loved were Blackfoot, and whatever was to come he would stand beside them.

"You cannot go back out there. And of course I will not change my mind. I have thought everything out carefully. We will surprise those redskins, and be back here at the fort inside a month."

"Let me ask you this, Uncle. Why do you suppose the largest part of the tribe has moved back into the mountains? Have you thought that they may know of your intentions?"

For a moment Benjamin Thatcher seemed to consider his words, but then as quickly he shook his head. No, he was sure, and he had already sent orders that the fort would be on the move in the morning. He would make short shift of these savages, gain his promotion, and then once again return to civilization. God only knew how much he hated this day-in and day-out life of dirt and bad food and incompetent bunglers. Once he received his promotion, as he had been promised he would when he was sent out here, he would go to Washington, and then he would be able to travel and live as he wished. "It does not matter what they know. We will overtake them and drive them from that valley."

"Then there is little more I can say." Nicholas started to the door after Sacred Eagle.

"I'll not be the one held responsible if the two of you go our there and get your hair lifted!" Thatcher shouted at his nephew's broad back. "Damn the insolent young pup," he hissed between clenched teeth as the door was slammed shut.

Sacred Eagle was furious as he rode through the front gates of the fort. His outrage heightened with each step Eagle's Wing took. And as Nicholas pulled alongside of him and the pair talked over all they had heard at the fort, they agreed that there was great need for them to hurry back to the Blackfoot village. There was little doubt in either mind that the major was speaking the truth and at this very moment the Crow warriors were sneaking about the Blackfoot camp in search of Silver Star. Sacred Eagle knew that if the Crow Indians went first to the valley, the alarm would have been sounded and their enemies quickly dealt with. But the fear in Sacred Eagle's heart was that the women would have left the village as had been planned, and that the Crow warriors would follow them into the mountains. There, it would be much easier for the enemy to hide and wait for the chance to capture his mother.

Kicking Eagle's Wing's flanks to spur him on to a faster pace, Sacred Eagle realized the full magnitude of what could be happening to his mother. He shouted to Nicholas that they would go first to the mountains.

The day wore on and Sacred Eagle and his mount seemed tireless as they galloped through the dense forest. Their pace never slackened. Beast and man seemed united by the fear of what was awaiting them. Nicholas had been forced to slow down earlier, for his mount, unlike Sacred Eagle's, did not have the strength to endure such a pace.

Night had set in, but a sliver of moonlight showed the way through the tall pines. Sacred Eagle at last slowed Eagle's Wing and, dismounting near a small stream, allowed his horse to drink and to nibble at the grass growing along the embankment.

This was where Nicholas found him at last. Sacred Eagle was sitting upon a fallen log and eating dried venison and a handful of dried corn.

With a sigh of relief the white man lowered his large frame to the ground. Patting his mount's rump, he let him go to where Eagle's Wing was feeding. "Damn! I thought it would be morning before I caught up with you."

Sacred Eagle smiled wearily at his friend. "We shall only rest for a short time." At Nicholas's look of torment, he added, "We will take it slowly through the forest at night. We cannot risk injury to our horses by their accidentally stepping into a rabbit hole."

This seemed to appease Nicholas, and as Sacred Eagle offered him his pouch of food, he gratefully accepted some sustenance.

It was only a short rest, and soon the two men were once again upon the trail leading into the mountains, hoping against hope that they would not be too late.

As the darkness settled over the forest the leader of the Crow warriors finally signaled to his men to halt and begin making camp. "We are far enough from the Blackfoot camp to rest for the night. The alarm will not be sounded until morning when they discover that the women are missing, and those that remain in the camp are mostly the old, and women and children. Any braves who dare to follow, we shall tend to."

The braves in his group clearly agreed with Spotted Elk. In a short time a fire was blazing and fresh meat was hissing and roasting over the open flames.

Sky Eyes's mouthpiece had been removed and

she had been tied to a tree. The braves ignored her as they settled down about the fire. Kalina had been left untied, and had offered to cook the venison. She had thought only of escape since she had been captured, and the only plan she could formulate was to try and win Spotted Elk's trust, somehow free Sky Eyes, and then try and find their way back to the Blackfoot camp. She had decided not to tell Spotted Elk that he had captured the wrong woman, that it was Sky Eyes's mother he had been instructed to kidnap. All her telling could do was to endanger their lives. It was best that they believed Sky Eyes was the one they wanted. She was younger and could endure better than Silver Star.

As Kalina turned the meat that was cooking on sticks over the flames, she looked toward Spotted Elk. "I will be glad to see my father and my brothers once again. I am sure my father will reward you greatly for bringing his daughter home safely."

Looking the woman over with an eye appreciative of her rare beauty, Spotted Elk did not miss the way her hide dress tightened about her shapely form as she bent over the fire. Perhaps the reward he would request would be this woman, he thought to himself as he watched her movements. He had one wife already waiting for him in his village, but many of his friends had more than one wife. And this woman before him was very

263

desirable. She would bring much satisfaction to him during the long winter nights ahead. "Perhaps your father would consider an offer for his daughter?" Spotted Elk said aloud. This drew Kalina's full attention. "After all, you have already been used by a Blackfoot." He seemed to spit the last word out.

Kalina straightened up, her dark eyes steady upon the face of Spotted Elk. As she read his thoughts within the depths of his eyes, she felt a shiver travel over her body. There was a certain cruelty in this warrior's manner that was easily seen. He did not have the tenderness of Sacred Eagle, and Kalina knew that a wife to this brave would be used without thought to her feelings or her desires. Again she thought of escape. She could not afford to let Spotted Elk take her back to her family, for she could not bear the thought that Pointed Arrow might allow this man to take her as his own. She realized that he and everybody else would think of her as defiled because she had been a slave to the enemy.

"Take the woman some food." Spotted Elk brought Kalina from her thoughts with his command, and quickly she took some of the sizzling venison from the flames.

As Kalina approached Sky Eyes, the tied girl said softly, with desperation in her voice, "Whatever are we going to do?" She also had done nothing but try to come up with some plan for their escape, but with her hands tied to the trunk of this tree, she could not get beyond her fear to reason out anything that could help them.

"Do not worry now. I will think of something." Kalina spoke quickly, as one of the braves sitting near the fire rose, came to the two women, and untied the bindings on Sky Eyes's wrist so that she was able to eat.

For a moment the warrior stood and glared down at the two women, but he seemed to find little to hold his interest, and went back to his companions.

Sky Eyes had little appetite, but when Kalina handed her the meat she took it. "I don't understand what all this is about," she whispered as she looked at her friend.

"These warriors were sent to capture your mother and bring her to the army fort. They plan to use Silver Star as a weapon against the Blackfoot."

"And they think I am a white woman?" Sky Eyes asked.

"Because of your pale eyes, they think that you are Silver Star."

"And what about you? How do you speak my tongue so well?" Sky Eyes felt truly mystified. "How could you have learned so quickly?"

"I will tell you everything when there is more time. All I can say now is that somehow the words of your people are known to me from a long time past."

Spotted Elk rose from the fire and started toward the two women.

"I will think of something to help us, do not worry," Kalina murmured.

"But why?" Sky Eyes had wondered since they had been seized at the river why this warrior woman would wish to help her. These were her own people. It would be easy for her now to return to her own village. "Why do you wish to help me?"

Kalina could not tell this young woman that to go back to her own people would mean that she would not be near Sacred Eagle. She could not tell anyone of the feelings in her heart for this girl's brother. All she could say was, "You are my friend. You offered me much with your friendship when I was but a slave."

"But if you return with me to my village, you will *still* be a slave." Sky Eyes stopped short; Spotted Elk was just a few strides away from them.

Kalina had no more time to talk with the other girl, but she smiled quickly. Truly, she had never been a slave. She could have fled the Blackfoot village anytime she had desired. She had been raised in the forest to trail and to track game. She could have easily slipped from Sky Eyes's village and made her way back to her father's lodge. But from that first moment when she had laid eyes on

Sacred Eagle she had been powerless to leave him. Her family, her home meant nothing to her any longer. All she desired lay in the keeping of the warrior who had claimed her heart along with her innocence. But all this she harbored in her heart, not daring to express her feelings. There was so much still unsettled between her and Sacred Eagle. Nothing and no one would be able to stand in the way of her sorting these problems out. She and Sky Eyes would escape these warriors, and then she would make her way back to the valley and to Sacred Eagle. Too much time had already passed.

"Go back to the fire and eat." Spotted Elk looked at Kalina before he once again tied Sky Eyes's hands to the tree. He had not forgotten the Crow woman's claim that the white woman was her friend. He would keep them apart if possible, for he would not have his woman being friends with a white eyes. He had determined that he would have this Crow woman for his own.

Kalina did go back to the fire, and forced herself to eat so that she would have strength when the time came for their escape. As she finished her meal the warriors began to split up, two going off into the bushes to stand guard while the others prepared to sleep until their turn to keep watch. Kalina took all this in and began to formulate a plan.

As Spotted Elk began to spread out his sleeping furs his thoughts strayed again to the Crow woman. Looking at her, for a time he contemplated ordering her to lie with him. But then what if he took this woman, and she spoke of it to her father and he then refused to give her to him? Was he willing to let go all his chances for this one night's pleasure? Lying flat on his back, he turned his head away from her beauty and thought of what he would offer her father for a bride price. She was worth little in his mind, for she had been used by his enemy—but would her father have the same opinion?

Spotted Elk had thrown a buffalo robe toward Kalina as she finished eating, and now she wrapped it about herself as she went across the camp and out of the firelight. Sitting with her back against a mighty oak, she shut her eyes and allowed herself to sleep for a short time.

The nodding of her head woke Kalina and she shifted, uncomfortable from sitting on the ground. She saw that all was quiet and everyone was asleep. It was deep into the night and the camp fire now only smoldering. Looking toward Sky Eyes, she saw that her head was drooping upon her chest as she sat against the tree she had been tied to.

Slowly, Kalina searched beneath her skirts for her hunting knife, keeping the buffalo robe about her so that if anyone was watching they would not see what she was doing. She clutched the handle of the knife and quickly slipped the sharp-bladed instrument up her sleeve.

As though just awakening she lightly rose to her feet. If anyone was looking, she hoped that they would think she was just going to relieve herself. The moment she was under cover of the brush that surrounded the camp, Kalina drew her knife into the palm of her hand, her sharp eyes looking about for one of the two sentries. On silent feet she drew closer to the brave nearest her. He seemed relaxed, and she was sure he had fallen asleep. With her blade now poised overhead, she took one careful step after another, until she stood only a few feet behind him. She thought of the tricks Pointed Arrow had taught her for combat with the enemy, and how to silently approach and overtake him. Kalina realized that it would be either this brave's life or her own. There would be no in-between. If she did not kill him, he would either kill her or return her to camp, and there would be no second chance for her and Sky Eyes to escape. She took the last step toward the Crow warrior and, without another thought, she brought her knife down, striking at the base of his skull and toppling the large man to the ground where he sat. Only a small grunt escaped his lips, proclaiming his last hold on life.

Unable to bear looking upon him, Kalina with trembling hands quickly pulled his knife, bow, and quiver of arrows from his side. Her dark eyes avoided his face. Not taking a moment longer than necessary, she slipped about to the other edge of camp, watching for the other sentry. When she saw him, she felt relieved, for he was lying on the ground, sleeping peacefully. He would live to face Spotted Elk when the alarm was shouted that the prisoner had escaped.

Approaching the tall pine where Sky Eyes was tied, Kalina easily cut her bindings and with a sharp, low warning, she woke her friend, pulled her to her feet and ran with her into the dense growth of the forest.

"We must hurry if there is to be a chance for us to get away." Kalina hissed softly. As Sky Eyes rubbed at her bruised wrists, Kalina started out at a hurried pace.

"Won't the sentry see us and call for their leader?" Sky Eyes asked as she followed close behind. As her eyes took in the large hunting knife tucked into the girl's waistband and the quiver strapped to her back, and the man's bow in her hand, she instantly regretted that she had asked. She had no desire to hear any grisly details about the warrior woman's deeds. It was different when a brave killed, and Sky Eyes had often listened in rapt attention as a warrior described his lethal duel with another warrior; but she did not wish to hear her beautiful friend's descriptive remarks about how she had won their freedom.

But if she thought Kalina was one to boast about her powers, she was mistaken. The dark-eyed girl only looked for a moment at Sky Eyes, and then turned once again and continued through the forest.

The pair were quiet as they quickened the pace through the darkness, freezing with panic every time a rabbit scurried or a large frog jumped, always thinking that they would come up against the fierce visage of Spotted Elk.

Kalina knew that they had to cover all the ground they could under cover of night, for with the morning's first light, the call would be sounded and the braves would be on their trail with a vengeance for blood. Their one hope was that they could somehow throw the warriors off their trail. Heading north toward the mountains, they did not stop to rest but kept going at a steady pace.

"Why didn't we steal one of their horses?" Sky Eyes gasped aloud as she tried to keep up with the warrior woman.

"Spotted Elk or one of those braves would have been awake as soon as we touched their animals. And just as quickly they would have had you tied back to the tree, and me . . ." She did not finish. She had killed one of their band and they would surely take her life even though she was a Crow woman.

Throughout the rest of the night the women ran for as long as they could and then walked fast. By morning they were both exhausted, their breath

271

coming in quick, shallow gasps, their sides aching and their hearts hammering wildly in their chests.

With first light, Kalina knew that they would shortly have to stand and fight for their lives unless by chance the Crow braves had somehow missed their trail and gone on ahead of them. Even as Kalina thought it, she felt that the chances of that were slim. Deep in her heart she knew that before the morning was over she would be fighting for her life and that of her friend. But still, they pushed themselves ever onward.

It was near noon when the first brave from Spotted Elk's band came into sight. As he sat astride his horse and his eyes caught sight of the women, a large grin spread over his savage, painted face.

Both women gasped aloud and stopped dead in their tracks as the man and horse suddenly appeared before them. He kicked at the sides of his mount as if to run them down. Kalina quickly pulled an arrow from the quiver upon her back. Drawing the bowstring back with the arrow in position, she took a steady bead and, exhaling, let the arrow fly.

Hitting its mark, the arrow entered the warrior's throat with a dull thud, flinging him from his horse and leaving him rolling upon the ground.

As though a morbid play were being enacted, for a few seconds Kalina and Sky Eyes stared at the writhing form. Then, pulling herself together,

Kalina took hold of Sky Eyes's arm and commanded her, "Go. Run as fast as you are able and don't look back. Keep going toward those mountains and you will find your people." She started to push the girl, but for a fleeting moment Sky eyes held back.

"I cannot leave you," she declared in strained tones.

"You must. I will be able to defend myself better if I do not have you to worry about. Do as I say, and perhaps you will be able to get back to Sacred Eagle and Nicholas." As Kalina said the name of her beloved, tears came to her dark eyes.

Sky Eyes did not know what else to say, for she feared that the warrior woman's words were the truth and she would only be a hindrance. She slowly nodded her head in agreement. First she hugged her friend to her, and then asked, "What is your name?"

A soft smile played about the petal-soft lips. "You have been a dear friend, Sky Eyes, and if we do not see each other again, I would have you know that even enemies can learn to love each other." Again she thought of Sacred Eagle, and for a moment she was tempted to tell the girl about the love she felt for her brother. But holding on to her pride and stubbornness, she kept her feelings to herself. "My name is Kalina," she whispered softly. As she said it she was filled with regret that she would never be able to tell Sacred

273

Eagle her name. She would never hear the husky tremor of his voice calling out to her in the throes of their lovemaking. Kalina knew that she could not realistically expect to hold off all the Crow warriors. The best she would be able to do was draw their fire and to detain them, giving Sky Eyes more precious time. But she also knew that she would do her utmost to kill more of them, perhaps even Spotted Elk himself, and then the other warriors might lose heart and give up the chase for the girl.

"Kalina." Sky Eyes softly whispered the name and then, with a final hug, she started running toward the mountains. She set herself a desperate pace, for she knew that the rest of the warriors would not be far behind this first one.

Sky Eyes had only been gone a short time before Kalina, hiding behind a large, rotten log, heard the sounds of horses' hooves. Having laid out both her knives and drawn her bowstring back to the ready, she peeked over the top of the log.

There before her was Spotted Elk with two of his warriors, their eyes searching the area for any sign of the women. As they had directed their mounts directly toward Kalina, she rose to a crouch and let loose her arrow, hitting the brave closest to Spotted Elk. The horses shied, and as they watched their comrade fall to the ground with an arrow protruding from his chest, Kalina seized the opportunity to ready her bow again.

Spotted Elk and the other warrior reacted faster than she had anticipated. With a shout they were off their mounts, the horses running into the forest and both braves hiding under cover of the forest growth.

Kalina hardly dared breathe as she tried to sight one of the two men. It all seemed to happen so quickly! Kalina barely had time to respond as the two braves, shouting war cries, sprang out from the cover of the pines and rushed toward her. Letting her arrow go at the first, Kalina saw that she hit her target in the side. As that man fell, she watched as Spotted Elk, his face contorted with a cast of death and hatred, run toward her.

Not having the time to retrieve another arrow and fit it into her bow, all Kalina could do was pick up the largest of the two knives. She rose to her full height and awaited him as he bore down upon her. Just as he was about to fling himself over the dead log, Kalina felt herself being pushed backward, and as she landed hard upon the ground she glimpsed a large form charging toward Spotted Elk.

The instant she regained her senses, she saw that the one who had saved her was Sacred Eagle. His fearless towering body bore Spotted Elk down upon the floor of the forest, and with a growl from deep within his chest he brought his war ax down upon his enemy's head.

It was over so fast that Sacred Eagle was standing beside Kalina before she could rise to her feet. As he helped her up, Kalina burst into tears, the full impact of the past two days hitting her with full force.

Sacred Eagle's strong arms encircled the girl, and with a deep feeling of possessiveness he held her tightly to his chest, inhaling deeply the scent of her flower-sweet hair. For a moment he held his eyes tightly shut as he again envisioned the sight he had come upon. He had heard the cry of the warriors as they had jumped from their horses' backs and charged his slave. Sacred Eagle had also dismounted, and had circled the area, never in his wildest thoughts expecting to be met with the sight of his warrior woman facing the two large Crow warriors.

While the warrior woman had shot the arrow and hit the first brave in the side, Sacred Eagle had come around from the back, pushed the woman to the ground, and attacked the Crow brave. Now he allowed himself to regain his breath and let his heart slow its rapid beating. His large hand soothingly stroked her long, dark tresses. He had felt his heart almost stop when he had recognized the woman who was standing bravely and fighting the Crow warriors.

Tenderly he kissed her brow. "You are safe now. No one will ever harm you again." He placed a long finger beneath her chin and made her look up into his face, his fingers gently wiping the

276

tears away from her cheeks. "Whatever are you doing here?" Suddenly it occurred to him that he could imagine the answer, and his anger began to surface. His hands tightened upon her forearms, and as he pushed her away from him, he demanded harshly, "Did you run away from my lodge?" All he could think was that she had tried to run away and had been found here in the forest by the three warriors.

Looking into his face, Kalina saw this written clearly—distrust and betrayal, there for her to see. Trying to pull away from him, Kalina felt a sob within her chest. Were his feelings for her so shallow? Did he think that she would flee him before they had reasoned out all that stood between them? She tried to shake his hands off her.

Sacred Eagle was not about to let her go, and as he jerked her back toward him, he felt the seam of her bodice give. The rent pulled the sleeve from the rest of the dress.

Feeling her own anger mounting, Kalina shrugged the hands from her shoulders. "I did *not* run away from your village. Your sister and I were kidnapped by these Crow braves and they were going to take us to the army fort. They thought Sky Eyes was your mother; and Spotted Elk, their leader, thought to take me back to my father."

Sacred Eagle's hands dropped as though he were touching flame, his face paling with each word she spoke. For a few moments they stood facing each other, and then, shaking himself, Sacred Eagle questioned her. "You speak my tongue so well? How is this? When I left you a few days ago, you said not a word of my language?"

"Because I did not speak did not mean that I did not know your tongue." Kalina was still angry with him for his harsh treatment and the words he had spoken to her.

"But how is this possible? Why did you not tell me that you knew the Blackfoot tongue?" He could not fathom why she would not have told him that she could speak to him in his own language. There was so much he could have shared with her, if he had known. Dismissing all she had said about the Crow warriors except the part about his sister, he then asked, "Where is Sky Eyes now?"

"I made her run toward the mountains in the hope that she would be able to get away from the Crow braves," Kalina admitted. At this moment she just wanted to rest. She felt totally drained now that she was safe, and arguing with this man held no appeal for her. Slowly she lowered herself to sit upon the log, a sigh escaping her lips as she did so.

"How long have you been out here?" Sacred Eagle inquired.

"Since yesterday afternoon when we arrived at the camp in the mountains. Sky Eyes and I were gathering wood and getting water, and Spotted Elk and his braves captured us." She did not add that she had had her own plans for leaving the mountains. It would do little good for her to tell of her plans to be at his side when he had to face the white men.

"But how did you get away from Spotted Elk and his men?"

"They kept Sky Eyes tied to a tree, but I had a knife hidden beneath my skirts. When they were asleep I killed one of the sentries and cut your sister loose."

Taken aback, Sacred Eagle stared at the woman before him. Finally he spoke. "You saved my sister's life and perhaps even the lives of many of my people. Why would you risk so much? Why did you not take this chance to return to your father?"

Her ebony eyes gazed at him. "I did not need Spotted Elk to take me to my father. Anytime I wished, I could have returned to my village on my own. As you have seen, Pointed Arrow, my father, taught me as he taught his sons how to hunt and track, and how to make my way back to my village without leaving any sign for trackers."

"Then why have you not escaped before now?" He knelt before her, hoping that her answer would be the one he wanted to hear. Was it because of him that she had not escaped? Were her feelings like his own? But before she could answer, Nicholas burst through the trees, his mount foaming from its long gallop.

"What has happened?" he asked as he saw Sacred Eagle kneeling before the slave girl and the large Crow warrior lying dead only a stone's throw from the pair.

"My sister and my . . ." Sacred Eagle stood, looked down upon the warrior woman, and almost laughed at the name he would give her. ". . . my slave were captured by the Crow scouts. My mother is still safe in the mountains. I think that we should hurry and reach Sky Eyes. She is making her way to the camp, but she has had enough of a scare and should know that she is safe."

Without another word, Nicholas kicked the sides of his horse and directed him toward the mountain path.

After helping Kalina to her feet, Sacred Eagle gave a shrill whistle, and within moments Eagle's Wing came at a gallop into the clearing, his nostrils flaring as he took in the odor of the Crow warrior and the blood that was seeping into the ground.

Taking Kalina's hand, Sacred Eagle lifted her onto the back of his stallion. And as the mighty beast would have risen upon his hind legs to unseat this unwelcome passenger, Sacred Eagle called out a harsh command. Hearing his master's voice so loud and demanding, Eagle's Wing instantly stilled, allowing the woman to sit up on his back. Then, as Sacred Eagle climbed up behind the woman, the horse seemed more at ease.

Following the path that Nicholas had taken, the pair upon the stallion sat quietly, close to each other, as they began to make their way after him.

It was only a short time before they came upon Nicholas with Sky Eyes held tightly in his arms. Wiping the tears from her cheeks as the couple approached them, Sky Eyes called out to Sacred Eagle. "Did Kalina tell you how she saved us from those Crow warriors? She was so wonderful, Sacred Eagle. She is such a dear friend. She risked her life for me. I shall always be in her debt."

Kalina could feel upon her the pale eyes of the man she loved, as he breathed her name next to her ear. She felt the very flesh on her body tingle with desire, for she had thought never to hear him say her name.

"Each moment that passes, I am learning more about my slave, sister. But let us keep going now, while there is still time to arrive at the village before dark."

For a moment Kalina thought of telling Sacred Eagle that she would not be staying in the mountains but would go to the valley with him. But upon reflection she decided that perhaps it would be better to travel with him to the mountains and let them deliver Sky Eyes to the camp. She would wait to broach the subject until they were alone in his lodge, after she had had more time to adjust to all that he had learned about her this afternoon.

As his strong arms encased her, she envisioned how, upon his sleeping couch, she would convince him to allow her to go to the valley and fight at his side. The flame of their desire would leave him powerless to refuse her.

Chapter Thirteen

In Sacred Eagle's chilled lodge, Kalina quietly started a flame in the fire pit. Sacred Eagle stood near the entrance flap, his thoughts inscrutable as his metallic gaze watched her every movement. They had not spoken since reaching the village. After seeing Sky Eyes to her mother's lodge and staying for a time to explain what had happened, Sacred Eagle had taken Kalina's arm and led her to his own tepee. Nicholas had stayed with Sky Eyes and was eating the evening meal with her and her mother. It was as though Nicholas feared that somehow she would be taken from him again, and he stayed near her to protect her.

Now, with Kalina in his own lodge, Sacred Eagle silently went to his sleeping couch and sat back against the headrest, his gaze never leaving Kalina as she began to prepare the food. He studied her, trying the sound of her name in his head. Knowing her name seemed to mean a lot to him.

Thoughts of her had plagued his every waking moment when he had been away from this village, and now he was still tormented while in her presence.

Silently he berated himself for his foolishness. The woman was his slave, his captive. He could do or say anything he desired to her, and she was powerless to do anything about it. But with this thought, he remembered what she had said: any time she wished, she could flee and return to her father. Was this the way of a slave? Were these feelings that he had every time he was in her presence the normal feelings between master and slave?

Her hands busy with the preparations for their meal, Kalina slanted Sacred Eagle a look, hoping to find his face softened now that they had reached his lodge. But as she glimpsed the stern, dark features, her heart sank. He was still angry with her for not telling him that she knew his tongue and because of the way she had spoken out about being able to return to her father. She had learned very little about men in her life, but one thing she had learned from her father and brothers was that a man's pride should not be trampled. And now that she had been given time to reflect, she knew that this was exactly what she had done.

Sacred Eagle's was indeed angry, but down deep he felt some guilt. Perhaps this woman had her own reasons for not speaking out and telling him that she knew his language. After all, just because he had taken her as his slave, was she meekly to tell him everything? And despite what she had said about fleeing him, had he not seen with his own eyes her courage and skill as she stood and fought the Crow? He knew that she was not like other women. Was this not one of the things that drew him to her so strongly? And after all was said and done, the fact was that she had saved his sister's life. She could have gone along with his enemy and saved herself, or she could have told Spotted Elk that he had gotten the wrong woman, and then the Crow scouts would have come back to the village and lain in wait for his mother. But no, she had fought and killed for his family. Did this not prove her loyalty?

Rising to his feet, Sacred Eagle caught up one of the warm buffalo hides from the sleeping pallet. Going to Kalina, he reached out and took her arm. "Let us go bathe." He gave her no choice in the matter.

"But I have just prepared our food," she protested, trying to draw back from him. For a moment she feared that he was going to inflict strange punishment upon her for her disobedience.

"It will keep till later." Sacred Eagle's strong, curt tone touched her, and unable to break his grip, she was pulled through the entrance flap and led down to the river.

The velvet sky was awash with stars. With a crescent moon lighting the way, the couple soon came to the river's edge.

Kalina shivered at the thought of being in the cold water, and as Sacred Eagle felt the tremors going over her, he chuckled deeply. "There is nothing like a cold bathe to cleanse the body and the mind." He turned her around and slowly began to unlace her deer-hide blouse. As he drew the garment over her head, an eager light entered his silver eyes. He savored the perfection of her rising and falling breasts, the nipples hardening with the first touch of the cold night air. "Beautiful," he breathed softly, and then with little haste he untied the horsehair belt that held her skirt. As the rest of her clothing dropped about her ankles, Sacred Eagle drew back and simply looked at her. She stood shivering, and he reached out and took the headband from about her forehead, allowing her long, silky black hair to fall about her shoulder, and strands to rest loosely over each breast. "Now you are perfection," he murmured.

Feeling the heat of a blush in her cheeks, Kalina stood quietly under his regard, her eyes unable to break away from his handsome face.

Sacred Eagle had worn a leather shirt and leggings, for the mountain air was much cooler than that of the valley. With nimble fingers he unlaced the leather tie at his throat and pulled the shirt over his head. He then reached down and pulled his leggings from his strong, muscular legs.

Standing a few feet from Kalina, Sacred Eagle seemed to take pride in his body as he felt the eyes of this woman roam freely over him, the cold air not seeming to affect him under the heat of her dark gaze.

Without warning, strong hands swept Kalina up and with long strides Sacred Eagle started into the river. Kalina shrieked and wrapped her arms about his neck as the cold water touched her buttocks.

Squirming to avoid the touch of the water did her little good, for Sacred Eagle threw himself into the depths of the river. Kalina came up from the freezing water gasping and shaking. And every time she tried to make her way out of the water, again and again he pulled her back and she came up splashing and breathless. At last she shouted, "If this is your punishment, I give up. I am sorry for all that I have said and done."

Sacred Eagle stopped his playful antics at these words. He had not meant their bath to be punishment. He had often bathed here in the mountains, in the chilled river. It had always invigorated him and cleared his mind of plaguing thoughts. Pulling her up close in his arms he said softly, " 'Tis no punishment, only a bath."

"Then I think I am well cleansed!" Kalina exclaimed between chattering teeth.

Laughing, Sacred Eagle relented and carried her to the river's edge. Pulling the buffalo robe about them, he stood in front of her and wrapped their bodies closely until they were dried. The breathtaking tension of naked body pressed tightly against naked body was more than either could bear. As Kalina felt the pressure of Sacred Eagle's stirring manhood, she softly moaned aloud with desire.

Still wrapped in the buffalo robe, Sacred Eagle reached out and tilted Kalina's chin up so that her face met his own. "Do you not feel much more alive and refreshed?" he smiled down upon her delicate, dampened features, delighting in the feel of her body as she pressed closer to seek out his warmth.

His smile was contagious, and Kalina began to grin, her head nodding in full agreement. "I feel wonderful now. I am afraid, though, that I find more pleasure in bathing during the day, when at least the warmth of the sun can take the chill away."

Sacred Eagle squeezed her naked body tightly against his own, and with this motion he stoked the building embers of their passion to flame. As he consumed the beauty of her face with his penetrating gaze, slowly his mouth decended over hers. His kiss was gentle at first but then slowly became demanding, all-consuming. Casting aside all her doubts and fears about their future, Kalina looped her arms about his neck. Her tongue circled and met his own, the contact sensual and more than inviting.

As his lips and tongue continued to relish hers, Sacred Eagle's hand moved slowly to her full, pressing breasts, feeling first one and then the other. A languid, passionate gasp escaped Kalina's throat as his hand casually dipped farther down. Finding the very core of her pleasure, his long, strong fingers caressed the center of her passion until he had her writhing in ecstasy against him, her head thrown back, leaving her sleek, creamy neck fully available to his hungry kisses.

His heated lips and tongue seared her throat and then regained and conquered her mouth, leaving her feeling as though she were drowning in his sweet, rapturous assault. He continued his fondling until he brought her to such heights of rapture that her body thrust upward against his probing fingers. Just when she was sure that she could take no more of this wondrous torture, Sacred Eagle allowed the buffalo robe to fall to their feet, and gently lowered her down upon the soft fur.

Their need for each other was overpowering, causing their racing passions to ignite quickly and fervently. He entered her with a powerful thrust.

Immediately Kalina wrapped her legs about his waist, drawing him in deeper. Sacred Eagle's hips began to move in rapid, circular motions, and meeting his thrusts, her slim hips converged with his. Matching him stroke for stroke, Kalina responded with such complete ardor that Sacred Eagle could barely restrain his urge to climax. Forcing himself to withhold for a while longer, he continued to make love to her until, wondrously, Kalina's body was racked with tremors as she achieved complete satisfaction.

At last able to fully surrender to his own needs, Sacred Eagle drew her shapely thighs up tightly against his own and released his seed deep within her trembling body.

Totally drained, Sacred Eagle tried for a moment to catch his breath as he held himself above Kalina. Shortly he rose up on his elbows and kissed her tenderly. "And are you still cold, my sweet?" he finally asked between kisses.

A sweet smile spread over Kalina's soft, kiss-swollen lips. "Always you tend to my every need. When I am hungry you feed me, and when I am cold you warm me. What woman could ask for a better master?" she teased.

When she said "master," Sacred Eagle felt his body tense. The word sounded out of place between them. After all, he seldom thought of her as his servant. She seemed so much a part of him, as much so as his breath or his need for sustenance. "You still have not told me how you come to know my tongue."

A soft sigh escaped Kalina's lips before she began to explain. "I am not truly sure how it is that I know your language. From the first, when you and your band attacked and you took me as your captive, your words seemed to come to me from a long time past. I knew what you were saying, and I was as surprised as you were when you first found out. I have pondered over and over in my mind how this could be, but I have no answer."

"Perhaps the Great Spirit gave you this gift of my language, as he knew that you would one day belong to me," Sacred Eagle ventured after a moment of reflecting over what she had said.

"Oh, so you still think I belong to you?" Kalina felt deeply disappointed over this statement. She had hoped that he felt more for her than a master did for his slave. She did not want to be the woman of his lodge, the one he turned to only when he needed a soft body to sate his desires. She longed to be the woman of his heart. But thus far he had proclaimed no such feelings toward her.

"You shall always belong to me!" Sacred Eagle declared warmly in her ear, tightening his grip upon her.

"And do I belong to you as perhaps your horse, Eagle's Wing, belongs to you?" She wished to explore his feelings, to make him declare aloud what he was feeling.

"You belong to me as the stars belong to the heavens, as the fish belong in the sea. Aye, Kalina, you belong only to me."

It was a tender moment. Kalina felt a tear fall from her eye. Where these the words one would speak to a slave? Was this man not sharing a portion of his heart? But still, she needed to know more. She ventured softly, "Can such a warrior as Sacred Eagle claim a Crow woman as his own?"

"My enemies took the woman my heart claimed with one hand, but with the other they have given my heart reason to keep beating. Crow, Cheyenne, Sioux—I care not, as long as you are here with me this moment. You are mine; that is all that matters." And so saying, his lips sought hers and tenderly partook of their sweet, tempting taste.

He breathlessly released Kalina's mouth and glimpsed the glazed, passionate look in her eyes. He laughed heartily and scooped her up into his strong arms. With the one hand wrapping the robe back about them, he boldly strode toward his lodge.

By the time they arrived, reason had returned to Kalina, and as Sacred Eagle put her down upon the soft furs of the sleeping couch, she asked, "Are you not hungry?" her eyes went to the fire that was still burning, and the bowls that contained their now cold dinner.

"In truth, I am starving—but only for the sweet tenderness of your flesh." His pale eyes traveled the length of her naked body as she lay back against the furs, his glance seeming to flame over her flesh.

Trying to control the dark blush that was now staining her cheeks, Kalina thought of what the morrow would bring. Unhesitatingly she spoke aloud. "You leave in the morning to go back to the valley and face the bluecoats. I want to be at your side to face this foe with you."

Sacred Eagle was taken aback by her words, and, slowly lowering his form to sit beside her on the pallet, he looked at her with disbelief. But as he studied the radiance of her beauty, he realized what a truly unusual woman she was. This woman he had made his slave was willing to fight beside him, claiming his enemies as her own. What more was she willing to do for him? he wondered silently. "You will stay here in the mountains where you are safe. I am not willing to risk losing you," he stated finally, hoping that she would not argue with him but do as he bade.

Rising up somewhat on the sleeping couch, Kalina retorted, "But *you* are willing to go and risk your life. Does it not matter that I would not have you in danger either?"

"It is different where I am concerned." He felt his irritation beginning to mount and wished she would be quiet and just let him love her as he desired. "A warrior is taught from his earliest childhood to fight and to defend his people from the enemy. You are a woman, and you belong here in my lodge where I know you are safe and warm."

Now Kalina wrapped a fur about her body and held the soft hide against her breasts, sparks of anger seeming to shoot from her dark eyes. "You say that only a warrior can fight for what he believes?" Sacred Eagle nodded his head, and she continued in heated tones. "I was raised in a like manner. From my earliest childhood I can remember holding a bow and a knife. I know how to hunt game, to gut and clean my kill, to track the enemy, and also how to quietly and cleanly kill those who would do harm to me or those of my heart. You say that I should stay here and keep warm in your lodge while you are fighting for your life? I say no! I cannot stay here in these mountains as you face the white eyes. I *must* go with you. I shall ride at your side."

Sacred Eagle knew that all she said was the truth. He had seen the proof for himself when he had watched her arrow hit the Crow brave, and he had seen the other warrior lying dead upon the earth some distance away when he had first come upon her in the forest. He had no doubt about her powers with weapons. But still, he was loath to risk her in the fight against the bluecoats. "No, you will stay here in the mountains with my mother and my sister." Thinking quickly, he added, "If all does not go well in the valley I will depend upon you to see that they are kept safe." He hoped that this would keep her satisfied.

For a few moments the pair upon the pallet looked at one another, Kalina discarding what he had just said. Why should she stay here and defend his mother and sister, when she would rather die a warrior's death next to him and travel the star path with Sacred Eagle at her side? But knowing that she would get nowhere by arguing with him, she kept her own council. She would do as she must, and he would have no say. As she had already tried to explain to him, she was her own woman. She would come and go as she pleased. And if he were angry, so be it. She would face his wrath as she faced all things in life. But she was determined that she would be at his side when he faced his enemies, the white men.

Not wishing this discussion to go on, and knowing that with daybreak he would have to leave her, Sacred Eagle wished only to hold Kalina in his arms. Perhaps this would be the last time he was able to touch her soft body and kiss her sweet lips. Perhaps upon the morrow he would meet death. He thought of Summer Dawn. He had always welcomed the thought of death, because in it he would be once again reunited with his wife; but now the thought did not seem to sit well in his mind, for to die would mean to leave Kalina. With these thoughts he felt more confused than ever. He wished he did not have to leave her here in the mountains, that they could take the time to sort out all the feelings that were swirling about them. Both sighing, the pair seemed to dissolve into each other's arms.

No more words were needed. They had made up their minds. All that could be shared now was the giving and taking of their passions. Her face was raised upward to his, and slowly his mouth came down to hers. At first their kiss was tender, and both seemed content just to feel the touch of the other's lips, the pressing of their naked bodies. Soon, however, their passions began to spiral, and as her soft lips parted, his heated tongue sought entrance, tasting the sweetness of her mouth.

"Kalina, Kalina." He savored the name like the rarest of wines. "I need you so much. I never seem to be able to get enough of your wondrous body."

Kalina moaned in response, for she was feeling the same overpowering need for their joining.

Gently he spread her firm thighs, and rising up, he knelt between them. Gazing down into Kalina's flushed face, Sacred Eagle smiled.

His smile set her heart racing. It was a smile of sensual, passionate desire, but there was something else plainly visible that left Kalina astonished. It was a depth of love so all-consuming and encompassing that it sent Kalina's heart racing with joy, and she knew in an instant that what they felt for each other was worth any risk she could take. One day, she knew, she would hear his declaration of love for her.

Sacred Eagle was joyfully surprised as Kalina took hold of his throbbing member and guided his penetration, which made them both tremble with a fiery longing for fulfillment.

Placing his hands beneath her hips, he brought her thighs up to meet his. "Sweet, sweet Kalina," he whispered, as her ardor caused wave after wave of desire to fire him onward.

Responding fully, Kalina arched her slim body beneath his, loving the feel of his penetrating hardness deep inside her.

His need now towering, Sacred Eagle's hips hammered rapidly against her, and matching thrust for thrust Kalina moaned provocatively, "Sacred Eagle . . . Sacred Eagle, you are mine and only mine." Her words were spoken in the Crow tongue for although she could not suppress them, she did not wish him to know the full extent of her feelings.

Sacred Eagle did not understand the words, but he did understand the meaning, and he kissed her fiercely.

Their need was now approaching its zenith, encouraging Sacred Eagle to move against her strongly and their thrusting sent them spiraling to love's wondrous climax, where they clung tightly to each other and were wonderfully fulfilled.

Tenderly, Sacred Eagle kissed her face, and with the final tremors of love's aftermath at last stilled, he cuddled her tightly into his embrace. "Sleep now, my beauty, for the morning will be upon us soon," he whispered near her ear. With a peaceful sigh they both fell into a trouble-free sleep.

Sacred Eagle awoke before the first break of daylight. Silently going about his lodge, he gathered his things and then, with Nicholas at his side, he left the mountain camp and followed the path down into the valley.

A contented smile played over Kalina's lips as she stretched out fully on the soft fur pallet, her blissful feelings about being with Sacred Eagle for the rest of her life filling her with a tranquil delight. Without opening her eyes she reached out to caress the dark tresses of the man who slept next to her. She opened her eyes with a start. Sacred Eagle was gone! She bolted into a sitting position as the full realization overtook her.

Looking about, she saw that his leather food pouches and extra clothing were gone. She had thought to try and convince him one last time to let her go with him, but now she would have to make the trip to the valley on her own.

But as she pulled her breechcloth and fur vest from the storage place, she thought of Falling Leaves. She had not seen to the older woman's needs now in three days. Was someone taking care of her? she wondered. Did the elder woman wonder about her whereabouts—and was she at this moment thinking about her? With a sigh she picked up the skirt and blouse that Sacred Eagle had taken off her the night before. They would do for the time being, she thought as she tied the leather strappings. She sat down and tried to mend the sleeve where it had been torn the day before.

There was no help for it. As soon as she had seen that Falling Leaves was taken care of, she would change back into the apparel she had worn in the Crow village. Hurriedly she made her way to the other side of the village and, calling aloud for permission to enter, went into the lodge.

Falling Leaves was resting upon her sleeping couch, and when she saw who her early morning visitor was, she grinned widely in welcome. "Come, daughter. I have missed you these past few days." She tried to sit up straighter.

Kalina smiled at the friendly old woman. Looking about, she made sure that there was plenty of firewood and that her water parfleches were filled.

Falling Leaves saw where she was looking and explained, "Silver Star has come daily to see that all is well with me. She is a kind daughter to our village."

Kalina went to the elder woman and, sitting down next to her, slowly began to talk to her. "Grandmother, I must leave once again for a few days, and I have come to make sure that you are all right and to tell you that I shall return soon."

The dark eyes that looked upon Kalina were full of questions. "You speak our tongue, daughter? How is it that a Crow slave can speak the language of her enemy?"

"It is a long story, Grandmother. I will tell you all when I return."

"I shall look forward to this story, then." She sighed as she lay back against her headrest. "I also have many stories that I would share with you." Her gnarled old hand took hold of Kalina's sleeve, and the hastily mended seam gave even further. "What is your name, daughter? I grow weary of thinking of you as Sacred Eagle's slave, and would put a name to the images you evoke within my thoughts."

Kalina smiled, loving this old woman more each time she saw her. "My name, Grandmother, is Kalina."

The old woman sighed aloud, and Kalina, sensing that something bothered her, asked, "What is amiss?"

"I had only hoped that somehow you would have the name of my lost grandchild." The words were barely a whisper, and as tears came to the dark eyes, Kalina's heart went out to Falling Leaves. Bending over her, she placed a kiss upon the weathered cheek. Then as she went to draw away from the old woman, Falling Leaves clutched at her arm. "What is it, Grandmother?" Looking down at her, she saw the old woman grow paler with each passing second.

"What is this?" The words were barely audible, but she pointed to the underside of Kalina's forearm. The girl turned her head to see what she was talking about.

"Oh, that is but the mark I was born with." Kalina turned her arm about, seeing for herself the small birthmark with the shape of a tiny arrowhead.

"Your mother told you that this was the mark given to you at your birth?" Falling Leaves's voice was soft.

"I never knew my mother. She died while I was very young."

"Did your father speak of this mark then?"

"My father said it was one of the signs that led him to teach me the ways of his sons. I was adopted into Pointed Arrow's family when I was five winters old, and when his wife died, he raised me as he did his sons. He claimed that the mark was a sign of my strength, for he said it was the sign of the knife."

Tears slid freely now down Falling Leaves's cheeks. Brushing them away, Kalina was shocked to hear her next words. "My daughter, Bright Lily, had a daughter who was called Morning Star, for at her birth the morning star shone its light down upon the Blackfoot valley. My granddaughter was with her mother the day Bright Lily was attacked

301

and killed by a bear. Morning Star was never found. She was but five winters old." And as her dark eyes penetrated into Kalina's, the old woman's next words astonished the younger woman. "My granddaughter had a birthmark on the inside of her forearm, in the shape of a small arrowhead."

Was this possible? Kalina wondered. But as everything seemed to flood her mind at the same time, she knew that the old woman was speaking the truth. How else could she have known the Blackfoot language? Had she not felt as though the words she heard from the mouths of her enemies were the same words as she had known long ago? Tears came to her eyes as the full realization of this discovery hit her. "You truly are my grandmother?" she asked softly. "Could it be possible that Pointed Arrow found me in the forest after the bear attacked my mother?" Kalina seemed to be talking to herself.

Falling Leaves nodded. "I felt the first moment I saw you standing in my lodge that you were my granddaughter. This old heart knew without being told that you were my Morning Star."

It had to be so, Kalina thought. Had she not been drawn to this old woman for no reason she could put a name to? Did she not feel a closeness to her that she had never felt for any other? As the full realization hit her, she wrapped her arms about the old woman. With tears coursing down her cheeks, she felt total joy in their reunion.

When the tears were finally dried, both women smiled with the knowledge that at last they had truly found each other. Fallen Leaves's hand reached up and brushed back the long strands of hair that had fallen in her granddaughter's face. "You must gather your belongings, Morning Star, and come back to my lodge. You are my grand-daughter, and no one shall ever call you a slave again."

Kalina laughed aloud with sheer joy, and after kissing Falling Leaves's forehead, she rejoined, "There is much that we shall have to learn about each other, Grandmother. So much time has passed since I was known as Morning Star. My name is Kalina now, and from this day forth, I shall be Kalina of the Blackfoot. But it will be a short time before we can share the same lodge. There is something I must do, and I shall be gone for a few short days." Kalina hoped that somehow she and Sacred Eagle would come to terms with their feelings for one another. Perhaps it would be her grandmother who would be moving her be-longings to another lodge. Kalina knew now that her love for Sacred Eagle was deep, and her desire was for him to think her worthy to become his wife.

"But Morning . . . Kalina," the old woman swiftly corrected herself, "we have only just found each other. Must you leave so soon?"

Smiling down upon her, her happiness clear upon her beautiful face, Kalina hugged her grandmother close. "Yes, I must. I shall have Sky Eyes see that you are cared for while I am gone." Kalina started to rise to her feet.

Falling Leaves took hold of her hand. "I shall tell all the village that you are Crow slave no longer. Now you are my granddaughter."

Kalina left the elder woman's lodge. For the first time in her life, she felt as though she truly belonged. In the Crow village it had been no secret that she had been adopted by Pointed Arrow. Perhaps this was why she had tried harder than others to please. She had always felt like an outsider. But no longer. She had found her grandmother. Even if Sacred Eagle did not wish to claim her for his love, at least he could no longer call her his slave. With this thought, she felt fearful. Was she not better off as his slave than to be nothing to him at all? What if he rejected her altogether when he learned that she was of the same tribe as he?

But no! she told herself vehemently. She would not allow him to cast her aside. She loved him too much. She would be his in whatever fashion he demanded. Slave or wife, she would be satisfied. And thinking thus, she started toward Sky Eyes's lodge.

Sky Eyes was just leaving the tepee when Kalina reached her, and as she saw the worried look on her face, Kalina asked, "What is wrong?"

Her usually healthy face looked drawn and pale, and the silver eyes gazed worriedly at her friend. "I must go to the valley. I must talk to Nicholas." Tears came quickly to her eyes.

"What is it, Sky Eyes?" Kalina halted the girl as she would have stepped around her, for Sky Eyes was determined to find a horse and ride down to where the fighting would be, in the valley.

"I had a vision last night." The girl seemed frantic.

"A vision about what?" For a moment Kalina wondered if the vision had anything to do with Sacred Eagle.

"I was standing atop a small hill, and when I looked out over the valley I saw lines and lines of the blue-coated white men. And as I looked toward the north, the tribes were gathered. As far as the eye could see, they sat astride their horses, their war paint smeared across their faces and their war shields held high in the air. My brother and my father were at the head of our people. I saw you also, Kalina," Sky Eyes whispered softly as she grabbed hold of her friend's arm. "At first I was not sure, but then plainly I saw you sitting upon the back of a large black horse. You wore the clothes you were wearing the day Sacred Eagle brought you to our village. I do not understand this, for you are but a slave. A slave could never be allowed to fight at the side of our braves, for fear that you would turn against our warriors."

"What else did you see in your vision? Why are you so upset?" Kalina disregarded what she was saying about her being a slave. She knew in her heart that she would be in the valley, fighting at Sacred Eagle's side, when the time came.

"As I stood upon the hill I felt a consuming fear of death. I saw Nicholas, and I also saw a warrior I could not view clearly. They were in mortal combat, but before I could see who was the victor, I began to fall from the hill. I could clearly see the floor of the valley, but as I opened my mouth to scream, a strong hand reached down and caught hold of me."

As she finished, Kalina asked, "Who was it that saved you from the fall?"

"I awoke, trembling and shaking, before I could see the face of the one that reached down. Oh, Kalina, I fear that the one who saved me was not Nicholas. If I do not warn him, he may be killed."

"I shall warn him for you," Kalina ventured softly. "I have come to request that you see to Falling Leaves. I am going to the valley as soon as I can get my horse. I will fight at Sacred Eagle's side."

"You cannot." Sky Eyes grabbed hold of the girl. "My brother will not allow it."

"He will have no say, for he will not know that I am there until it is too late for him to send me away."

"But what of Nicholas?"

"When I see him I will tell him to take care, that you worry over his life." Kalina was now impatient, for Sacred Eagle had told her that the army troops had left the fort and she knew that the fighting could start at any time. She, too, harbored a fear for the one she loved, and she knew that she had to be there in order to be certain that he was safe.

"I will go with you." Sky Eyes was adamant. "My mother will care for Falling Leaves, as she has in the past. But I must go and make sure that Nicholas is safe."

There was little time to argue with the girl, but Kalina knew that Sacred Eagle would be furious with her if anything happened to his sister. "The only way I will allow you to come with me is if you promise that you will not go near the fighting. You must stay hidden, out of danger, and I will send Nicholas to you the first chance I have."

Sky Eyes would have agreed to anything just as long as she was able to go to the valley. Eagerly she nodded her head. "I will do whatever you say."

"Tell your mother that we are going to hunt and gather walnuts. See that she goes to Falling Leaves's lodge, and then meet me at Sacred Eagle's lodge."

Sky Eyes turned and hurried off to do as she

was bid, and Kalina made her way back to Sacred Eagle's lodge. Changing into her breechcloth and fur vest and gathering her weapons, she went to get her horse and Sky Eyes.

There were only a few braves left in the village, and those that were there were down by the river, gambling. None seemed to notice as the two women rode out of the village.

Chapter Fourteen

The Blackfoot valley was teeming with activity as Sacred Eagle and Nicholas rode into camp. Thousands of tepees had been set up along the river, and men, women and children rushed about the area. Four different tribes had come together in the valley to hold off the attack of the white man. The tension could be felt throughout the entire village.

Only Star Hawk had thought to send the women, children, and elders of his village up to the mountains to keep them out of danger. The other chiefs had brought their entire tribes with them. Sacred Eagle was thankful for his father's foresight. There were children running and playing, women cooking and watching the smaller children, and old men sitting about out in the open, gossiping and renewing old acquaintances. There would be much loss of life if the defenses did not hold up and the army made its way into the heart of this valley.

Looking out over valley's floor, Sacred Eagle could see the dust rising thickly into the air. The young braves and old warriors were holding practice war games to hone their weapons and skills. Their shouts and war cries filled the air and set Sacred Eagle's heart pounding with the expectations of what the morrow would hold. He thought about the white major at the army fort; how foolish he was! If he could see the number, might, and skill of his enemy, Major Thatcher would have second thoughts about the invasion.

It was late afternoon and the entire encampment was making ready for the fight that Star Hawk calculated would occur late the next morning. The scouts he had sent out were at this very moment following the long line of troops through the forest near the valley.

Drums had been beaten throughout the day, and several warriors were now dancing near the large center campfire, beseeching the spirits to direct their hands and their lives, asking for the skill to fight to victory or to die with honor.

Nicholas and Sacred Eagle dismounted before the lodge that was used for communal ceremonies. War councils were often held within, and they noticed two braves sitting near the entrance flap as sentries, their hands busy as they worked on their weapons, making sure that each arrow was straight and their bows firm.

Sacred Eagle nodded his head toward the two as they looked at Nicholas. The two sentries were from a different tribe, and were wary of the large, golden-haired man who wore the clothing of an Indian but whose skin, though tanned, was still obviously white. Knowing Sacred Eagle well, neither spoke out as Nicholas followed his friend into the lodge.

There were hundreds of warriors sitting inside, the higher-ranked chiefs near the fire and those of lesser rank, or younger braves and warriors, cross-legged in the outer circles.

Drums pounded within the lodge as well as outside, and the higher-ranking chiefs were speaking over them. They were telling of the influence of the white man upon their lands and of the diseases their families had contracted because the white men had been allowed to travel through their villages. They spoke loudly and fiercely about the injustices that had been inflicted upon them these past years, the treaties and promises that had been broken, and the lies they had been told. Shouts of agreement were given, and the tempers of all within the lodge were heightened. One chief told of an entire Cheyenne village being wiped out because of the pox that had been brought to the village by some trappers two winters past.

Star Hawk was sitting in the center of the ring of high chiefs. As he nodded his head in agreement with chief Flaming Arrow, who had just spoken, his dark eyes fell upon his son and the white man who would soon be a part of his family. He had been waiting for the pair to return with the information they would have been able to learn on their trip to the white man's fort. He motioned for them to make their way through the circles of men and to sit beside him.

It took several moments for the two to reach Star Hawk and sit next to him in the warmth of the blazing center fire. The warrior who had been talking when they came in continued telling the group about the devastation he had witnessed farther north, when the white man's army had attacked a tribe in the early hours of the morning. The village had been unsuspecting and awoke to the sound of gunfire and mounted troops galloping over their lodges. The women and children had run screaming in an attempt to escape, and the warriors had tried to gather their weapons and defend their village; all had been cut down by the white man. The snow had been soaked with the blood that had flowed that morning. A few had escaped into the forest—only a few out of hundreds.

As the warrior finished speaking, murmurs could be heard about the white man who had just joined the group. Star Hawk listened, then rose slowly to his full height. His long, feathered headdress and the silver and black paint smeared across his face held everyone in thrall. The entire lodge quietened as he solemnly looked about.

"My son and his friend have just come back from the white man's fort. They sought information about the attack that will soon be upon us. We will listen to my son, Sacred Eagle. His words will tell us much, and we shall use our wisdom to plan our strategy."

As Star Hawk paused, the murmurs again reached his ears. Turning back toward the main group, he sighed. "The white man with my son is called Nicholas Prescott. He is a friend of my people."

"No white man is the friend of the Blackfoot," came a bold voice through the murmurings.

Sacred Eagle looked toward the warrior who had spoken, understanding his feelings fully, for the white man had proven himself unfaithful again and again. "I say this man is a friend." His voice thundered, and quiet prevailed. "At the end of this war between the bluecoats and my people, he shall become the husband of my only daughter. My wife, Silver Star, is also white, as most of you know. She, like Nicholas, has proven herself to be loyal and true to the Blackfoot. She is a mighty healing woman with great medicine. Nicholas befriended my son when he was in need, and now he offers us his help. He was sent here by men in Washington who care what is taking place in this valley between our tribes and the white man. He has sent these men word of the steps we must take to protect our people and our lands. He will fight at our side tomorrow when the white men attack. He will stand against his own blood, for he is as one with my people."

There were more murmurings, but now many were in agreement with Star Hawk. As the chief sat down, his son rose to his full height. Throughout the entire Blackfoot nation all knew of the mighty Sacred Eagle, and as he stood before them, there was a respectful quiet as he began to speak.

"My father, Star Hawk, has been wise in guiding me in my youth and as a young warrior. He speaks the truth when he tells you that Nicholas Prescott is a friend to our people. Not all white men hate the Indian. Not all wish to rob us of our lands and our heritage. I would wager my life in faith that this man can be trusted."

Numerous heads nodded, and many seemed to relax at Sacred Eagle's words. Even Nicholas felt touched by what he had heard.

"It is not the time to fight with those who offer us their friendship. The day is close when we shall have to stand together and face our enemies as a united front." Shouts of agreement sounded throughout the lodge at the young man's wise words.

"The evil bluecoats are coming at this moment toward our valley, and we shall have to stop them.

The major at the fort, the leader of the bluecoats, cannot be reasoned with. He hates the Indian because of his skin color, and will not turn from this confrontation. He underestimates our strength and number and expects to find a sleeping village here in our valley." For a moment Star Hawk stood silent, thinking. Then he went on.

"The white major sent several Crow scouts to the mountains to capture my mother and bring her to this valley. They intended to use her as a bargaining tool with my father."

Star Hawk, his features turning pale, rose at his son's side, his fists clenching and his dark eyes seeking his son's in his need to know all.

Sacred Eagle smiled reassuringly at his sire. "His plans were foiled, for instead the Crow scouts found my sister, who has the same pale eyes as my mother. Thinking her the one they were sent to capture, they stole her and my slave." He saw the desperation on his father's features and quickly eased his fear. Laying a hand upon his arm, he said, "All is well now, for my slave, who is also known as a warrior woman, had a hidden knife. In the dark of night, she killed one of the Crow scouts and freed my sister. The next day, having taken the scout's bow and arrows, my slave defended herself and Sky Eyes by killing two more of our enemies. Then Nicholas and I came to her defense and killed the last Crow scout."

Star Hawk sighed with relief and the lodge grew

loud as they spoke curiously about this woman who was Sacred Eagle's slave. Sacred Eagle raised his hands for quiet. "When the major hears that his plans have been ruined, his anger will be great. He will not change his plans when he hears that he will not have my mother as a pawn to aid his cause. He is swelled with his own importance and strength. This will only add fuel to his hatred of our people. We must be ready, for there are many bluecoats under his command."

After a pause, Star Hawk added, "This morning I sent a large band of my own braves to the forest near the army fort. Tomorrow they will begin their attack. They will burn the fort to the ground and clear our lands of the threat of the white intruder. It is up to us to do the rest."

Shouts were heard again, and as Sacred Eagle sat down next to his father, Star Hawk softly questioned him further about Sky Eyes and Silver Star. After being fully assured that the women were safely in the mountain camp, Star Hawk began to make plans with the higher chiefs to be ready with the first light of the next morning. They would not wait until the attack came, but would be mounted on their horses, ready for their enemies. In this fashion, surprise would be totally on their side, and they would have victory.

For the rest of the afternoon the communal lodge roared with the fervor of the warriors and chiefs as they spoke about the white man. They built up their spirits to the boiling point in preparation for the next day.

Major Benjamin Thatcher sat atop his sorrel stallion and stared imperiously at the detachment of soldiers who rode in a long line behind him. He called to Corporal Patterson, "Has there been word yet of that damned Crow scout and his useless braves?"

"No, sir. I sent out a small detachment of officers this morning to scout the area, but Spotted Elk has not been seen."

"He should have brought the white woman to us by this morning at the latest. Tomorrow we shall reach the valley. I hoped to have had the bitch before we entered their home territory." Looking at the junior officer, Thatcher scowled. "We'll make camp soon. It's impossible to see in this damned forest when the sun lowers," he said. Everything was against him, he thought as he swiped at an insect that was buzzing by his ear. "If that redskin doesn't show up by morning, we'll go on as planned. With or without the woman we shall bring this Star Hawk to his knees and drive him from the valley. And if the scout does show up late, be sure and tell Sergeant Hadely that those red devils are not to receive any of the payments promised. I'll not have them getting drunk on the army's whiskey if they pull in here after the fighting is over."

"Yes, sir," the corporal answered swiftly. "I will tell Sergeant Hadely right away to be on the watch for the scouts and the woman."

"Good, good; and have a couple of those boys set up my tent. I think we'll camp up here in this clearing." He pointed ahead a short distance. "My arse is bloody well throbbing. This blasted beast feels like a rocking chair. After we beat those red heathens I'll expect a more comfortable horse for the return trip to the fort."

"Yes, sir." Dan Patterson saluted, showing none of the irritation he felt at the major's constant complaints. Why the man hadn't stayed behind at the fort and allowed someone else to be in charge, he would never know. Kicking the sides of his horse, he shouted out the orders to the men to break camp and to set up the major's tent. This would be a long evening for him, he knew, for the major would get little sleep with the attack only hours away. He would have to bear every insult and complaint that the older man wished to vent upon him.

As the night came on, the army troops settled down for a few hours' sleep, their minds filled with visions of plunder and the loot they would be capturing to take back to families and friends at home. They lay there, wrapped up tightly in their blankets, thinking of how righteous their cause was—the Indians were too far beneath them

318

to merit any regard. Not one of them realized that at that very moment, the Blackfoot tribes were making final preparations to fight them in the morning.

The drums beat now with a loud insistence, and the shamans and the elders called out to the Great Spirit and the fathers of the past to honor them with victory and to guide their young warriors.

As the village throbbed with life, Sacred Eagle, after looking over his containers of war paint and making sure his weapons were within reach, lay down upon his sleeping pallet and tried to get some much-needed rest. As his eyes closed, his thoughts traveled far from this village to the quieter, more peaceful mountain, and to his mother, his sister, and Kalina.

As he thought of Kalina, his heart beat faster. He could imagine her lovely features, her soft skin and apparently gentle ways, and he was filled with a longing to be there in the mountains at her side. She was like no other woman. She was all things to him, strong and dependable, gentle and loving. She filled his mind with peace; with her, war and fighting did not exist. He smiled with these thoughts. His warrior woman, a woman who could stand before a trained warrior and defend herself, softened his heart. He would be more than glad to see the end of tomorrow's battle;

319

then on the back of Eagle's Wing he would leave this valley and reclaim Kalina. It was time that their feelings were spoken aloud, time to put a name to this raging within his heart.

As he felt his senses dull with sleep, a soft call brought him from his near-slumber. Medicine Wolf, his tribe's shaman, entered, bearing over his arm a pure white eagle-feather cape.

Sacred Eagle sat upright when he saw the cape. The dim light of the pit fire gave the shimmering white feathers an iridescent glow.

Sitting down next to the sleeping pallet, Medicine Wolf began to speak softly. "This day, with the Great Spirit guiding my steps, I went to the hiding place of this sacred cape. I thought to bring it to you upon the morrow, for in past days the shaman of the village kept the cape in his care until war came to our tribe. But as I went to place the cape in the special place that had been appointed, I was led to bring it to you instead."

Sacred Eagle listened, not reaching out to touch the sacred cape for fear that the power it contained was too overwhelming.

"There is much power in this cape. Soaring Eagle, the mighty war chief of days long past, knew well of the magic that the wearer possesses. It will make you invincible before the enemy. I can feel the force that throbs with a powerful surging even as I hold the cape."

The dark gaze of the shaman probed deeply

into Sacred Eagle's eyes, as though trying to read his thoughts. Sacred Eagle's face concealed none of his awe.

"I shall tell you a story of the mighty Soaring Eagle." Medicine Wolf seemed to relax, the cape now draped over his lap. As he began to tell of the Blackfoot war chief, his face became animated and he seemed to relive the days of old.

Sacred Eagle had heard all the stories of Soaring Eagle as a child at the knee of his own grandfather, Golden Eagle, but now he paid close attention to each word that the old man said. The story of people and days of old was very precious to his people, and they were always willing to hear a good storyteller recite his own version.

"Years and years ago, when the people did not have horses but hunted on foot, they went to war against their enemies armed only with their cunning and their sureness of the forest near their camp. Our tribe had a chief in those days called Swift Buffalo, and he had a son named Soaring Eagle. It was Soaring Eagle who left his village when he was a young man, in search of his vision. He traveled far, seeking that which the Great Spirit would show him. His steps took him far from his village, and he came to a place in the earth where the Great Spirit had stamped his foot. Today we call this place a canyon. And at the bottom of this great hole in the earth, he saw a sight that held him still. There was a great beast, the color of the night sky. Soaring Eagle followed the path made by the animals that fed and watered in the great hole, and soon he was standing near the great beast.

"The black beast snorted aloud with the presence of one of the people, but he did not bolt. He stood and eyed this strange being, and Soaring Eagle gazed upon him. Soon the beast took a step toward the young man, and then another. It was only a short time before the brave was reaching out a hand and touching the nose of the mighty animal.

"As Soaring Eagle won the trust of the beast, the mighty animal reared up on its hind legs and gave a shrill cry, and soon the canyon was filled with more of the strange creatures.

"That night, as Soaring Eagle slept upon the floor of the canyon with the strange animals all about him, he had a dream. He was sitting upon the back of the large, black beast, and behind him other braves of his village were seated upon the backs of more of the animals. Soaring Eagle awoke sweating, his heart beating at an accelerated pace.

"He knew that the Great Spirit had led him to this place and gifted him with this sacred vision. When he returned to our tribe, he was riding the large, black stallion, and the rest of the great herd followed into the center of the village behind him.

"Soaring Eagle became a mighty war chief, his

power and strength known to all in the Blackfoot nation and throughout all the other tribes. He and his black stallion became a legend of the people. The shamans from all the Blackfoot tribes gathered together one spring day, and with their womenfolk they made the cape and headdress from the sacred eagle's feathers. They put all their power into the cape, and in those days the shaman's power was stronger than any power known to the people. They anointed and blessed each feather, and they kept the cape and headdress in a special place until the call to war was sounded. Then Soaring Eagle wore the sacred articles, and no harm could befall him. The people were victorious, never knowing defeat while Soaring Eagle was their leader. When the Great Spirit wished him to sit at his feet and he died, the cape and headdress were secreted in a special hiding place. Only the shaman of our tribe knew this hiding place, and the secret was handed down to me as a young man." Medicine Wolf sat quietly when he had finished his story.

Sacred Eagle's silver eyes looked with great wonder upon the cape in Medicine Wolf's lap. Surely there was no stronger power in all the land than that which the Great Spirit and the Grandfathers were now offering to him.

Rising from the floor of the lodge, Medicine Wolf took the cape in his hands and, with a swift movement, laid the abundance of white feathers

323

around Sacred Eagle's shoulder. "You are worthy of this gift, Sacred Eagle. You will defeat the enemy, and you will be untouched. The Great Spirit knows that you will need all your strength and all the power that this cape can lend you. That is the reason for his directing me to your lodge. Allow it to be your blanket for this night. Let its power saturate your being." With this, the old man turned and left the lodge.

Lying still and hardly daring to breathe, Sacred Eagle felt the pressure on his body of the hundreds of eagle feathers sewn into the large cape. For many, many years this cape had been lying in secret and waiting for the one that was worthy to be its wearer. At this moment, full of the responsibility for the cape lying on his body, Sacred Eagle was unsure of his own worthiness.

From the center of his soul, he heard the words, "The Great Spirit knows all your abilities, your fears, and your strengths. He makes no mistake in choosing whom he claims as worthy." With a sigh, Sacred Eagle relaxed, allowing a feeling of total contentment and peace to consume him. He felt as though his body did not belong to him. He was as light as air, each muscle and fiber of his being saturated with a charge that spiraled him upward. He was as light as down, his thoughts racing to a place that knew only a higher sense of satisfaction. With this overwhelming feeling pulsing through his body, he slept. His dreams took him to another day, another time, when the people knew no threat of the white man, when they could roam the forest, the plains, and prairies freely, chasing the herds of wild buffalo and singing songs of life and death. And in these dreams he became a fuller part of himself and his people. He was charged with the cares of all the Blackfoot, and he pledged to be their bringer of victory.

The activity of the Blackfoot camp began with the first rays of dawn's light. Kalina cautioned Sky Eyes once again to stay where they had spent the night. Near the outer edges of the forest, close to the river, a small knoll rose slightly above the floor of the valley, and upon this hill the two women had spent the night, wrapped tightly in their buffalo robes.

Now, ordering the girl to stay here out of danger, Kalina mounted her horse and started slowly toward the village near the river. She swallowed nervously as she viewed the unfamiliar tepees, but she had a strong sense of determination and did not falter or turn back. Dressed in her warrior woman's garb, she was resolved to find Sacred Eagle and fight at his side. She cast from her mind her fear about Sacred Eagle refusing to allow her to fight. He would have little choice in the matter. From the knoll where she had left Sky

Eyes, she had watched as all the Blackfoot nation's warriors left the village. At this very moment they were forming their lines of defense.

As Kalina watched, the valley floor swarmed with mounted men. Her heart beat wildly in her chest as her dark eyes scanned the throng, looking for the one she desired. She did not see Sacred Eagle though, and actually she was thankful, for as she slowly directed her horse through the groups of warriors, she feared deep within her soul that as soon as Sacred Eagle saw her he would demand that she return to the village and remain with the other women and children.

Chilled by the morning air but trying to ignore the prickling of gooseflesh running up and down her arms, Kalina held her head high as more than one eye was cast in her direction. The warriors wondered who she was and what she was about, but each was too busy with his own worries, and none bothered to halt the woman wearing only breechcloth and vest. Kalina's quiver was full of arrows and her bow was slung across her chest. She wore the headband of the Blackfoot, and the painted designs smeared upon her horse's rump and forelegs were the sign of the Blackfoot.

As she approached the edge of the valley's floor, her eyes were drawn to a long ravine, and there she viewed a magnificent sight. All the Blackfoot high chiefs had gathered, their headdresses of different brilliant colors splendid in the morning light, as they held the reins of their prancing horses. Their faces were streaked with war paint and their mounts were also colored with vermilion. Kalina's heart seemed to all but stop, as her dark eyes caught sight of the one who had claim to her heart.

Sacred Eagle sat astride his prancing, huge, white horse, his strong hand easily holding Eagle's Wing under firm control. About his shoulders and down his back, resting upon the flanks of his mighty steed, he wore the splendor of the eagle cape. Upon his head rose up a magnificent head-dress of the same brilliant white feathers. None could compare with him or his stallion. As Kalina looked at his face, she could see even from a distance that his lips were moving as though he were in communion with the Great Spirit. His features were streaked with his sacred sign, the white eagle. Three streaks upon his right cheek were of pure white, and the other side of his face was painted red, for the blood of the mighty fathers before him. He wore only a breechcloth, and upon his chest was tied a porcupine breast-plate dyed red and white. He looked invincible. His high-strung horse was snow-white, with circles of red vermilion running down each of his legs, his long, sleek neck painted with circles of the same hue. Upon the stallion's mighty chest was Sacred Eagle's handprint in coal black, proclaiming the oneness of man and beast.

Kalina held her own mount still as she witnessed this spectacular sight. As though drawn by an outer force, the silver eyes that had been closed in prayer opened and stared at her.

Sacred Eagle was more than surprised as his eyes focused upon his slave. He took in quickly the nature of her attire and her weapons, and a scowl stole over his handsome features. At a slight pressure from his legs, Eagle's Wing slowly left the ravine and the other chiefs and started toward the warrior woman. And as Kalina looked at the man she loved, his features clouded darkly with anger.

Holding her chin high, Kalina awaited him. It was an effort to stop her hand from trembling as she held her mount still.

"What is this, Kalina?" he asked, his voice sounding hollow and strained.

"I have come to fight at your side, Sacred Eagle."

For a second it looked as if he might smile, but then his displeasure was shown by a dark scowl. "You will return to the mountains. I told you that I would not risk you here in this war."

"I will stay and fight." Kalina was adamant, determined not to be threatened or bullied.

"Then I will have you taken from this valley and held safe until this war with the bluecoats is over."

"I will kill whoever dares to take hold of me or

my horse." Her dark eyes flashed angrily at those of silver.

Seeing that she meant what she said, Sacred Eagle felt his irritation mounting. "You are my slave, and I *command* that you turn from this valley."

It was upon her tongue to tell him that she was not a Crow slave but in fact the granddaughter of Falling Leaves; but something stilled her words, and with a tilt of her chin she responded, "Indeed, you have mastery over me." She left out saying that the mastery she spoke of was over her heart, not over her person. "But I will not obey you in this one thing. I will not leave this valley until I am sure that you are unharmed. I have been trained in the ways of war and will be worthy to sit my mount at your side." Her dark eyes beseeched him as she added softly, "Do not send me from you, Sacred Eagle."

Feeling the full force of those eyes piercing through to his heart, Sacred Eagle took a moment before he asked, "And this beast, too? Has she also been trained in the ways of war?" A slight smile now touched his sensual lips. Reaching down her hand, Kalina lightly patted the mare's graceful neck. "She is all I have, and has proven herself fit. Neither she nor I will falter at your side."

Even as he spoke Sacred Eagle thought himself insane. "You will ride behind me. I shall have one of the younger braves go back to the village and get you one of my horses that have been through the ordeal of battle before."

Tears stung in Kalina's eyes as she realized that he was indeed going to allow her to stay near him. "I will ride at your back, then," she softly conceded.

Turning his stallion about, Sacred Eagle rode back to the chiefs. As the eyes of all those in the valley watched, the beautiful warrior woman slowly followed behind, pulling her mare up behind him as he took the path along the ravine.

Calling out to one of the braves sitting in attendance upon the many chiefs, Sacred Eagle instructed him to go back to the village and bring back the large black stallion from his herd of horses. And as he felt the dark gaze of his father upon him, he looked for a moment at Star Hawk and then turned to see the woman riding behind him. He knew that he had made a poor decision, but as he had looked into her dark eyes and heard her desire to remain at his side, he had been unable to refuse her. He would answer to his father later for this folly, but realized that he did not care what anyone said about his slave. He would watch over her today, and in his heart he knew that he would always watch over her. She was his, and he knew that the word "slave" was not as binding as what he felt for her in his heart. When this war with the bluecoats was over, he would have to make some decisions about this woman. He knew now that he could not live without her, nor was satisfied to have her as his slave. He wanted them to be more than master and slave. Even if he had to leave his village, go into the mountains with this woman at his side, and live a life separate from his tribe, he would do it. He would no longer live without her. He wanted her for his mate. She was the woman who would be the mother of his children—not a slave, not one that was being forced to do his bidding, but a woman willingly in his embrace because of the love between them.

The arrival of his black stallion pulled him from his thoughts. Sacred Eagle watched as Kalina changed horses, her ebony gaze holding his as she sat astride the mount. Sacred Eagle found himself lost in the depths of her stare.

The morning slowly drew on. Several young braves came riding quickly through the valley, calling that the bluecoats had been sighted coming through the forest and that they would soon be at the edge of the valley.

Whoops and war cries greeted this news, and war axes and shields were drawn. Kalina, too, laced her war shield from the side of her horsehair saddle, and pulling her bow into her hand, she readied herself for what was to come.

It seemed to happen quickly after the braves rode through the valley. The bluecoats appeared from the forest and the warriors heard their shouts when they saw the entire Blackfoot nation gathered together for this great battle.

Major Thatcher looked with disbelief as his troops pulled out of the forest and into the valley. To the north lay lined ranks upon ranks of Indians. They were mounted and looked as though they had been awaiting their appearance. Major Thatcher shouted for Corporal Patterson to get the troops in line to defend and attack. But even as he gave the orders, he knew in the pit of his stomach that he had made a terrible mistake. He had expected to be met not with such a force, but with a sleeping village. The warriors in the valley far outnumbered his troops. "Damn!" he swore aloud. If only those Crows had gotten that woman to him before now, he would have had some form of leverage. Now all he could do was try and overpower these savages. If his troops retreated, those heathens would cut them down before they were a hundred yards into the forest.

Not liking what he was seeing, Harry Hadely approached the major. "What do ye think, sir? I thought most of the village had moved to the mountains. How the hell did they know we would be coming here? And what shall we do now?" He knew that it would be futile to stage an attack against such odds. Even though there were over fifteen hundred soldiers in his party, he could see that they were far outnumbered. And then, as his eyes went to the ravine where the Blackfoot chiefs sat boldly staring toward them, he pointed a finger in their direction. "Look over there, sir!" He could not believe his eyes as he looked at a tall Indian sitting upon the back of a huge white stallion. "Do you still think we should try to overtake them?"

"What the blazes do you *think* we are going to do, Sergeant? We came here to do a job, and by God we're going to do it." He swallowed nervously as his eyes also found Sacred Eagle and the other war chiefs.

"But, sir," Sergeant Hadely began, seeing little reason to jeopardize the lives of the men in this command, "perhaps you could speak with them, and they will allow us to go back to the fort. You can't expect us to fight off the whole Blackfoot nation."

"They won't listen to any talk now. They're wanting a fight, and won't be satisfied with anything less." Corporal Patterson rode up at that moment.

"Damn those Crow scouts' hides for letting us walk into this mess," the sergeant shouted, his blue eyes watching the rows of braves. As the line of war chiefs rode out from the ravine, he gulped back his breath. "Looky there, Major," he gasped as the colorful group rode proudly before the rows of readied warriors.

"Get the men ready to charge!" Major Thatcher yelled, knowing that the moment was upon them.

"Yes, sir." The corporal saluted and shouted to the men to prime their rifles and hold at the ready.

"Get them going, Corporal. Let's chase them red devils straight to the pits of hell," Thatcher commanded, and struck out at his horse with his riding crop.

Corporal Patterson called to his men to charge. As one, the fifteen hundred men started to ride over the valley floor, their rifles aimed and their shots sounded loudly.

At the shout to charge, Star Hawk's loud war cry sounded out through the morning air.

The soldiers had time for only one shot apiece, and many of these went wild as the young men faced their savage, bloodthirsty adversaries. None had thought that the day would begin as it had. They had imagined easy victory and a quick finish to a day's work.

With no time to reload, the bluecoats tried to fend off the burst of attacking Blackfoot with only their sabers and the bayonets attached to the barrels of their rifles.

The Indians seemed to converge from all sides, driving the soldiers to the middle of the valley. Their piercing war cries and raucous shouts filled the ears of the all but defenseless men of the army.

With attacking fury, the Blackfoot hacked and hit out at the white men. Their war axes, swinging

334

high through the air, were brought down on the heads of their opponents. Their knives flashed dangerously in the morning sunlight as they found their mark in white flesh.

Kalina followed closely behind Sacred Eagle, in the very thick of the fighting, striking out at any white man that came within reach. Her dark eyes were fixed constantly upon the white eagle cape. As one of the soldiers in a last burst of strength tried to attack Sacred Eagle, she struck with a bold swipe of her war ax and knocked him from his horse, the hooves of her mount trampling him and snuffing out his last breath. Kalina gave no thought to the man; she had only Sacred Eagle in her mind. She must make sure that he remained safe.

Sacred Eagle kept an eye upon Kalina, too, making sure that no harm came to her. Each time she came into contact with one of the soldiers. He watched as she boldly vanquished him; he was always ready to come to her aid. Then as he turned and the white man tried to attack him, he saw Kalina knock the man to the ground below her horse. Sacred Eagle threw her a smile of love and thanks. She smiled in return, and then Sacred Eagle, his war cry bursting from his lips, was again in the fray, his mighty white stallion pawing at the horses of his enemies, its teeth bared as it hit out at animal and man alike.

As the battle raged on, Nicholas, fighting as

335

fiercely as any brave, drew close to Kalina and Sacred Eagle. As he came closer, Kalina pointed to the knoll where she had left Sky Eyes, and called to him the whereabouts of the woman he loved.

The fighting was over within a short time. One by one the bluecoats fell to the ground. The Indians finished them all off, leaving no survivors. Nicholas watched with sadness when he saw his uncle fall from his mount under the attack of a ferocious warrior. It was then that he turned his horse from the battle.

Nicholas knew that it was over for the army. They had made a terrible mistake, and had paid with their lives. By this time the army fort would have been overtaken and burned to the ground. The Blackfoot had proven their strength and their will to survive.

Kicking at his horse, he rode to where Kalina had said he would find Sky Eyes. His need was great to have her softness held closely against him. It had all been such a waste. If only his uncle had listened to him. If the white man was not so greedy, all of this could have been avoided. As he came to the small knoll, his green eyes looked about, and as he halted his horse he saw Sky Eyes stepping forth with Thunder Spirit at her side. The warrior's hand grasped her arm, his features fierce as he glared at the white man upon the horse.

"I swore that I would get even, white man. Now you will die!"

All the anger that had built up within Nicholas over the past hours now erupted. "Let Mary Jean go," Nicholas shouted as he jumped from his horse, his chest heaving with unbridled fury. He had thought he had finished with this man, and now he realized that he should have killed him that day in front of the whole village.

"Her name is Sky Eyes, white man." Thunder Spirit thrust her away and she fell to the ground. "Now I will restore my honor and claim this woman for my own," he spat, as he held a sharp, glinting knife in one hand and his war ax in the other.

With no weapon but the knife strapped at his waist, Nicholas charged Thunder Spirit as though attacking a great, fierce beast. His fist shot out and hit Thunder Spirit on the jaw, sending him sprawling on the ground.

Sky Eyes hurriedly got to her feet, her silver eyes wide with fear as she backed away from the two men. Thunder Spirit quickly jumped to his feet, and the two circled each other like wary animals on the scent of fresh blood.

Again it was Nicholas who charged. This time Thunder Spirit struck out with his war ax, hitting Nicholas's chest and leaving a deep gash across his ribs.

Further enraged, Nicholas clenched his fist and

337

slammed it into Thunder Spirit's face with all his might, his wound seeming to hinder him little. As the pair rolled upon the earth, Thunder Spirit tried to gain entry with his knife. Sky Eyes clapped a hand over her mouth, backing further away from the fight and the threat to the life of the man she loved.

Nicholas avoided the attack, and matched his strength against that of the larger warrior, his own knife now in his fist as he tried to strike at a vital mark.

With a burning sensation running down the length of his side and up the inner side of his arm, Nicholas brought his blade down sharply, finding his target as he felt the strength of his adversary waning. He saw that he had pierced Thunder Spirit's chest. With one final thrust he again brought his knife down, ensuring that never again would this man threaten the woman he loved.

Sky Eyes watched, blinded by tears, as the fight raged between the two men, the flowing red blood seeming to add to her hysteria. When she saw the glinting of steel in the sunlight, her entire world seemed to darken. She felt as if she were falling, sinking into an abyss of destruction and whirling bodies and flashes of red.

When Nicholas reached Sky Eyes she fell into his embrace, her head thrown back and her eyes fluttering. "You are safe, my love," Nicholas whispered breathlessly, trying to wake her from her faint. "Nothing will ever harm you again. Everything is over. You are mine from this day forth."

Slowly his words penetrated the recesses of her mind, and Sky Eyes was pulled along a long dark path to reality. "You won?" she whispered, her eyes looking past him at Thunder Spirit, lying still upon the ground. "You are truly here?" Tears rolled down her cheeks.

Grinning through the pain he now felt, Nicholas said, "Aye, you are here in my arms, and shall never be far from them again. I will take you far away from all this hatred and fighting. As soon as your father allows, we will be wed, and then we shall go to Rosebriar. You will love it there, my sweet. It is so beautiful and peaceful."

Pulling his head down to her own, Sky Eyes kissed his lips fiercely, savoring the feel and taste of him. "I would travel to the ends of the earth with you, my love," she said softly.

As the warriors took care of the dead and wounded, Sacred Eagle led Kalina toward the riverbank. Dismounting, he held out his hand to offer her his help in dismounting.

Gratefully, for she was now bone weary, Kalina let herself slip to her feet.

Tenderly he pulled the quiver from her shoulder and walked her toward the river. Bending, he cup-

339

ped his hand and brought water to her face to wipe the splatterings of blood away from her beautiful features.

Lacking the will to resist his ministrations, Kalina allowed Sacred Eagle to tend her for a time. She sat down upon the soft grass and sighed aloud.

"My beautiful warrior woman." He spoke softly. "My entire body is filled with desire for you. It is as though you took a spark and threw it high into the night, and that is when I was born. Your flame set me into being. Your love has made me reborn."

Not sure that she was hearing him correctly, Kalina stared into his bronzed face. "You are not angry with me for coming here and demanding that I be allowed to fight with you?"

"Angry?" Sacred Eagle smiled. "I feel only love for you." He spoke aloud all the feelings that had recently been raging within his soul. "I care not that you are a Crow slave. If my tribe refuses to allow me to wed you, we shall leave my village. We shall go high into the mountains and live a life of peace and happiness."

Tears sprang quickly to Kalina's eyes. She had doubted that she would ever hear such a declaration of love from this great warrior's lips. "But you are mighty in the eyes of your people. Would you leave them, and all that you will one day be, for me?"

"You are all that matters." Sacred Eagle breathed aloud, his lips descending to cover hers and drinking of the sweetness that only she could bestow. "You are my heart." His embrace encased her in that moment. "I lost one love to the enemy; I will not lose another, even to my own people."

Kalina's heart rose up to the very heavens at this heartfelt declaration. Tenderly she kissed him, showing all that she felt for him. "I have prayed to the Great Spirit that one day I would hear these words from your lips." She smiled widely as she dashed away the tears upon her cheeks with the back of her hands. "You need not leave your people though, for I am not a Crow slave."

Sacred Eagle looked at her, not understanding. "In my heart you are no longer a Crow slave," he agreed; but he could not say that his tribe would fully agree.

"No, no, you do not understand." Kalina sat up straighter and, taking his hands into her own she tried to explain. "Truly, I am not a Crow slave. My grandmother is Falling Leaves. I am the daughter of her daughter, who was killed so long ago. My Blackfoot name is Morning Star."

Astonished, Sacred Eagle could only stare at her.

"It is true!" She turned her arm about and showed him the birthmark shaped like a small arrowhead. "Falling Leaves saw this mark and de-

341

clared that it was the same as her lost granddaughter's."

"But what of your family in the Crow village?" Sacred Eagle's mind was now catching up to what she was saying.

A smile lit up her features as she said, "I was adopted into Pointed Arrow's family when I was five winters old. Falling Leaves lost her granddaughter when she was also but five. Kalina of the Crow and Morning Star of the Blackfoot are one and the same."

As the full meaning of what she was saying hit him, Sacred Eagle gave a loud whoop. Grabbing hold of her, he swung her up into his arms, twirling her about in the air with his happiness. "Nothing can stop me from claiming you as my own then," he declared in his joy.

Laughing aloud in complete abandon, Kalina retorted, "Only my grandmother can give such permission."

But this did not dampen Sacred Eagle's joy. "I will ply the old woman with gifts and love. She will not refuse me." He continued to swing her about, and then pulling her up tightly against his chest, he kissed her hungrily, his hands roving over her near-naked body. Then, with a deep moan in the back of his throat, he pulled himself away. "We must go this very day to the mountains and approach Falling Leaves. I can wait no longer to claim you as my mate. My body aches, even now, after all we have endured this day, to make you one with myself. I long to reclaim your soft body next to mine." Again his lips settled over hers, and with longing Kalina wrapped her arms about his neck.

Her happiness was complete. It had taken her such a long time to admit her own feelings for this man, and now at last he had allowed his heart to lead him. They would share a lifetime of happiness, side by side. Nothing would ever stand between them, for their love would always endure.

Epilogue

It was a velvety dark night, awash with the dazzling brilliance of millions of stars, the full moon casting its shadows throughout the Blackfoot valley. The entire tribe was gathered in the center of the village, and as they watched, Kalina and Sky Eyes stepped toward the middle of the group. Both women were dressed in bleached white dresses that had been patiently stitched with beautiful designs. Their long, flowing black hair fell loose down their backs, held from their faces with hairbands that matched their dresses. Near the blazing fire, the two women stood quietly before Medicine Wolf and Star Hawk.

Looking away from the two women, the villagers glanced toward the outer circle of the group as Sacred Eagle and Nicholas approached. They were also dressed with care, bleached hide shirts and breeches covering their tall forms, their stances proud and tall. Nicholas, with pride clear on his features, walked to where Sky Eyes stood and tenderly placed her hand within his own. His grass-green eyes beheld the beauty of her lovely face and his heart filled with joy. Sacred Eagle also walked to the woman of his heart. His long hair was braided on the sides of his face and hung loose down his back. His face, unlike Nicholas's, was painted in the colors of his war paint, displaying to all his pride and his honor. And as he reached Kalina's side and drew her hand into his own, his smile stirred her features to a glowing radiance.

Star Hawk bestowed a paternal look of love first upon his daughter and then upon his son. "This night I stand before you as a proud father. I will watch as our shaman says the words that will join you with the ones of your heart and know that from this night forth, you will be changed. Always know this, my children: wherever you are and whatever you do, your mother and I are here and offer you our guidance. As a pair you came into this life, and now as a pair you will be joined and then step apart, as is the will of the Great Spirit. Your steps shall be led by the ordained destiny that has been plotted out from the beginning of time. Be happy, my children, for you are loved."

Sky Eyes brushed the tears from her cheeks and Sacred Eagle solemnly nodded his head, knowing that the words his father had spoken had cost him much. Not only was his only daughter about to join and leave his lodge, but she would be leaving with Nicholas tomorrow for New Orleans and then for England.

Star Hawk stepped aside, and the shaman took his place in front of the couples. As he said the words that would join them for all time, the villagers listened to each word he chanted. At last he called for the Great Spirit to bless both unions. When he finished, Sacred Eagle turned toward Kalina, all the love and adoration he felt for this woman showing on his face as he placed silver bracelets on each of her forearms. The bracelets were etched with the design of an eagle.

Admiring the bracelets, Kalina pulled a silver amulet from the small pouch tied at her waist. She had planned her gift carefully to be something special between herself and Sacred Eagle, and as she held out the necklace, he saw that the painting on its smooth surface was of a warrior riding a white stallion and an Indian maiden riding a black.

The significance of the design was not lost upon Sacred Eagle. He knew well that as his mate, Kalina would always ride at his side. She would be the soft, gentle woman of his lodge and mother of his children, but she would also be his friend and ally when he went out hunting or in times of war. Bending, he allowed her to secure the necklace about his neck. As she finished he pulled her tenderly into his arms and kissed her lovingly. This drew shouts of approvals from the villagers.

Nicholas had also had bracelets made for his wife. He had fashioned their design in the sign of her parents. Two stars were fashioned upon the clasp, and in between them were two tiny emeralds, signifying the color of his eyes and the depth of his love. "I love you with all my heart, Mary Jean," he whispered softly in her ear.

Allowing Nicholas to pull the bracelets over her wrists and lock the clasps, Sky Eyes turned her hands this way and that with admiration. With a satisfied smile she also removed the beaded pouch tied at her waistband. Pulling open the drawstring, she drew forth an intricately designed headband, its stitching depicting the story of their meeting and their courtship.

Nicholas looked at the work with fascination, and then with a large grin he wrapped his arm about her shoulders. "Wife, you are a treasure." He kissed her lips softly. No other gift could have meant more to him, for he knew that she had taken great care and consideration with each stitch. "My heart is brimming with love for you. I shall make you happy forever."

Sky Eyes saw the love shining upon the features of her husband, and as she looked about at her village and for a moment shared the wonderful togetherness with her brother, her eyes filled with tears of joy. This moment was meant to be. Destiny had swept up the stormy rapture of their love and had overcome all the obstacles that had stood in their way. Her steps would take her far away from her family, but fate had long ago set their paths, and love would guide them.

ROMANCE REIGNS
WITH ZEBRA BOOKS!

SILVER ROSE (2275, $3.95)
by Penelope Neri

Fleeing her lecherous boss, Silver Dupres disguised herself as a boy and joined an expedition to chart the wild Colorado River. But with one glance at Jesse Wilder, the explorers' rugged, towering scout, Silver knew she'd have to abandon her protective masquerade or else be consumed by her raging unfulfilled desire!

STARLIT ECSTASY (2134, $3.95)
by Phoebe Conn

Cold-hearted heiress Alicia Caldwell swore that Rafael Ramirez, San Francisco's most successful attorney, would never win her money . . . or her love. But before she could refuse him, she was shamelessly clasped against Rafael's muscular chest and hungrily matching his relentless ardor!

LOVING LIES (2034, $3.95)
by Penelope Neri

When she agreed to wed Joel McCaleb, Seraphina wanted nothing more than to gain her best friend's inheritance. But then she saw the virile stranger . . . and the green-eyed beauty knew she'd never be able to escape the rapture of his kiss and the sweet agony of his caress.

EMERALD FIRE (1963, $3.95)
by Phoebe Conn

When his brother died for loving gorgeous Bianca Antonelli, Evan Sinclair swore to find the killer by seducing the tempress who lured him to his death. But once the blond witch willingly surrendered all he sought, Evan's lust for revenge gave way to the desire for unrestrained rapture.

SEA JEWEL (1888, $3.95)
by Penelope Neri

Hot-tempered Alaric had long planned the humiliation of Freya, the daughter of the most hated foe. He'd make the wench from across the ocean his lowly bedchamber slave — but he never suspected she would become the mistress of his heart, his treasured SEA JEWEL.

Available wherever paperbacks are sold, or order direct from the Publisher. Send cover price plus 50¢ per copy for mailing and handling to Zebra Books, Dept. 2757, 475 Park Avenue South, New York, N.Y. 10016. Residents of New York, New Jersey and Pennsylvania must include sales tax. DO NOT SEND CASH.